The
CHRONICLES
of
UNCLE MOSE

Library and Archives Canada Cataloguing in Publication

Russell, Ted, 1904-1977.
The chronicles of Uncle Mose / Ted Russell ; edited
by Elizabeth Miller.

Originally published: Portugal Cove, N.L. : Breakwater Books, 1975.
ISBN 1-894463-88-9

1. Fishers--Newfoundland and Labrador--Fiction.
2. Newfoundland and Labrador--Fiction. I. Miller, Elizabeth Russell
II. Title.

PS8535.U86C4 2006   C813'.54   C2006-900997-X

PRINTED IN CANADA

Cover design: Adam Freake

MIX
Paper from
responsible sources
FSC
www.fsc.org   **FSC® C016245**

This paper has been certified to meet the envi-
ronmental and social standards of the Forest
Stewardship Council® (FSC®) and comes
from responsibly managed forests, and veri-
fied recycled sources.

FLANKER PRESS
ST. JOHN'S, NL, CANADA
TOLL FREE: 1-866-739-4420
WWW.FLANKERPRESS.COM

15 14 13 12 11   5 6 7 8 9 10 11

      Canada Council   Conseil des Arts
Canada   for the Arts   du Canada   Newfoundland Labrador

We acknowledge the financial support of the Government of Canada through the Book Publishing
Industry Development Program (BPIDP) for our publishing activities; the Canada Council for the
Arts which last year invested $20.1 million in writing and publishing throughout Canada; the
Government of Newfoundland and Labrador, Department of Tourism, Culture and Recreation.

The CHRONICLES of UNCLE MOSE

Ted Russell

Edited by
Elizabeth Miller

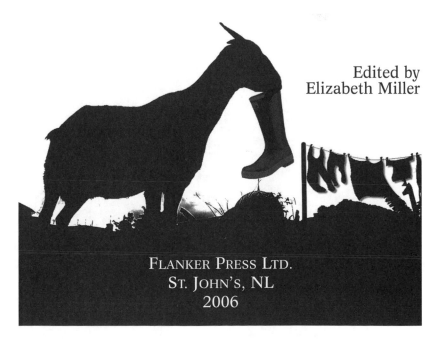

FLANKER PRESS LTD.
ST. JOHN'S, NL
2006

To Naomi and Tamsyn –
with love from Betty-bat

CONTENTS

PREFACE

The Chronicles of Uncle Mose debuted in Newfoundland on CBC Radio in November 1953. Created and narrated by Ted Russell (1904–1977), each story comprised a segment of approximately six minutes on *The Fishermen's Broadcast*. Continuing uninterrupted until 1961, the monologues aired initially once, later twice a week. In 1958, Russell rewrote some of the episodes for a national program, *Come All Ye Round*, a fact that explains the existence of several of the stories in two versions.

Each episode began with what quickly became a familiar phrase – "And now the Chronicles of Uncle Mose," spoken by CBC announcer Harry Brown – followed by a short excerpt from "The Sealer's Ball" played on the organ by Bob MacLeod. Ted Russell would then speak to the radio audience as Uncle Mose. He did not cultivate a special voice for this purpose, but read his scripts in the slow, deliberate pace with a slight Conception Bay accent that was part of his normal speech pattern. Reading in what appeared to be spontaneous conversation (though the scripts were actually carefully constructed and timed to fit the slot allotted by CBC), he succeeded in establishing a bond of familiarity and intimacy with his listeners.

An initial objective of the *Chronicles* was to provide a

1

means of communicating relevant information to fishermen living in isolated communities along hundreds of miles of coastline. Uncle Mose would keep fishermen up-to-date on the latest news of interest: current fish prices, new government regulations, local problems, and general matters of policy. But the series soon became much more. Drawing on his nearly fifty years of experience as a teacher and a magistrate living and working in outport Newfoundland, Ted Russell brought to his stories a wealth of insight into the nature of rural life. Before long, many of the characters – Grampa Walcott, Grandma, Skipper Joe, Aunt Sophy, Jethro Noddy, and King David – took on a life of their own and became household names.

One can find in these stories the many attributes that mark Ted Russell as one of Newfoundland's great writers: a mastery of the art of storytelling, a profound understanding of human nature, and a deep respect for the dignity of the traditional way of life. The most enduring appeal of these tales lies in Russell's sense of humour. Perhaps most popular are the tall tales, an integral part of Newfoundland's oral tradition. Most of these were stories that Ted Russell himself had heard during the forty years he spent in the outports. Though he was fully aware of the hardships of outport life (after all, he served as a magistrate during the dark days of the 1930s), his essential vision of life was comic. Usually whimsical, though at times satirical, Ted Russell successfully captures the incongruities of life in an isolated community confronting the effects of change.

The Chronicles of Uncle Mose were set in the 1950s in Pigeon Inlet, a fictitious community that was beginning to experience change yet still adhered to the traditional way of life and its concomitant values. A composite of the many communities with which Russell was familiar (notably Coley's Point, Pass Island, Harbour Breton, and Fogo), Pigeon Inlet was typical of hundreds of outports scattered along the rugged coastline of Newfoundland and Labrador and dependent almost entirely for their existence on the inshore cod-fishery. This fishery, with its economic uncertainties, its reliance on the unpredictable ocean, and its demand for hard work, helped to mould the characters of the outporters. Isolation from the outside world also fostered close ties and a meaningful interdependence.

The first appearance of the *Chronicles* in print came in the late 1960s in the *Newfoundland Quarterly*. Then in the 1970s, Breakwater Books issued two collections of the stories: *The Chronicles of Uncle Mose* (1975) and *Tales from Pigeon Inlet* (1977). These, along with several smaller collections issued during the 1990s by Harry Cuff Publications, have long since been out of print. Meanwhile, Kelly Russell has released several of the stories on various media: LP recordings, cassette tapes, and CDs.

In preparing this present collection, I have engaged in some light editing. Using where possible the invaluable *Dictionary of Newfoundland English*, I have provided glosses for several words and phrases that are likely to be unfamiliar to many early-twenty-first-century ears. I have also clarified a few topical references. However, I have not made a single substantive change, not even with respect to occasional remarks about women that might by today's standards seem somewhat belittling. In such cases, fidelity to the text and its historical/cultural validity has trumped political correctness.

Elizabeth Miller
Toronto
March 2006

PIGEON INLET

I SUPPOSE BEFORE I BEGIN tellin' you about the people who live here in Pigeon Inlet, I ought to say somethin' about the place itself. Well, there's not much to tell. Even though you've never seen it, you must have seen dozens of places just like it. We're all fishermen here and, apart from our gardens and Levi Bartle's sawmill, there's nothin' except fish. We've got as good a harbour as you'd care to see, deep water, good holdin' ground. And if anybody ever wants to build a fish plant, we've got the perfect place for it, right at the mouth of Bartle's Brook.

We're right in the middle of a stretch of coast about forty or fifty miles long, with five or six smaller places spread out along the shore on each side of us. The people from these places might possibly move into Pigeon Inlet if ever we get one of those fish plants we hear so much about these days. One of these places is a goodish-sized place almost as big as Pigeon Inlet. The name of that place is Hartley's Harbour. It's about six miles from here and the Hartley's Harbour people think there's no place like theirs. I bet that if ever a fish plant comes to this shore, *they'll* want it in Hartley's Harbour. They think they're the capital of the shore. They've already got the District Nurse stationed there, which they would never have had except for skulduggery. Anyway, they're goin' to be unreasonable enough to want the fish plant, but you watch out. They won't get it. We will. That is, if one comes.

Now to get back to the people of Pigeon Inlet. I'm goin' to tell you about the Executive of our Fishermen's Local. Skipper Joe Irwin is our President and Bill Prior is Vice President. I'm the Secretary and Sam Bartle is Treasurer. Grampa Walcott is our Honorary President. We had to give Grampa some kind of a title or it'd break his heart. I'll tell you about him first.

Grampa Walcott is the oldest man in Pigeon Inlet. He's eighty-two years old, but smart as a cricket and wants to be into everything. He's only a handful and you'd think the wind'd blow him away, but no matter how stormy the night, he can get to the Lodge* meetin' or a local meetin' as well as any of us. He went fishin' when he was seven or eight years old and hasn't had a summer ashore since. That's seventy-five summers fishin'.

Of course he doesn't do much fishin' now. But he always supervises the drawin' for our salmon and net berths every spring in April. We always give him Number One berth, the one right at the mouth of the Inlet, the one easiest to get to, and he always fires the gun at twelve o'clock every May the tenth when the rest of us claim our berths. He's quite a character. He couldn't read or write until ten years ago when the Adult Education teacher was here. He always used to say he expected to live to ninety, but since he learned to read he says he's goin' to reach the hundred mark. He says he's got more to live for now.

There's not much to tell about Sam Bartle. He's in his

thirties, the youngest of the five of us. He's able to turn his hand to almost anything and could give up the fishery tomorrow if he wanted to. But he doesn't want to unless he's got to. In fact, he worked in St. John's winter before last and could have got a steady all-year-round job, but he turned it down and came back to Pigeon Inlet to continue fishin' in the spring. The way Sam explained it was that he couldn't get a place for his family to live. He could get two or three rooms but he wants room enough for his young children to kick around in and he couldn't find that in St. John's for love nor money. So he came back to his fine big house and his fishin'. Besides, fishin' is in his blood and he doesn't intend to give it up unless he's goin' to be starved out of it.

Bill Prior is about the same, only a few years older, and a bit more tied down to the fishery. Bill is the ablest man on the shore. There's a crossbeam down in Levi Bartle's fish store where you're allowed to write your name in lead pencil, provided you've got a fifty-six-pound weight hooked onto your little finger while you're doin' it. There are three names on that beam and Bill's name is the highest of the lot.

As for me, Mose Mitchell, I'm not really a Pigeon Inletter at all. I'm from the Sou'west Coast. Went Bank fishin' when I was sixteen and got a bellyful after thirty-four years of it. I had neither chick nor child. So I jacked up and came to St. John's. Couldn't stand the dust and smoke and noise and used to get heartsick whenever I looked out the Narrows. Then one day I met this fellow, Joe Irwin. He was short-handed, carryin' a load of freight north to Pigeon Inlet, so I shipped with him and came here and I've been here ever since. Not married yet, but there's still time. Only in the prime of life yet. Guess I'll end my days here – especially if we get that fish plant!

Our President is Skipper Joe Irwin, the man who brought me here three and a half years ago. Joe is about my age, fifty. The prime of life, like I said. He's as good a man as ever water wet. His schooner is the only one in the place. She's lyin' up all the year, except when he takes a load of dry fish or lumber to St. John's each fall and brings back a load of supplies. He used to go to Labrador fishin' in her till he had to give it up. It got so that the more fish he'd catch, the more money he'd lose. Like he said in our Executive meeting one night, "Boys," he said, "I was like a mouse tryin' to chew his way through a twelve-inch partition. The harder I'd gnaw, the further I'd go in the hole." Another time when he was takin' out his last load of Labrador fish and a round-tripper from the *Kyle*** asked him what made it so thin and squat-lookin', Skipper Joe nearly lost his temper. He said, "Ma' am, if you'd been in the hold of my schooner for the past two months with twelve hundred quintals of fish on top of you, you'd be thin and squat-lookin', too." Anyway, he's finished with the Labrador fishery and he's settled down to shore fishin' like the rest of us.

* Lodge: the Orangemen's Lodge, a Protestant organization

** *Kyle*: a steamer which during the 1950s served primarily the Labrador coast

ALGEBRA SLIPPERS

IF THERE'S ONE SURE PROOF that times are gettin' more civilized than they used to be, it's the way business is carried on nowadays. Years ago, accordin' to Grampa Walcott, 'twas somethin' awful, and to prove his point, a thing which Grampa is always ready and willin' to do, he tells this story about how he got the pair of swile*-skin slippers that he's been wearin' now for nigh on thirty years (of course he's had three new pair of soles and two new pair of uppers in 'em during that time, but they're the same pair of slippers). He likes to treasure 'em because, he says, they remind him of the one and only time he ever got the better of old Josiah Bartle, who was the merchant here thirty years ago.

And even then, he said, he'd never have got 'em only for a thing called Algebra. When I asked him what in the world Algebra was, he said he didn't know, but it must be a wonderful fine thing to help a poor man like him get the better of a shrewd old bird like Josiah Bartle.

'Twas along about the middle of April 1931, says Grampa, when Liz, his missus, told him the molasses keg was empty and he'd better go down to Josiah's store and get some. Grampa wondered how he'd pay for it, because 'twas too early in the spring to get credit on next summer's account, and he certainly didn't want to disturb the bit of gold he had in the sock. 'Twas then Liz reminded him of his two swile-skins. True, one of 'em had some shotholes in it, but the other was perfect and between 'em they ought to fetch enough molasses to tide 'em over till credit time. So, takin' his empty molasses keg and the two swile-skins, off he went.

Skipper Josiah the merchant was glad to see him, business bein' what it was that time of year, and told Grampa how lassy was current price – a dollar a gallon. Likewise, swile-skins was current price – a dollar a skin. Grampa asked him what about shotholes, and Josiah told him they was current price too – ten cents off for every shothole. Grampa had no trouble figgerin' he'd get one gallon for the good skin and part of a gallon for the shotholey one. When Josiah came back from inside where he kept his swile-skins, lassy, and things like that, he said right friendly like, "Here you are, Ben. Here's your keg, with your half gallon of lassy." Grampa was took aback and said it ought to be more than that.

Josiah rubbed his hands friendlier than ever and said, "No. Half a gallon is exactly right. You see," he said, "two swile-skins at a dollar each is two dollars. Then fifteen shotholes in one of 'em at ten cents a shothole, that's a dollar fifty. Take that off the two dollars and you have fifty cents left, and with lassy a dollar a gallon, here is your half gallon."

Grampa knowed there was somethin' wrong. He said there was nar shothole at all in one of 'em and he asked Josiah to give him a gallon for that one and give him back the holey one. But Josiah explained how he couldn't do that, because the two skins went together in what he called in business a package deal, where the good points of one had offset the bad points in the other. Then Grampa wanted to call the whole thing off and go home again with his two skins and his empty keg, but Josiah said no. Business was business, and what was done couldn't be undone, or the business world'd never know where it stood. Then Grampa made a remark, but Josiah threatened the law on him for it. So all that was left for him to do was to go home.

When Liz, his missus (Grandma she is now), tipped up the keg that night to full the molasses dish, she noticed there wasn't much in it, so she wormed the story out of Grampa and give him twenty-four hours to go back to Josiah and get his rights or else she'd do it. Of course, a thing like that'd disgrace Grampa completely. So he spent nearly all that night layin' awake thinkin' up a scheme. Next mornin' he had it, and went over to Uncle Phineas Prior to get his help in carryin' it out. Uncle Phin was only too glad to do it.

And so late that evenin', Grampa visited Josiah's store. Phin Prior with two or three more had just started an argument about the big profits merchants made. They asked Grampa's opinion, and he went even further than the rest and said that merchants often sold things for ten times what they paid for 'em. Josiah got mad and poked his snout right into the trap. He told Grampa he'd been glad to sell him anything he had for ten times what he'd paid for it. "All right then," said Grampa, "Sell me back that swile-skin that got the fifteen shotholes in it."

Well, what a hullaballoo. Everybody wanted the particulars and they all agreed Josiah hadn't paid nothin' for it. So bein' as how ten times nothin' was nothin', Josiah was bound by his word to give it back to Grampa for nothin'. If Josiah had given it right then he'd have been better off, but he couldn't bear to get the worst of it. So he said he wouldn't be guided by people with less book-learnin' than he had. Then who should come in but the schoolmaster, and they put the thing square up to him. And, said Grampa, 'twas the schoolmaster that brought up this business about Algebra.

Accordin' to Algebra, said the schoolmaster, Josiah hadn't just paid nothin' for the swile-skin with the holes, he'd paid fifty cents less than nothin', because he'd took fifty cents off the good one on account of it. Algebra called that a minus fifty cents, and ten times that was minus five dollars, which again (accordin' to Algebra) meant that Josiah had to give Grampa back the skin and five dollars besides, and Grampa went home happy.

Liz wasn't so happy though. She said if that was Algebra, 'twas no better than Bingo, and she made Grampa give the five dollars to the Church Organ Fund. But she let him keep the swile-skin, and that's what he made the pair of slippers out of that he wears to this very day. He calls 'em his Algebra slippers and says that, whatever Algebra is, there's no doubt 'tis a true friend to the poor man.

* swile: seal

THE DISTRICT NURSE

NOW I'M GOIN' TO TELL YOU how the District Nurse came to be stationed at Hartley's Harbour instead of here in Pigeon Inlet where she ought to be.

We wanted her here and Hartley's Harbour people were unreasonable enough to want her there. The Government couldn't please everybody, so they told her to spend her first three months in Hartley's Harbour and the next three months with us. Then she could decide for herself, and they'd build her dispensary in whatever place she picked.

We in Pigeon Inlet figgered out we couldn't lose – for three good reasons. First, a nurse'd want a nice clean store to do her shoppin'. We had that. Levi Bartle's store in Pigeon Inlet is away ahead of Lige Grimes's old place in Hartley's Harbour. Second, she'd want a good boardin' house, and we had that. Aunt Sophy Watkinson's boardin' house was famous all along the coast, while in Hartley's Harbour she'd be lucky if she didn't starve to death at Aunt Sarah Skimple's. Third, and most important of all, she'd probably want some nice company her own age, and that was our strongest point. The Hartley's Harbour boys are all right in their own way, but not to be compared with young Lloyd Walcott, a handsome, strappin' young fellow, just like myself thirty years ago. What more could a nurse want?

Well, in November she came down on the boat to Hartley's Harbour and we saw her on the deck of the steamer. Just out from England she was. Pretty little thing, but awful skinny. Anyway, if she didn't starve in the next three months, we'd fatten her up when we got her up in the Inlet in February. We were so sure of gettin' her now that we began to pick a place to build the dispensary.

We wouldn't have been so sure if we'd known that Lige Grimes had just given up chewin' tobacco. He had cleaned up his store and put up a big notice. It read: *No Smoking or Spitting Allowed. By Order of the Hartley's Harbour Nurse's Committee.* The hypocrite! But we didn't know that till 'twas too late.

At last, one day in February the nurse moved in by dog team, bag and baggage, to start her three months with us. She looked thinner than ever, but Aunt Sophy was ready with a big supper for her and young Lloyd Walcott dropped in accidentally during the evenin'.

Our Committee had a lot of meetings from then on and Grampa Walcott always had somethin' good to report. Nurse's appetite was good and she was gettin' fatter every day. She liked Aunt Sophy, and young Lloyd was up there every night. Grampa walked in on them in Aunt Sophy's livin' room one night. He chuckled when he reported this to us and said that courtin' was the one thing that hadn't changed in the last sixty years.

In May the first steamer came and the nurse had to go back to St. John's. She said she'd have to report to the Government before decidin' where her headquarters would be, but we were sure we had her. Why, she looked a good thirty pounds heavier than she had three months ago. Levi Bartle even bet Lige

Grimes a hundred dollars that we'd get her. I don't hold with bettin', especially with fellows like Lige Grimes.

Well, we got our shock a week later, when me and Skipper Joe were sittin' down in Levi Bartle's front room listenin' to the Gerald Doyle News Bulletin.* The Bulletin was about three parts over when we heard this: "Nurse Plumtree, who is in St. John's on official business, is returning by next boat to take up residence in her new headquarters at Hartley's Harbour."

We looked at each other. There must be some mistake. The Bulletin continued: "Nurse Plumtree looks very fit and healthy after her winter in the North. She laughingly admitted to a reporter from this Bulletin that she had put on too much weight during the past three months, but that she intended to diet from now on till she had reduced to her normal weight."

We stared in amazement. What was he talkin' about? The Bulletin continued: "Our Hartley's Harbour correspondent informs us that Mr. Lloyd Walcott of Pigeon Inlet has just accepted a position as bookkeeper with the enterprising firm of Elijah Grimes of Hartley's Harbour. Mr. Walcott will be taking up his new duties shortly." I looked at Levi Bartle out of the corner of my eye. His face had turned white as a sheet.

The Bulletin continued: "Mr. Grimes has just been awarded the contract to build the new nurse's dispensary in the up-and-coming town of Hartley's Harbour." I looked again. Levi's face was turnin' from white to red – dark red. The reader continued: "The nurse's committee of Hartley's Harbour gratefully acknowledges receipt of a generous donation of one hundred dollars from Mr. Levi Bartle, a popular businessman of the little settlement of Pigeon Inlet. This money will be spent by the committee for liquid refreshment at a time to be given in her honour when she arrives shortly to take up her permanent residence in Hartley's Harbour. It is expected that a good time will be had by all." I looked again. Levi's face was purple now – a deep, dark purple. Me and Skipper Joe Irwin tiptoed silently from the room and out through his back door.

You'd think that much of a victory would have satisfied the crowd from Hartley's Harbour. But no! They had to rub it in a bit harder. A few days later, Levi Bartle received somethin' in a big flat envelope and wondered who was sendin' him a calendar in May. It was postmarked "Hartley's Harbour" and in one corner of the envelope was written: "You can hang this up in your store now we're finished with it." Levi opened the envelope and found – yes, you've guessed it. It was a cardboard notice showin' signs of wear and tear. On it was written in big letters in indelible pencil: *No Smoking or Spitting Allowed. By Order of the Hartley's Harbour Nurse's Committee.* Poor Levi was fit to be tied.

Well, that'll show you what we Pigeon Inlet people are goin' to be up against when we try to get a fish plant in Pigeon Inlet instead of in Hartley's Harbour. But we'll do it. Yes, sir! You watch!

* Gerald Doyle News Bulletin ("the Bulletin"): a radio news program (1932–66) which provided not only news but personal messages for those living in isolated communities

TV

ONE OF PIGEON INLET'S greatest drawbacks is that we've got no TV. We hear tell now and then how the outside world pities us in our misfortune and they're tryin' to get to us just as soon as ever they can. But in the meantime there we are, cut right off. Apart from Levi Bartle the merchant, and young Bill Irwin, who won a scholarship and is up at the University, I'm the only Pigeon Inletter that's ever seen TV, and I think it's almost a Christian duty to tell the rest about it so as they won't feel too bad about what they're missin'.

'Twas when I was up in St. John's last fall with Skipper Joe in his schooner, takin' out our load of dry fish and loadin' up with general cargo whatever was offerin', that who should happen down on the wharf this evenin', but Uncle Bill Bobbitt, a man I hadn't laid eyes on since we was dory* mates with Captain Angus in the old *Bluenose.* I'd heard about Bill afterwards, how he'd had his own schooner fishin' out of places like Lunenburg and Gloucester. But now he told me he'd swallowed his anchor and was retired and livin' right here in St. John's – up on the higher levels. He give me the name of the street and his number.

He asked me to come up that night and I said yes, I certainly would, and what a great yarn we'd have about old times. I thought he looked kind of took aback at that and said somethin' about TV. But I paid no heed to that, not knowin' any better at the time.

Anyway, after supper that evenin', I put on my other shirt and up I went. I found the street all right and the number, but I figgered there was nobody home 'cause 'twas all dark. But havin' come that far I thought I might as well knock, makin' sure of course that I didn't strike my knuckles on that little brass thing on the doorpost. By and by, after I'd knocked three or four times the door opened, and what a relief. 'Twas Uncle Bill. 'Twas the right house after all. I started to tell him how I thought I'd lost my way, but all he said was "Sh-sh..."

Well I shushed all right. Then I whispered to ask him was there anybody dead. "Not yet," he said, "but they soon will be when Two Gun Buck gets after these fellows what's tryin' to steal the cows." For a minute he had me frightened and I told him perhaps I'd better not come in. But he shushed me again and steered me in through a doorway into what I s'pose must've been their parlour – that is if you could see it.

As it was, all you could see was a place about the size of the bottom of a biscuit box over in one end of the room all lighted up like the screen when Jabez Tacker from Hartley's Harbour used to show a movie picture. Only this was smaller than Jabez's screen and 'twas makin' a louder noise owin' to it bein' up closer.

Well I couldn't see anybody, not plain that is, but I figgered they was there watchin' this lighted-up biscuit box thing. So, to show my good intentions, I bid 'em all the time o'day and remarked on how glad I'd been to run across Uncle Bill, my old friend from way back. But all the reply I got was a lot of shushes from all directions, and Uncle Bil still steerin' me flopped me down in a chair and whispered to me to watch the TV.

So that's what it was. Well I'd heard about it and now here was my chance. So I watched it. But it didn't take long before I remembered I'd seen it before. 'Twas the same thing Jabez Tacker showed us three falls ago. Only when he showed it, it used to break every few minutes, whereas now 'twas spliced up proper, and besides the weather was fine when Jabez showed it, whereas now 'twas snowin' to beat the band. I remarked to Uncle Bill that if the snow kept up they'd have to put away the horses and get out the komatik,** but that brought on more shushes, even from Uncle Bill, so I kept quiet for a spell. Then all at once it dawned on me how I might help 'em all out, and get a chance to have a yarn with Uncle Bill besides. So I told 'em how I'd seen all this afore and how 'twas the fellow with the big black moustache that stole the cows, even though right now you wouldn't think butter'd melt in his mouth. But 'twas all right I said, the girl found out about him in time and didn't marry him after all, especially bein' as how Buck killed him with twenty-five or thirty bullets from his Six Shooter.

Well, that put the fat in the fire. Somewhere in the room a youngster started to screech about how that bad old man had spoiled everything. So I whispered again to Uncle Bill to ask him how much longer they'd be watchin' TV that night and he whispered back, till after the late show in about six more hours' time. I said I think I'd better be goin' but he whispered to me to wait for the weather forecast. So I waited. I wished afterwards I hadn't, 'cause this fellow's face come on the screen – after the cows had gone – to tell us that there was a region of high pressure approachin' the Northeast Coast that would affect our weather for the next forty-eight hours.

Well, knowin' what high pressure done to poor Skipper Lige Bartle, I figgered Skipper Joe ought to know 'twas comin', so I excused myself as best I could and got out. Uncle Bill shushed me out as far as the door, but I could see he was anxious to get back to his TV. He asked me didn't I think it was a wonderful thing. I agreed with him, then hurried down to wake up Skipper Joe and warn him to get goin' next mornin' early, before that high pressure struck us.

* dory: small, flat-bottomed boat with sharp bow and stern

** komatik: long sled adapted for winter travel and hauled by dogs

AUNT SOPHY

WHEN I STARTED THIS, IT was my intention to keep women out of it, but keepin' women out of anything is easier said than done. Nobody can talk very long about Pigeon Inlet without bringin' Aunt Sophy Watkinson's name into it, so this might be as good a time as any to tell you about her.

Aunt Sophy, as everyone calls her, is a daughter of Grampa and Grandma Walcott. She got good learnin' when she was growin' up and was a schoolteacher for two or three years before she married Tom Watkinson. Poor Tom was drowned on the Labrador a couple of years later and Aunt Sophy supported herself and her little girl, Soos, by keepin' boarders. She's got the best boardin' house on the coast and, besides, nobody in Pigeon Inlet would think of takin' in a boarder unless Aunt Sophy sent to tell them she was filled up. The Clergyman, the Magistrate, the Mountie, the Welfare Officer, the Nurse, and the Fish Inspector all stay there when on their rounds, and then in summertime she gets a few travelling agents. Then again, in late years we've had a few sports come to catch salmon in Bartle's Brook. But I'll tell you more about that another time. Let's get back to Aunt Sophy.

Now, 'tis just as well for me to own up to it, because you'll find it out sooner or later, that there's a lot of talk around

Pigeon Inlet about me and Aunt Sophy. Especially since her daughter, Soos, married Bill Irwin and went with him to Corner Brook, where Bill works in the cement mill. There's Aunt Sophy livin' by *herself* and there's me livin' by *myself* and I suppose people must have somethin' to talk about. Anyway, they don't mean no harm, but there's no truth in any of it, at least not yet.

Of course, me and Aunt Sophy are civil to each other and bid each other the time of day when we meet and all that. Then again, a month ago Aunt Sophy remarked to Skipper Joe Irwin's wife about "that poor Mr. Mitchell up there livin' by himself with no one to cook his meals or sew on a button for him." Of course, Skipper Joe's wife told everybody – includin' me.

Now, I'm not the best cook in the world, but I can sew on a button as well as the next one. Still, I've managed to go around all the past month with a button off the jacket of my best suit and a dozen times out of the corner of my eye I've seen Aunt Sophy lookin' at it and I could see that her fingers were itchin' to get out her needle and thimble. All right, too! That's a good way to have her.

Then again, we're about the right age, although to tell the truth, I can't seem to find out exactly how old Aunt Sophy is. Everyone knows my age. I'm fifty-... well, the prime of life. But how old is Aunt Sophy? Tell me that!

She dropped a hint by accident the other night when we were talkin' about last year's Coronation. She said she still had the badge that was given out to all the schoolchildren at the Coronation in 1910. Then she caught herself, blushed a bit and said that of course it wasn't only schoolchildren that got those badges, there was also a few extra given out to take home to the babies and the children that were too young to go to school. That night after I was in bed, I got to thinkin'. If Aunt Sophy was goin' to school in 1910 when she got that badge, she must be fifty at least. But if she was a baby at the time and her big sister brought it home to her, she might be as young as forty-three. A big difference. A real big difference.

Next day I made the mistake of askin' Grampa Walcott. "Grampa," I said. "On a fair shake, how old is your daughter, Sophy?"

"Mose," he said, "of course I know the answer, bein' as how I'm her father, but the way I figger, Soph's age is Soph's own business."

Well – that was that, but next night I tried another tack. I was sittin' down with Grampa and Grandma Walcott in their front room and there was the old family Bible lyin' on the table. I figgered that a peep at the fly-leaf of that Bible'd tell me Sophy's age all right, so I reached over unconcerned like to pick it up, when Grandma quicker than you'd believe possible for a woman her age forestalled me. "Here, Mose," she said, "if you're in the mood for readin' a bit of Scripture, take this small Bible. That big one is kind of clumsy to hold up." And that was that.

But for all her good points, Aunt Sophy's got her faults. There's a lot of things we men get fun out of that Aunt Sophy don't approve. I'll give you an instance. One evenin' last winter I heard over the radio that the Mountie had gone to St. John's for three or four weeks. So I went and borrowed Sam Bartle's five-gallon keg. I figgered what Mounties don't know'll never hurt them and I was goin' to put down a little drop of – but perhaps I shouldn't talk about such things. Anyway, comin' home with the keg under my arm, I met Aunt Sophy.

"You must be a dear lover of molasses," says she.

"No," says I, without thinkin'. "Don't use a gallon in the run of a year. Why, Aunt Sophy?" says I.

"You must be layin' in a five-years' stock," says she, lookin' hard at the keg. "You must think the price is goin' up," says she.

There was a look in her eye that made me feel like I haven't felt since Granny caught me stealin' bakeapple jam. I flustered a bit, then I looked at the keg under my arm as if 'twas the first time I'd even seen it.

"Bless my soul," says I.

"Yes?" says she.

"Sam Bartle's molasses keg," says I. "How did I ever get hold of that? I must've taken it by mistake."

So I turned tail back to Sam Bartle's and I didn't get that keg until two nights later, when everybody in Pigeon Inlet (especially Aunt Sophy) had gone to bed.

RABBITS

I WANT IT UNDERSTOOD THAT Grampa Walcott, our oldest citizen, is a truthful man. If such a thing is possible, he's *too* fond of the truth. He's so fond of it that sometimes he stretches it a bit to make it go further. Like last fall, the night that fisheries man was here from the mainland boardin' at Aunt Sophy's and he invited me, Grampa, and Skipper Joe up for a yarn and to share his hospitality.

The trouble was, his hospitality give out about half past nine, but Skipper Joe disappeared for a minute and come back with a gallon jug. By that time, the yarn was well under way so nobody, not even the mainland man, noticed the difference. Or, if he did, he certainly give no sign of it.

He was a Mr. Mc... a strange name, but no matter now, because by that time he was insistin' we'd call him Bill. Anyway, it settled down to where he and Grampa were doin' most of the talkin'. Me and Skipper Joe just put in a "ha" or a "ho" every so often, 'cause with Grampa present, we could take the night off and leave it to him to uphold the reputation of Pigeon Inlet.

Grampa said that the stupidest animal in the woods was the beaver, an animal stupid enough to put his head into a snare and keep on pushin' ahead into it instead of backin' out. Bill informed Grampa that the beaver was highly thought of on the mainland, bein' a sort of symbol of the average Canadian, and that Newfoundlanders, bein' new Canadians, shouldn't speak disrespectful of their national animal. Besides, he said, the beaver was very industrious.

Grampa said bein' industrious only made it worse, and that the best thing a stupid animal could do was to be lazy, and thereby do fewer stupid things. Bill said as how the beaver was very useful to humanity, and Grampa said yes, but only by bein' skinned. As a new Canadian, he hoped that wasn't the case with most of his fellow countrymen. But to be patriotic, said Grampa, he'd take it back about the beaver. Besides, there was another animal in the woods almost as stupid, the rabbit. And he hoped that, as a Canadian, he was now on safer grounds. Bill assured him he was, so the talk settled down on rabbits. They both agreed, as good sportsmen, that 'twas downright shameful to take advantage of a rabbit's stupidity by snarin' him, and Bill told how one time up on the mainland he'd actually killed and skinned a rabbit with one shot of his bow and arrow. The arrow'd pinned the rabbit's ears to a tree, and it had been goin' so fast that it jumped right out of its skin.

Well, fortunately, the jug was makin' the rounds at the time, so Grampa had a minute to recover from *that* one. But one good swig and he was ready.

One solitary rabbit, he said, wasn't worth the time a man'd waste crouchied* down with a bow and arrow waitin' for him to come along. "Bill," he said, "I had a better plan years ago. I'd find an old tree stump in the woods, with a crank in it, stick a head of cabbage down in the crank, then scatter a handful of pepper over the stump and go home and go to bed. A rabbit'd come along, tug at the cabbage, stir up the pepper, start to sneeze, and he'd sneeze so much he'd beat his brains out agen the stump. Next mornin'," said Grampa, "you'd hardly see the stump for the dead rabbits piled around it."

Well, that'd have finished most visitors we have come here, but I'll say this for Bill, he had it about him. He signalled for the jug, and thereby got a chance to refresh hisself for another try. "Grampa," he said, "the only thing wrong with the scheme of yours is that it *kills* the rabbit, and the only true and sporty way with rabbits is to catch 'em alive. My favourite way back home," he said, "is to get a box about the size of an egg crate, with a door in one end and a head of cabbage in the other. The rabbit comes along, sees the cabbage in the far end of the box, goes in through the open door, tugs at the cabbage, which has a string fastened to it, and when he tugs, the string pulls the door closed. You come along next mornin' and there's your rabbit, alive in the box."

There was only one left in the jug, and for me or Skipper Joe to have touched that would've been as bad as if an Israelite had broken a piece off the handle of David's slingshot. So Grampa downed it.

"Bill," he said, in a half-hurt tone of voice, "I didn't know we were talkin' about *live* rabbits. But since we are, let me say there are two things wrong with your way of catchin' 'em. First, you catch only one at a time. Then, you lose a whole cabbage by it. My way used to be to dig a deep hole either in the ground or the snow, and bury a empty molasses puncheon** so that the open end'd be just flush with the surface.

Then," said Grampa, "I'd trim a bit off the head of the puncheon, fasten a iron rod to it, and lay it across the open end, so that 'twould tip up or down as soon as anything touched it. Right fair in the centre of that puncheon head, I'd fasten a head of cabbage and I'd go home and go to bed. A rabbit'd come along, see the cabbage, and step on the head of the puncheon. 'Twould tip down, and he'd drop in, and the contraption'd come back into place, to wait for the next rabbit."

"I s'pose," said Bill, "the puncheon'd be full of live rabbits next mornin'?"

"Not only that," said Grampa, "but I'd have to come early. Otherwise, after it got full, the cover couldn't tip down, and the rest of the rabbits that hadn't got caught'd eat that head of cabbage. And part of the game," said Grampa, "was to cook that same cabbage with your rabbit dinner."

We went home after that. Bill wished us good night, and said that if ever he was here for another talk, perhaps, after all, we'd better discuss beaver.

* crouchied: squat, bent down close to the ground

** puncheon: a large cask for liquids, fish, etc.

JETHRO NODDY

ONE THING I'M ALWAYS AFRAID of is that I'll get you tangled up by tellin' you about too many people at the one time. There are two more characters I've got to tell you about before you can get a proper insight into the goin's-on in Pigeon Inlet. In a way, these other two characters are related, although one of' 'em is a two-legged character and the other is a four-legged character. The two-legged one is Jethro Noddy and the four-legged one is Jethro's billy goat, King David.

I think I'll tell you about Jethro Noddy first, although in some ways King David is a more interestin' character.

When I told you a while ago that the men in Pigeon Inlet were the finest and hardest-workin' in the world, I've got to own up that I was forgettin' about Jethro Noddy. I suppose every place has got one odd one – who's not quite so hard-workin' and industrious and independent as the others. I know they've got one in Hartley's Harbour and they had one in the place where I lived on the Sou'west Coast. In bigger places they've probably got two and in a place the size of St. John's I wouldn't be surprised if they had three or four. Anyway, Pigeon Inlet got Jethro Noddy.

Now, let's be fair to Jethro. 'Twould be a sin to call him

lazy because off and on he can work as hard as any man in the Inlet. Only he don't stick to it, and when he gets a few quintals of fish caught or a few dollars earned he slacks up right away. I can't guarantee the truth of this, but Levi Bartle, the merchant, tells how he wanted his fish store swept out one day and he asked Jethro, "How would you like to earn a dollar?" And Jethro said, "No, thank you, sir, I've got one." That story mightn't be exact gospel, because Mr. Bartle stretches it sometimes, but 'twill give you an idea.

And it wouldn't be fair to call Jethro a good-for-nothin'. After all, he's got a wife and eight children. But he's no good on his own. He's got to be workin' under someone else, and even then you've got to watch him. Joe Irwin tells a story about how Jethro was helpin' him build a wheelhouse on his boat and Skipper Joe saw Jethro usin' a hammer to drive in a two-inch screw. Skipper Joe bawled at him and asked him didn't he see the slot in the head of the screw.

"Oh, yes, Skipper Joe," said Jethro, as he give the screw another belt with the hammer.

"Isn't that slot there to be used puttin' the screw in?" asked Joe.

"No, sir," said Jethro.

"What's it there for, then?" bawled Joe.

"For takin' it out, sir," said Jethro.

Like I said, he's not much good on his own. This spring he's salmon fishin' with Luke Bartle. Then he'll be a share-man* in Skipper Joe Irwin's trap skiff. After that you'll see him and his biggest boy out in their punt on fine days handlining in shoal water. Other times you'll see him goin' in over the hills with his trout pole. Then he'll pick up a few dollars if any sports come to fish for salmon in Bartle's Brook. They all want him for guide because he seems to know all the salmon in the pools just as well as if he was one of 'em. Oh, he'll get by, all right. It might be a tight pinch – but he'll do it.

The clergyman was preachin' a few Sundays ago about bein' happy. He said it wasn't always what you had in this world that made you happy. It was what you could learn to do without. That fits Jethro sure enough.

I'll never forget how Jethro put one over on me one day last spring – and my leg is not too easy to pull. I was busy tryin' to finish a herring net and I had a few turn of birch wood in my backyard that I wanted to have sawed and clove. So I thought I'd ask Jethro to do it. 'Twas near the middle of the month, so I figgered the Family Allowance was runnin' short and he'd need a dollar or two. So I said:

"Jethro, how much will you charge me for sawin' up that bit of birch wood?"

Jethro looked at me, then at the pile of wood, then back at me. "How much?" he said.

"Yes, how much?" said I.

He looked at the wood again – walked around it – you wouldn't know but what he was a qualified scaler. Then he looked back at me. "'Bout three parts of a cord, isn't it?" he asked.

"'Bout that," said I. "Now, how much will you charge?"

"Nuthin'," he said.

"Nuthin'?" said I.

"Not a cent," he said.

"But," I said, "Jethro, you can't do that. It's kind and

neighbourly all right, but you with a wife and family – you need a dollar or two like the rest of us. What'll you charge for sawin' it?"

"I won't charge nuthin' for sawin' it," said he.

"Why not?" I asked. "You must have a reason."

"Yes," he said, "Mose, I've got a reason. The reason why I'm not goin' to charge 'ee anything for sawin' it – is that I don't intend to saw it." And off he went.

Well, like I said, Jethro's a character. There's no harm in him and his only fault is that he's the owner of the other character I've got to tell you about – the four-legged one, King David the billy goat. If you think Jethro Noddy is a character, wait till you hear about King David.

* shareman: member of fishing crew who received a stipulated proportion of profits from a voyage

KING DAVID

I'VE MENTIONED KING DAVID before, but perhaps I ought to give more particulars so that everybody'll know who he is. Grampa Walcott says 'tis hard to believe that there's anyone in the world that don't already know all about King David. But like I tell Grampa, it's a big world.

Now, anybody that didn't know any better might say that King David is only an old billy goat, like sayin' the Atlantic Ocean is only water. King David is more than just a goat. I wish I could express it. But 'tis like I heard two round-trippers say last summer down on the Government wharf when the *Kyle* was in. They was takin' snaps of him (from a safe distance) and one of 'em said didn't King David add a tone to the place and the other said yes, but she'd call it atmosphere. And if strangers that barely know him think things like that about him, what must we think of him here in Pigeon Inlet that have knowed him as far back as anyone can remember?

Grampa Walcott says it must be over twenty years ago since King David ever left the place even to go in over the hill. Before that he used to be missin' for a day or two every fall while he made his little annual visit to Hartley's Harbour, but late years he appears to have the same opinion of Hartley's Harbour as the rest of us. So day after day you'll see him here, generally formin' a picket line all by himself alongside any house where his nose tells him there's pork and cabbage cookin'. Naturally, every other good goat in the place respects his picket line until he's had his pick of the vegetable scraps that are put outside the door. Then he sort of decertifies himself and the others move in.

How old is King David? I dunno. Nobody appears to know. What I mean is that nobody in Pigeon Inlet remembers a time when King David wasn't here. Even Grampa Walcott says that as far as he knows King David was always here. Of course he had to be born sometime, but whenever it was, nobody had an idea he was goin' to live so long. Otherwise they'd have marked his birthday down, perhaps not in the family Bible, but somewhere. But then, who'd have thought it. No doubt he wasn't much different from the other goats, but look at him now!

Jethro Noddy owns King David, that is if it is correct to say that an animal like that can be owned by anybody. But it is Jethro's goat's house that he goes to every evenin' to lie down. Jethro thought for a spell that he ought to get some recognition from the authorities. 'Twas back when we got Confederation and recognitions was easier to get than they are now. Jethro applied on King David's behalf for somethin' on the grounds that, since everybody was bein' looked after, why not King David who certainly was a senior citizen. His neighbours all told Jethro that he wouldn't get anything, but like Jethro said, there was no harm in askin', and besides, with an election goin' on at the same time, who knows? Well, he got nothin', even though Grampa said he could give an affidavit about King David's age. Jethro even decided to get a grant out of somethin' called "Historic Sites and Monuments" 'cause, like he said, if King David wasn't a historic site, he had never seen one. He wrote three or four letters before he even got an answer, and when he did, it said there was a lot of goats like King David over in a place called the Rocky Mountains, and if you give it to one you have to give it to all. Like Jethro said, 'twas poor satisfaction. He'd seen pictures of those Rocky Mountain goats and they were not to be compared with King David.

I asked Grampa once how King David come to get his name. Grampa said he was christened by a young clergyman that afterwards went away to the First World War and never come back. In those days, there was no fence could stop King David and no law neither. Skipper Jonathan Briggs (Pete's father) had court work over it the time the goat jumped in over his fence and devoured all his cabbage. Skipper Jonathan had a lawful fence, but then as Uncle Sol Noddy claimed and proved in court, the goat had a lawful yoke. Skipper Bob Killick, the magistrate, suggested as how Uncle Sol might use a bigger yoke, but Uncle Sol said such a thing would be downright cruel and, rather than do it, he'd have to get an opinion from the Supreme Court.

But this clergyman who seen the fence what the goat jumped over – yoke and all – said he ought to be christened King David after a famous character in the Bible who was a wonderful great hand for jumpin' over walls. Grampa asked him wouldn't it be disrespectful comparin' an old goat to a character in the Bible and the clergyman said 'twas a Christian duty for someone to give that goat a name, 'cause up till then everybody was callin' him by whatever name first come to their lips, and some of the names wasn't fit to be called on a fish culler.*

I asked Grampa how come King David hadn't gone the way of all goats and made a Christmas dinner for the Noddy family years ago. Grampa explained 'twas just another example of puttin' things off till 'twas too late. Uncle Sol was actually goin' to have him for Christmas one year, but one day that fall King David broke into Joe Prior's dog pound where he kept his team for carryin' the mail wintertimes. Well, says Grampa, after poor Joe with the neighbours' help had rounded up his dogs from where they were scattered, we examined King David lookin' for what the newspapers called "minor cuts and bruises." But these dogs hadn't left a dent on him.

'Twas then, said Grampa, that in spite of hard times Uncle Sol figgered that even if King David could be killed for Christmas, which was doubtful, one thing certain is that no oven could roast him. So since then we've let nature take its course.

* fish culler: person who sorted fish into grades by quality and size

Dogs

TODAY I'M GOIN' TO TELL YOU somethin' about the dogs in these parts, and especially about the damage they've done. Of course, dogs never have done and never will do half the damage to people and property that is done every year by motor cars, but still they do get into mischief sometimes. The worst case in the history of Pigeon Inlet was what happened to Sam Bartle's wife Maggie about three or four winters ago. There's no doubt about it, Maggie got a good nip from one of Fred Prior's dogs and it might have been a lot worse if Fred hadn't been right alongside when it happened. Fred got rid of the dog that did it and Maggie's leg healed up all right, so that was that.

'Twas only the following winter that Maggie took sick one night and Fred Prior went with his dog team through a blizzard to Hartley's Harbour for the nurse. Then the next day Fred took her to the mercy flight airplane at Pummelly Cove Pond. She got to Gander Hospital just in time. Doctor said her appendix was ruptured, and another hour would've been too late. There must be ten or a dozen people alive today in Pigeon Inlet who'd have been in their graves long ago only for dogs. So when we go abusin' the dogs for the few times they bite somebody or somethin', let's give 'em credit for the good things they've done. Like Grampa Walcott says, there's two sides to every account and Maggie Bartle agrees with him.

And now I must tell you about one dog that tried to bite once too often and met his match. He was foolish enough to tackle King David. Of course, any self-respectin' Pigeon Inlet dog would have had more sense than to tackle King David, but this was a Hartley's Harbour dog and he didn't know any better. Well, he soon learned.

It was one day last winter when Sam Grimes come up with his dog team to bring the nurse up to Phil Watkinson's wife on a confinement case. Sam had his dogs hitched on under Phil's flake while the nurse was doin' her duty, and a crowd of us men were standin' around by Phil's stage door waitin' for news. Phil was hopin' that, bein' as how he's got all girls so far, there might be a change for the better this time, when who should walk along by Sam Grimes's dog team but King David.

Sam has got all his dogs named after different products he hears advertised over the radio. There's Ex-Lax. That's his leader. Then Flydead, Whiffit, Dimp, Vicks, Dragon's Blood, Life Saver, and three or four more of them. They're a great team and Sam brags that his leader is the fastest-movin' thing on the shore. Well, this dog, Whiffit his name was, got wind of King David, which wasn't much trouble, chewed off his traces, and took to go after King David down the road. King David just quietly turned round and faced him, while we fellows instead of interferin' just watched the fun. After all, Whiffit was a sort of foreigner from Hartley's Harbour, and besides, whatever he was goin' to get was no more than he deserved for bein' what the newspapers'd call the aggressor nation.

Whiffit circled around King David and tried to bite him in the hindquarter. Though what good he hoped that'd do was more than we could figger, because King David's hindquarter is certainly too tough for a dog to chew. But, be that as it might, King David was too smart for him and the next thing we heard was a string of yelps from Whiffit as King David put the horns to him.

Whiffit ran up under Sam Bartle's flake for refuge with King David after him and that's all we saw of the fight. We could hear Whiffit's yelps for a minute or two, and then out he come with his tail between his legs and made a beeline up the hill straight for Hartley's Harbour. King David come out just afterwards chewin' his cud as if nothin' had happened and went on about his business down the road. We were all so interested that we didn't hear Aunt Sophy until she called out to us three or four times to tell us that Phil's wife had a nine-pound boy.

Sam Grimes told us a month later that he had to make away with Whiffit because every time his dog team'd get near Pigeon Inlet, Whiffit would stop pullin' ahead and try to sheave* astern. Phil wanted to call his boy David, but when his wife found out the reason she wouldn't hear of it.

Fred Prior can tell yarns by the hour about his experience with dog teams. Fred believes that dogs can understand human language and that if you cuss on 'em they'll go faster. There's one yarn he tells about the time he brought the clergyman from Pummelly Cove – but perhaps I'd better not tell that one. Anyway, I've just got time to tell you one of Fred's yarns. Fred was bringin' a travellin' agent on his komatik from Hartley's Harbour one year first week in April. 'Twas a chilly day and the agent was a cranky kind of fellow, findin' fault with everything.

Well, Fred had an old bearskin that he used to keep his passengers warm and he tucked his bearskin around the agent with the fur part, of course, on the outside. They hadn't gone a mile before the agent bawled out to Fred.

"Stop the dogs," said the agent.

Fred brought the dogs to a halt. "What's the trouble, sir?" he asked.

"Turn this bearskin the right way," said the agent. "Don't you know you always ought to use a bearskin with the fur part turned in toward your passenger?"

Fred did as he was told, but just as he was tuckin' the rug around the agent with the fur part on the inside, Fred began to chuckle to himself.

"What are you laughin' about?" asked the agent.

"Well, sir," said Fred, "I'm laughin' to think what a fool that bear was. He wore that skin all his life and I don't suppose he knew first or last that he had it on inside out."

Like I said, Fred Prior is a character.

* sheave: turn or reverse direction

Airplanes

SOME PEOPLE ARE AFRAID OF some things and other people are afraid of different things altogether, and generally speakin', most of us are a bit scared of anything we're not used to. Take airplanes, for instance.

I've heard tell how some places in Newfoundland no bigger than Pigeon Inlet see airplanes passin' overhead two or three times a day. I suppose we're a bit off the track, because we hardly ever see one like that, and up till a few years ago, except for the boys who'd been off to war, the people in Pigeon Inlet weren't much used to airplanes at all.

Now, of course, 'tis different. Every once in a while we see planes goin' overhead takin' some poor sick person to a hospital, and a scattered time one pitches right here in our harbour. Sometimes it brings fish experts lookin' for information. Other times it's to bring a doctor or to take away a patient. So we're gettin' a bit used to airplanes now, but some of us are still a bit scared, as I'll tell you in a minute or two.

Now, as you know, there are two kinds of machines we see flyin' around. One kind got its crankshaft stuck up through the roof and I understand they're called helicopters, but we generally don't bother – we call 'em all airplanes. Like Uncle Bobby Tacker said the first time a helicopter come to

Hartley's Harbour to pick up a sick woman. Next day Uncle Bobby come up to Pigeon Inlet and we asked him wasn't there an airplane down around his place yesterday.

"Well," said Uncle Bobby, "in one way 'twas what you might call a airplane and in another way it wasn't. To tell the truth," he said, "'twas a airplane, but 'twas only a young one – not fully growed and it wasn't able to fly proper. I allow," said Uncle Bobby, "'twill take that one two or three more trips before it can fly end on, the way 'twas intended to."

Then there was Aunt Paish Bartle. When they went to take her away to the hospital the fall before last, she said no, she wasn't goin' to get aboard that thing. After a spell they persuaded her, but first of all they had to promise they'd let her sit up by the door. "Because," she said, "I'm not goin' to take any chances. If," she said, "we get up there in the sky and anything goes wrong with that thing, I don't intend to run any risks. I want to be right by the door so that I can open it and walk out."

Grampa Walcott was worse than that. The same fall, Grampa took an awful pain and we figgered 'twas his appendix, so we wanted to wire for an airplane. But Grampa said no. He said he'd skippered his own schooner for fifty years and had put in many an hour hove to on a lee shore. But he said the trouble with those airplanes, you were always on a lee shore and you couldn't heave 'em to under a double-reefed mainsail if anything went wrong, or drop an anchor neither.

Anyway, 'twas lucky that Grampa's appendix was all right, and all he had was a pain in the belly. So we didn't have to get the plane after all.

But the worst of all as far as airplanes was concerned was Jethro Noddy. It happened the fall before last, late in November. There was a draft of wind in from the Southeast peckin' snow and there was a few birds flyin', so most of us were out in our rodneys* tryin' to knock down a bit of fresh meat, makin' sure of course not to kill any of these turrs** by mistake. Then the wind chopped from the Nor'west smack off shore and we all scurried for the harbour. It wasn't until the rest of us were in safe and sound that we noticed Jethro Noddy was missin'. He'd been off by himself, outside of most of us, and he hadn't been able to make the land.

Well, there it was, gettin' dark and blowin' too hard for anything to go out after him. All we could do was wire for an airplane to come and then we did what we could to cheer up Jethro's missus and try to make her believe she'd see him again, in this world. The forecast said the storm was likely to last three days.

Well, next mornin' the airplane arrived to search for poor Jethro. We told the pilot that Jethro's only chance for salvation was an island about three miles off. 'Tis small and low-lyin' and bare as the palm of your hand. If Jethro hadn't managed to get ashore there, he was a goner for sure. The pilot said if Jethro was on Murre Island he'd drop him a bundle of grub and dry clothes and then go for a helicopter to bring him home.

Three days runnin' that airplane searched before it give up, but all it ever saw was Jethro's punt (or one like it) upside down on Murre Island. No sign of Jethro or any other livin' thing. So we hoisted the flag half-mast and the plane went back to Gander.

The wind died away that night and next mornin', when I looked out through my bedroom window, what should I see but Jethro rowin' his rodney in the harbour – as unconcerned as you please.

Yes, like he told us afterwards, he'd been scared to death for fear the airplane would see him and come down to take him aboard. So he'd spent the last three days crouchied under his punt until he was sure the plane was gone back to Gander. Besides, he said, he had a few turrs that he'd shot by accident, and what these airplane fellows didn't know – well, they couldn't tell the Mounties.

* rodney: small round-bottom boat with square stern

** turrs: seabirds hunted as food

MAKIN' A SHOW
OF OURSELVES

WITH GRAMPA WALCOTT GONE off to Nova Scotia aboard the salt-bulk schooner that left here last week, there's hardly anything goin' on here worth talkin' about. And if I hadn't almost made a show of myself berry pickin' last Saturday, and if Skipper Joe hadn't made a show of hisself by bustin' out laughin' in church last Sunday, I wouldn't have any news at all.

First of all, let's take Skipper Joe's case, laughin' out loud in church right in the middle of the sermon. I know 'twas an awful thing for him to do and it goes agen my grain to publish it, another man's downfall, but bein' as how the story has spread to Hartley's Harbour already and goodness knows how much further, Skipper Joe give me permission to tell the whole story in the hope that once you got the rights of it you won't be too hard on him.

Now there's two things about Skipper Joe you've got to understand before I go any further. In the first place, you can be with that man day in and day out for years and never see him crack a smile. 'Tis not that he's not just as happy inside as anyone else, but well, he says, it's the fault of the salt water. There's been so much of it beat into his face during his lifetime that it's all stiffened up. But that's a misfortune, because a good-tempered man like Skipper Joe ought to smile, otherwise the fun in him will get all bottled up and when it breaks loose 'tis like an explosion like it was last Sunday in church. But I'm comin' to that.

Another thing about him is the way he follows the sermon, listens to every word and follows the meaning right from beginning to end. It's what you might call a good habit for a man to have. He's the only one I know that has it. But as it turned out, that's what led to his disgrace last Sunday night and, to make it worse, the clergyman was here personally and the place was packed.

Well, the clergyman was preachin' his sermon, and no mistake it was a humdinger. In between spurts of almost dozin' off, I was followin' kind of close, here and there. It was about what a useless thing noise was, how some people talk too much. I glanced over at Aunt Emma Jane Bartle out of the corner of my eye to see how she was takin' it, but she was lookin' as unconcerned as you please, perhaps not hearin' a word he was sayin'.

Then I must have lost track for a minute, knowin' of course what he was sayin' didn't apply to me, when the next thing Skipper Joe burst out with this laugh what almost shook the kerosene lamps loose from their moorin's. He couldn't seem to stop. Then he grabbed his cap, stuffed it into his mouth, and got out through the door somehow, but some of us left behind and sittin' near the door could swear we heard him at it again all the way down the hill.

Well, as soon as the hymn started, Skipper Joe's missus got

up and went out, but whether it was in shame or to see if Skipper Joe had gone off his head, we didn't know. Then, the minute church was over, I hurried out to see how he was gettin' on, and I could see Emma Jane Bartle hurryin' home, no doubt to get to the telephone to tell the news to Hartley's Harbour.

Well, I found Skipper Joe down in his stage, where he'd gone to get clear of his missus and to hide away until the worst of it was over.

"Skipper Joe," I said. "Whatever in the world made you do it? Was there somethin' in the sermon struck you as funny?"

"Uncle Mose," he said, with his head hung down miserable-like, "'twas a wonderful sermon. All that about noise bein' not much use, and people talkin' too much without sayin' anything worthwhile. And then best of all was the part about how the most beautiful things and the most wonderful things goin' on in the world don't make any noise at all. Like he said, did any of us ever hear a flower bloom, or a dawning break? All very well, but then he asked did any of us ever hear yeast workin'. And," said Skipper Joe, "when I thought of the hours I spent with my ear right down close to my keg listenin' to it tiss, then how could I help laughin'."

Well, maybe he could help it and maybe he couldn't, but for sure I couldn't help what happened to me last Saturday. I can't describe it 'cause I don't know myself exactly what did happen. I do know that Aunt Sophy and the two girl teachers she got boardin' with her wanted to go up in the Arm berry pickin', and with Grampa gone nothin' would do them but I had to take them up in motorboat, then bide up there with them for protection, they said.

But if the truth was told, I needed the protection more than they did. In the first place, there was no need of goin' in half as far as we did, because there was plenty of berries right out by the landwash.* Then, why did these two girls get separated from me and Aunt Sophy away in the woods? They said they got lost, but I noticed they were back to the motorboat before we got back and they were gigglin' behind my back all the way home and castin' hints about what was me and Aunt Sophy doing in there by ourselves so long and Aunt Sophy not sayin' a word to stop them.

Come to think of it, what *was* me and Aunt Sophy doin' in there by ourselves? Aunt Sophy was pretendin' that she knew the way back to the boat better than I did, and then the two of us by following what she called the short cut, we got astray. So that between walkin' and sittin' down takin' spells, it was goin' on for dark before we got back.

And I've heard Aunt Sophy's mother, Grandma Walcott, brag about how Sophy knows the berry pickin' grounds like the palm of her hand. It goes to show. A single man isn't safe in these parts, not even at such a harmless thing as berry pickin'.

* landwash: the seashore between high- and low-tide marks

OPERATIONS

I SUPPOSE ONE OF THE MOST aggravatin' things that can happen to a man is to have an operation and not to be able to tell everyone about it. I had a little operation myself last week, and bein' as how the nature of the operation was – well, I can only talk about it to what you might call a select audience like Grampa Walcott and Skipper Joe and Pete Briggs, and I make sure that they won't spread it any further. 'Twasn't much to it, and since I can't give all the particulars, perhaps I shouldn't mention it at all, so as not to give a wrong impression.

Like the wrong impression Emma Jane Bartle got when she married Luke. She was Emma Jane Grimes then, livin' in Hartley's Harbour, and Luke had just come back from overseas where he'd been in the war. He'd been wounded – not very serious but enough to talk about, and one night when he and Emma Jane was courtin', he promised her that after they got married he'd show her the place where he got wounded in the war. Well, Emma Jane misunderstood him and went around braggin' about as how Luke was takin' her to France on their honeymoon. She said afterwards she was some mortified when she did see the place where he'd been wounded, especially as how Luke never did pretend to be much of a hero anyway.

But while I'm on the subject of operations, and even though my own isn't worth tellin' about, I might say that we've had some awful important operations in this place. Perhaps the one that comes foremost to my mind is Uncle Benjy Bartle's. Uncle Benjy is the sexton in our church, a job that he's had for years now ever since the time he got back from the hospital where he'd had the operation. The way the congregation figgered, the few dollars that goes along with the sexton's job would be a great help to poor Uncle Benjy, considerin' the awful handicap he had to go through the rest of his life with. And even now that he's gettin' his Old Age Pension and could do without the salary, people figger 'twould break his heart if he had to give up bein' sexton and so he holds on to the job in spite of his shortcomin's.

Besides, we're used to him, but it must seem odd to strangers meetin' him first. Why, only a week or two ago there was some round-trippers come ashore for a walk from the coastal boat and, wantin' to see all the sights, they walked into the church to have a look around. Uncle Benjy was sweepin' out the church porch, gettin' her ready for next Sunday. The visitors got a bit of a start when they spotted him because he only got the one eye. That's what his operation was about. But he went inside with them while they looked over the church and everything went all right till one of 'em asked him how many people the church could seat. Uncle Benjy scratched his head for a minute and said he didn't know. They must've thought that strange because they asked him again how come he didn't know. And Uncle Benjy said nobody knowed how many the church could seat 'cause they'd "never had 'en vull."

But to get back to his operation. 'Twas ever so many years ago that he went away to St. John's to the hospital and had the eye took out. And when he got back he was a hero. It even took the wind right out of poor Aunt Polly Bartle's sails because, even she, with all her operations had to admit that she'd never had anything to compare with this. And so wherever Uncle Benjy went there'd be a crowd to fuss over him and tell him what a wonderful experience he must've gone through. Now up till that time, nobody ever took much notice of Uncle Benjy and so all this was a bit new to him and he couldn't help likin' it.

Perhaps that's why one night when a crowd of the neighbours was gathered in his kitchen askin' him what the operation was like and didn't it pain somethin' awful, Uncle Benjy spoke up and said, "Boys," he said, "you don't know the half of it, and bein' as how you're all so interested, I might as well give you the whole story. I wouldn't tell this," he said, "but you'm all so interested that I can't keep it from 'ee any longer. Do you know," he said, "that when a doctor takes out one of a man's eyes, he got to take out both of 'em and put the good one back in again after?"

Well, that was somethin'! If Uncle Benjy was a hero before, what about now? Uncle Benjy went on to explain that a man's eyes was so connected up inside that that's what had to be done. Of course, with the bad eye gone, the doctor had no trouble tightenin' up the nut on the other one to fit it in place.

"And did he take out your two sure enough?" someone said.

"That he did," said Uncle Benjy.

"Are you sure?" they asked.

"Sure I'm sure," he said.

"But how do you know?" they asked him.

"'Cause," said Uncle Benjy, "I seen the two of 'em plain as anything on the table."

Well, 'twas only a week after that he got the job as sexton of the church, 'cause like Grampa Walcott said afterwards, a man like that was entitled to the best the community had to offer.

EELSKINS

EVER SINCE I CAN REMEMBER, I've heard people talkin' about what they call "the vast untapped resources of Newfoundland" and how, if they were properly tapped and handled, we'd all be well off. Especially around election times, the crowd tryin' to get in always blames the other crowd for neglect of those "untapped resources" and promises to tap 'em good and proper once they get in charge. I've even heard politicians go so far as to promise *two* jobs for every Newfoundlander, just by the proper handlin' of these resources.

Most of us have great faith in our politicians, and so we've waited and are still waitin' for them to turn on the tap. But once in a while you find a ordinary common Newfoundlander tryin' to do somethin' his own self. A good example is Uncle Matty Rumble who lives up in Rumble Cove, about five or six miles from Pigeon Inlet.

Uncle Matty lives alongside Rumble Cove Brook, and up and down that brook right past his door twice a year swims what he considers one of our "vast untapped resources" – eels, thousands of 'em. Oh, they don't all get by him, because, like he says, he dearly loves a meal of fried eels, and bein' as how they'll fry in their own grease, it's a savin' on fatback.

But that's not the important thing. It's the eelskins, and a few years ago Uncle Matty figgered that if he could save up all the eelskins and find a market for them, he'd stand a fair chance of endin' up – well, perhaps not a millionaire, but a thousandaire for sure.

Well, the upshot was that one day last year Uncle Matty come down to Pigeon Inlet and told me confidential-like that he had a barrel chock full of pickled eelskins and was lookin' for a buyer. Lige Bartle, our local merchant, naturally wasn't big enough to swing a deal that size, so Uncle Matty had been writin' letters to Job Brothers and Bowring Brothers, two firms that he'd heard a lot about, but they didn't seem interested. Another outfit he'd heard tell of was the Christian Brothers, but with a name like that he didn't expect they'd be in the fish business anyway.

But Uncle Matty wasn't licked yet. No, sir. Just as he was in Bartle's shop goin' to buy some rope to make a tacklin' for his pony for the winter, the idea struck him. Why waste money on rope? Why not make a tacklin' – completely out of eelskins? Then by next year this time he'd be turnin' out eelskin ropes by the hundreds. So he went home and made a complete outfit all ready for when the time come to tackle up his horse and slide and go in for a load of firewood. The eelskins he used hardly made a dent in his barrel, so he figgered if this worked out he'd be able to supply all the lumber camps in the country.

So early one winter's mornin' he tackled up his outfit. The eelskin ropes were a bit stiff from the frost, but that didn't matter very much and off he went. His slide path went in straight from his house, upgrade a little, for about a mile.

There he cut his load of wood and put a bit extra aboard to give his new outfit a proper test, and started off for home. He walked alongside his horse's head and never bothered about lookin' back. The horse seemed to find the goin' a bit heavy and Uncle Matty was kept busy encouragin' her to pull harder, so they made slow but steady progress towards his house at the other end of the slide path. Meanwhile, 'twas gettin' warmer every minute.

What Uncle Matty *didn't* know was that the warmer it got the more the eelskins stretched. And so, when he got his horse by his back door and looked around to admire his fine load of wood, there was no load to be seen, not a stick, not even a empty slide. Lookin' back into the distance, all he could see (or thought he could see) was two white threads about the size of #40 sewin' cotton straight along the slide path and about two feet off the ground. His eyesight wasn't good enough to see his slide-load of wood, but be knowed very well where it was – right at the other end of these two threads.

Well, Uncle Matty figgered to himself, if eelskin ropes stretch during the day, they'll shrink up again when it gets frosty again that night. So he made the horse go round and round his house five or six times, tied a knot in the two threads with another eelskin, put away his horse, went into the house, and had his supper. 'Twas gettin' frostier every minute and Uncle Matty went to bed and to sleep, knowin' full well that by the time he woke up next mornin' his load of wood'd be by his back door.

That must've been a bitter frosty night. Not that Uncle Matty minded, but his old dog was awful restless and Uncle

Matty had to heave the bootjack at him to make him settle down. Apart from that Uncle Matty slept like a log. He always said a good night's sleep was a fittin' reward for a hard day's work, although once or twice he almost woke up thinkin' the house was shakin', but he was used to that happenin' often on windy nights.

Next mornin' he woke and blew a hole through the frost on his kitchen windowpane. And sure enough, there was his load of wood right by his back door. It had worked! That's what come of a man usin' his brains as well as tappin' some of those vast resources the politicians kept talkin' about. Why, he might even end up bein' a politician himself.

But his biggest surprise was yet to come. After he hauled on his clothes and went outside he found that his load of wood hadn't budged an inch from where he left it yesterday. But his house! His house had shifted a mile into the woods during the night. Rememberin' how he hove the bootjack the night before, Uncle Matty was ashamed to look his old dog square in the eye for days.

SAFETY

I SUPPOSE 'TIS ONLY NATURAL, but sometimes I can't help thinkin' that the kind of laws we dislike most are the ones that are made for our own protection. There was a fellow in Pigeon Inlet last summer inspectin' passenger boats to see if they was properly equipped with lifebelts and one thing and another that the law says they ought to carry for the protection of whatever passengers they might happen to have. He didn't bide here very long because, like he soon found out, there's nobody here makin' a regular business of passenger carryin', although anybody'll take anybody else in motorboat to the hospital or the nurse when there's an emergency. But he was a nice, friendly man and I couldn't help askin' him how he was makin' out with his job of tryin' to make us fishin' people safety-conscious, and accordin' to what he told me, he got an awful job on his hands.

In the first place, he says, the travellin' public don't seem to care whether they're protected or not, and if he was to hang up a boatload of passengers just because the boat had no oars, no sails, or fire extinguisher and no lifebelts, the people that'd give him the dirtiest looks would be these very passengers (includin' women and children) that he's tryin' to protect. They don't seem aware of the kind of things that can happen until one of 'em happens, and by that time 'tis too late.

In the second place, the authorities whose job it is to enforce the law and even prosecute those who break it don't seem to take these safety laws as serious as they might. Let a man have a loaded gun aboard his car, or a trout a half-inch below the legal size, and they're down on him like a thousand of bricks. But let another man set out with a boatload of passengers and not have any of the things that the law says he should have for their protection and these same authorities likely as not'll pretend they don't notice it.

As for the men who operate the passenger boats, this fellow told me that in all fairness he had to admit that most of 'em were quite ready and willin' to carry out whatever safety precautions the law told 'em to. After all, like he says, a man who spends a lot of money on a good boat and engine and intends to make a livin' in the passenger business would be very foolish not to spend the other few dollars for proper safety equipment to keep him on the right side of the law and make her safe, not only for his passengers, but for hisself as well. But there's still a few that don't seem to recognize a risk even when they're takin' one, and to prove his point he told me a story about somethin' that happened to him a few years ago when he first come around on this job of safety inspection. Naturally the law was new then, and nobody knowed about it, so each boat was equipped accordin' to each boat owner's idea of safety.

The one he hired to take him around was no better than the rest, so he thought he'd convert that crew first, not only for his own protection but to sort of set a good example.

Well, they done all he told 'em to and set out on their trip. Like the two men aboard the boat told him, they were safety-minded and they figgered this new law was a wonderful fine thing.

Well, the first night, they anchored in a little cove where there was no livyers and after supper they started playin' cards on the cabin table by the light of the kerosene lamp that was hung overhead. After a spell, he got tired playin' cards and decided to turn in to his bunk, and perhaps read a book till he got sleepy. They offered to shift the lamp up nearer to his bunk but he told 'em no, to keep it where it was for 'em to play cards by. Then they said they had nar other lamp aboard, but they could fix up a candle for him and he said all right. So he got into his bunk and they stuck the candle into the bunghole of a keg and propped it up by his bunk where it give him all the light he wanted for readin'. He noticed when they were settin' it up that the bunghole was a bit too big for the candle, but after softenin' it a bit they got it to stick in place all right.

By and by the two-man crew finished card-playin', blowed out the lamp, and turned in. He noticed his candle was almost burned down but thought he'd finish the chapter he was readin', 'cause 'twas an adventure story and awful excitin'.

But just then, as one of the men was already snorin', the other one spoke up and said, "Mister, is you gone to sleep yet?"

"No," he said. "Why?"

"'Cause," said the fellow, "I just thought of somethin'. You'd better blow out that candle before you dozes off. You see, we might run across a few turrs on this trip and all our bit of gunpowder is in that keg."

"Well," said the inspector, "there never was a candle blowed out any quicker than that one. And come to think of it, I never did finish that chapter from that day to this. The adventures in it didn't seem so excitin' after that."

GRAMPA'S ONLY
SICKNESS

ON SATURDAY NIGHT I WAS up to Grampa and Grandma Walcott's house, listenin' to Grampa's new radio. There they were – the two of them – in their own little parlour with their slippers on, not a care in the world, better off than they ever were in their lives, listenin' to the News Bulletin. By and by, when the news was finished, Grandma said, "Turn it off, now, Grampa, until the Gospel Singer comes on." Grampa switched it off and we began to yarn.

"Grampa," says I. "I can't figger you out at all."

"How's that, Mose?" says Grampa.

"Well, Grampa," says I. "Here you are and Grandma. You've worked hard all your lives. But now – what with the pension and all – you needn't work anymore. Why is it you still keep on fishin'? You caught twenty-five quintals last summer, didn't you?"

"'Bout that, more or less," agreed Grampa.

"But why do you bother about fishin' at all?" said I. "You don't have to. And Grandma doesn't have to help you."

"No," said Grampa, "in one way we don't have to work anymore. But there's other ways of lookin' at it. In the first place, we like work. Perhaps we're old-fashioned. But we think that while people are workin' they're really livin'. But after they give up workin', well, they're more or less just lyin' 'round waitin' to die."

"And," chimed in Grandma, "in Pigeon Inlet there's no other work for Grampa to do, only catch fish, and there's no other work for me to do, only look after him and help him make his fish."

"But the Old Age Pension?" said I.

"Yes, Mose," said Grampa. "The Old Age Pension is a blessin' sure enough, and I'm thankful for it. But as far as I can see, somebody got to work and produce somethin' or else there'd be no Old Age Pensions and no money to pay Old Age Pensions with. So, I feel that I ought to help these people who've got to work by doin' a bit of work myself. I sort of feel that it's a way for me to say 'Thank you' for my pension – and Grandma's, of course."

"But suppose you got sick or crippled up with rheumatism," said I. "What then?"

"Ah," said Grampa, "that'd be different. Then I'd have to give it up. But I'm not sick or crippled neither."

I looked at them, Grandma readin' away at the *Family Herald* while Grampa looked at his watch to see if it was nearly time for the Gospel Singer. "Ten minutes yet," he said.

"Grampa," said I, "were you and Grandma ever sick in your lives?"

Grampa chuckled while Grandma tried to look angry by glarin' at him over her spectacles. "Grandma was," he said. "She was laid up five times since I married her."

"Five times," said I. "When was that?"

"Hush your foolishness," said Grandma, but Grampa paid no heed to her.

"Yes," he said, "five times. Three girls and two boys."

"Oh," I said.

"Now," said Grandma. "Tell Mose about the one time you were sick."

"Aw, never mind that," said Grampa. "'Twas not worth talkin' about anyway. Just a pain in the stummick."

"If you don't tell him," said Grandma, "I will."

So I got the story out of them bit by bit – the story of Grampa's one and only spell of sickness – and then, as he said, 'twas only a stomach ache. Here's the story the way I got it.

It was one night in the Christmas season about ten years ago. Grampa and Grandma finished their dinner about one o'clock and there was some cabbage and gravy left over. Grandma was goin' to throw it out to the pig, but Grampa persuaded her to put it away in a bowl on the pantry shelf for him to eat suppertime, about six o'clock that evenin'. Meantime, Grampa was goin' out for an hour or two with Captain Lige Bartle, Skipper Joe Irwin, and the boys who were makin' a celebration. Grandma warned him to be home by six o'clock or the pig'd get the cabbage and gravy. She wouldn't leave it lyin' around a minute later. Then after Grampa went out, she washed the dishes, washed her night-cap, and put it to soak in a bowl of starch right alongside the bowl of cabbage and gravy on the pantry shelf.

Grandma waited until seven o'clock before she lost her patience. Then she grabbed one of the bowls (the cabbage and gravy, she says) and emptied it out into the pigsty.

Grampa tiptoed home around twelve o'clock that night and didn't light a lamp for fear of wakin' Grandma. But he was hungry. So he groped his way to the pantry, and gobbled down (so he says) the cabbage and gravy he found in the bowl. Well, that's the night he had the awful stomach ache, and he twisted and turned all night until it passed off towards daylight.

Next mornin' Grandma found that her nightcap was gone. The question was – who ate it, Grampa or the pig? Grampa always maintained it must have been the pig, and of course the pig can't speak to defend himself. Grandma maintains it was the cabbage and gravy she gave to the pig.

I'm inclined to believe Grandma. After all, the pig didn't give any sign that he had a stomach ache, while Grampa that night had the only one he ever had in his life – and by all accounts, an awful one it was.

Uncle Sol Noddy
and the Law

A FEW DAYS AGO, GRAMPA Walcott and I got to talkin' about the youngsters nowadays and how they are not half as bad as we fellows were when we were their age about forty years ago. I'd like to tell you what he had to say about it.

"Mose," he said. "The difference between the boys here in Pigeon Inlet and the boys in these bigger places that you hear about over the radio is that the boys here have got somethin' to do. Now that they go to school more regular than they used to, they can always find somethin' to occupy their time. There's rabbit slips to tend to in winter. Then in over the hills troutin' in the spring, while in summertime they can always get plenty of activity around the boats and engines.

"Now, take St. John's," said Grampa. "I remember when my daughter Mary was bringin' up her family there. Her young fellow, Jim, had her worried to death. He was always gettin' into mischief and she was beginnin' to figger he'd never amount to anything. Until what happened? He started to sell newspapers in the mornin's and it made a little man of him. Of course," said Grampa, "he was a little man all the time, but he hadn't had any way of showin' it.

"Boys," said Grampa, "are much about the same every-where. They need somethin' to occupy their minds and keep 'em out of mischief. And here in Pigeon Inlet, they've got a better chance to keep occupied than in a bigger place.

"And," said Grampa, "it's not only the youngsters that are gettin' more sense. It's the grown-up people, too. Of course," he said, "that's only natural. Better boys'll grow up to be bet-ter men. You take the men here in Pigeon Inlet. We've got a lot more sense than we had forty years ago."

"That's right, Grampa," said I. "I remember how you've told me before about how the people here killed off all the lobsters back then. We wouldn't be as foolish as that nowa-days."

"No," said Grampa, "indeed we wouldn't. And not only that. We're wider awake in a lot of things. Forty or fifty years ago, we had to believe whatever someone told us. Take the price of fish. I remember one year just after I got married the price of fish dropped right down to next to nothin' – and we had a bad time that winter. All the reason we got for the price of fish bein' so low is that there was cholera in the market. Imagine that! Cholera in the market. There's a lot we still don't know about fish markets, but someone'd have to give us a better excuse than that nowadays."

"But, Grampa," said I.

"Yes, Mose," said he.

"Grampa," said I, "when you talk about how much more sense the men have got now than what men had years ago. Aren't you forgettin' somethin'?"

"What?" said he.

"What about Jethro Noddy?" said I.

"Ah, yes," said Grampa. "There's Jethro Noddy. And lookin' at Jethro makes it hard for any man to figger that the world is gettin' better and that men are gettin' more sense. But," said Grampa, "did you know Jethro's father, Uncle Solomon Noddy?"

"No," said I.

"Of course you didn't," said Grampa. "Uncle Solomon died before you come to Pigeon Inlet. Uncle Solomon was a hangashore.* And the one good thing you can say about Jethro Noddy is that he's a better man than his father was. True enough, Jethro is no better than he ought to be, but at least he's not a hangashore like Uncle Solomon was."

"Uncle Sol must have been pretty bad," said I.

"Bad was no name for it," said Grampa. "Listen while I tell you about the time he was up before court for nettin' Bartle's Brook.

"In those days," said Grampa, "we used to salt our salmon and sell it by the tierce, and 'twas always a surprise to us how well Uncle Sol used to do with the salmon. Then we got to rememberin' that Uncle Sol's oldest daughter, Luce, was married to the river warden, and Uncle Sol always had a good chance to know what nights the warden'd be on Bartle's Brook and what nights he'd be down to the river in Hartley's Harbour.

"Anyway, one night the policeman was in the place and he hid away by the path and watched Uncle Sol and young Jethro come home from Bartle's Brook with a brin bag full of salmon each. He followed 'em back on their second trip and found 'em with their net out in Pummelly Pool. Well, the magistrate come next day and fined Uncle Sol ten dollars or thirty days. Uncle Sol asked if he could have a bit of time to pay the fine, because this was the time of year when a poor man had the best chance to earn a few dollars. The Magistrate allowed him a month and Uncle Sol said he figgered that'd be time enough. So that was that.

"Well, less than a week later, Uncle Sol had another tierce of salt salmon packed in his stage. He sold it to the Tradin' Company for ten dollars and paid his fine.

"Now," said Grampa, "what people wanted to know is – where did he get his salmon? All that week it had been a blank for the rest of us. And another thing we noticed. Uncle Sol's son-in-law was away all that same week – awful busy on the river down in Hartley's Harbour."

* hangashore: idle, mischievous person

LOGGIN'

LOOKIN' AT PIGEON INLET these days, you wouldn't think that the people here make much money out of the lumber woods – and we don't. The only loggin' done nowadays is when somebody cuts a stick or two for his own use and saws it in Levi Bartle's sawmill. Levi says he only keeps the sawmill there as a convenience to the public. He used to let us saw our stuff on the halves, but now oftentimes he tells a fellow to go right ahead and just pay for the gasoline. That's about all the loggin' we have any connection with – except for cuttin' firewood.

Years ago, though, accordin' to Grampa Walcott, 'twas a different story and there used to be no less than three different kinds of loggin' where a fisherman could pick up a few dollars to help stand against a poor fishery and tide him over the winter.

In the first place, there was the pulpwood cuttin' every winter and Grampa says 'twas a bad day for the coast when they started cuttin' pulpwood summertime instead of wintertime. After that happened, a man had to be either a lumberman or a fisherman. He couldn't be both of it. But before that, almost half the men in Pigeon Inlet used to go in over the line every fall as soon as fishin' was over, and come back just in time to get ready for fishin' again. 'Twas a great help! Then, in the second place, there was cuttin' sawlogs. Back forty years ago, old Josiah Bartle, the father of our present merchant, Levi Bartle, used to saw a lot of lumber every year and employ a lot of Pigeon Inlet men every winter cuttin' sawlogs. In the third place, old Josiah for four or five years runnin' had a contract for pit props. Cuttin' sawlogs and pit props for Josiah didn't pay quite so well as pulpwood, but 'twas nearer home and a lot of fellows preferred it for that reason.

Grampa loves to get into arguments with younger men about conditions in the lumber woods nowadays compared to what it was forty or fifty years ago. One thing he agrees on is about the flies. Grampa says anyone can have the lumber woods for him, since it's a summertime job, in among the flies. He'd rather haul up a sixty-pound graplin a thousand times than cut one stick of wood in summer. But except for that one thing, he thinks loggers nowadays got a picnic compared with back then. One day last week, we got into an argument down in Skipper Joe Irwin's net loft and finally we got Grampa started tellin' us yarns about lumberin' years ago. Here's one that he told. Of course, I'm just tellin' you what he told us. I'm not prepared to guarantee the truth of it.

'Twas around forty or fifty years ago, said Grampa, that old Josiah Bartle had a contract to cut pit props for four or five years runnin'. First year, they cut the props just above Bartle's Brook, only two or three miles away, so they could go in every mornin' and come home each night. But, by the third year, they had to go in about eight or ten miles. So they told Skipper Josiah if he wanted 'em to cut pit props that distance from home, he'd have to put a camp in there, a place where they could sleep at night and eat before and after the day's work.

Skipper Josiah begrudged the expense but he realized he had to do it, so he built the camp and hired Solomon Noddy, Jethro's father, to be the cook. So, accordin' to Grampa, one Monday mornin' late in November, Josiah took his crew, about ten of 'em, into the camp so as they could start wood-cuttin' right away. When they come to examine the camp, they was stunned. But Skipper Josiah didn't give 'em much chance to criticize. He started right in.

"Now, boys," he said, "there's your camp. 'Tis not a mansion, but there's a nice floor to sleep on. 'Tis dry, and 'tis as clean as you mind to keep it. Besides, as you can see, there's a stove for Uncle Solomon to cook on and keep you warm and comfortable."

"But, Mr. Bartle," said one of the fellows.

"Yes, yes," said Josiah. "What is it now?"

"You've got no windows in it," we said.

"Windows!" barked old Josiah. "What do you want with windows in a loggin' camp? Never heard the like. Windows in a loggin' camp! Nonsense!"

"I don't know," said Jonathan Briggs. "Seems to me there's windows in all the houses I've ever seen. To let the light in."

"Yes, but not in a proper loggin' camp," said Josiah. "The way it is, men, you'll all be up and out of it before daylight and you won't be back to it till after dark. Then Sundays you'll all be gone home anyway. So, how will you know whether there's any windows in it or not?"

And, said Grampa, do you know he never put windows in that camp first or last.

"Grampa," said I, "I suppose he was right. You didn't miss the windows, did you?"

"No," said Grampa, "we didn't. That is, the rest of us didn't except for poor old Solomon Noddy, the cook, who was in the camp all day long and Sundays too. Mostly in the dark, because 'twas too cold to leave the door open and Skipper Josiah was too stingy to allow him enough kerosene oil to keep the lamp lighted in the daytime. So Uncle Solomon had to put up with the dark and try to get used to it."

"Did he get used to the dark?" I asked Grampa.

"Yes, Mose, he did," said Grampa. "In a way of speakin', he got too well used to it. Without knowin' it, that first winter, he got to be like a cat – able to see better in the dark than in the light. In fact," said Grampa, "a funny thing happened in his house the first night after he got home. That night, his missus went across the road to visit a neighbour and when she come back 'twas pitch dark in the kitchen, but she could hear Uncle Solomon hammerin' away with his tack hammer, so she struck a match to light the lamp. Uncle Solomon bawled at her to blow it out. He was tappin' a pair of boots and he asked her how in the name of goodness she expected him to see how to do it if she lighted the lamp. So she had to blow it out again while he finished the job. He gradually got over it, though," said Grampa, "and by the middle of the summer, he could see just as well in the light as he could in the dark, or perhaps better."

My Suspicions of Skipper Joe

I GOT A SUSPICION THAT Skipper Joe don't want to see me get married. I don't know why, because he's a married man and as happy as most married men can expect to be. Now, if 'twas Lukey Bartle instead of Skipper Joe I'd understand it and figger that poor Lukey, married as he is to Emma Jane, was doin' it with good intentions. But Skipper Joe! Still I've got this suspicion that he's doin' his best to put a pothole or two on the path of true love between me and Aunt Sophy. Only I wish he'd come straight out with it and no back doors, instead of bein' what the storybooks call "subtle."

Take for example that night two or three weeks ago after I'd given Aunt Sophy the bakeapples I picked in on the Big Brown Bog, for her to jam up for me on the halves. Well, that evenin' just before suppertime, I was passin' her house when she come out to her gate and said, "Uncle Mose," she said, "I'm doin' up the bakeapples after supper. What about droppin' in some time tonight to get your share?"

"What time," said I, "will they be ready?"

"Oh," she said, "around ten o'clock or thereabouts."

"Well now," said I, "I'd love to, but 'tis kind of late for me to come callin'."

"My, Uncle Mose," she said, "after how you worked to pick those berries, you not only deserve your share of jam, but you're entitled to come for 'em any hour you wish. I'll be expectin' you," she said, givin' me the pleasantest look I've ever seen on a human face.

Skipper Joe happened to walk along while we were talkin'. He just passed the time o'day and kept right on walkin', but as things turned out afterwards, I know he must have heard every word we said, especially that bit about me goin' up to Aunt Sophy's house that night at ten o'clock.

Anyway, that evenin' just before dark a crowd of us were standin' around on Levi Bartle's wharf yarnin' about one thing and another. I watched my chance and slipped away to go home. Skipper followed me and, instead of goin' home, he came right to my door. "Uncle Mose," he said, "I s'pose there'd be no harm in me droppin' in for a minute."

"Well," said I, "Skipper Joe, you're always welcome, but I got somethin' special to do later on tonight."

"Oh that's all right," said he, "I only want to talk to you for a minute."

Well, we went into the kitchen, and I remember glancin' at the clock on the mantelpiece. I could've swore 'twas half past nine, but when I come back from the bedroom with the lamp from where I'd left it after the night before, I looked at the clock again and 'twas only half past eight.

"Yes," said he, "I've been noticin' how fast the evenin's are closin' in."

"I think," said I, "I'll turn on the radio to make sure my clock is not slow."

"Yes, said he, "but not yet for a minute, I've got somethin' to talk to you about."

Well, that turned out to be a long minute. Skipper Joe is not usually a very talkative man, but this night he could talk the leg off an iron pot, and every subject he brought up, he wanted my opinion on it too. Time passes quick that way, but by half past nine (by my clock) I was beginnin' to wish the cats had him. Then, a quarter to ten, Skipper Joe said, "My! Look at the time, I must be gettin' home."

As soon as he went, I crawled into a clean shirt, screwed down the lamp, and set out for Aunt Sophy's. I didn't go far – no further than my own back door, and then I stopped, because Aunt Sophy's house was in darkness. And so was every other house in Pigeon Inlet – except my own. Well, I went back in and did what I should have done long before. I turned on the radio and found 'twas exactly eleven o'clock. So I set my clock right by puttin' her on an hour and went to bed.

Next mornin' 'twas too windy for fishin', so after breakfast I went see Grampa Walcott. 'Twas my intention to tell him the whole story and ask him to explain to Aunt Sophy and tell her how sorry I was. But no sooner was I in Grampa's house than over she come and 'twas no trouble to see that she had her dander up. She took no more notice of me than if I'd never been there, but she laid three bottles of bakeapple jam on the kitchen table.

"Father," she said, "if you ever run across somebody by the name of Uncle Mose, give him these. They're his share –

like he was promised." Grampa pointed towards me and tried to head her off, but she wasn't to be stopped. "Tell him," she said, "if you see him that there's someone in this world that believes in keepin' promises, even if he don't."

"But Soph," said Grampa, "don't you see Uncle Mose?"

"No," said she, "I don't see him. And that's only half the story." And out she flounced and went home.

Well, I told Grampa and Grandma the story and they agreed I should go right over and tell it to Aunt Sophy. Like Grampa said, "Soph got a temper, but she's not one to bear malice."

So over I went and knocked on her back door. I heard her say, "Come in." So, cap in hand, in I went. 'Twas kind of dark in the back porch, and the second step I made I heard the squawk from the cat. I'd trod on his tail again. Aunt Sophy opened the inside door, grabbed up the cat, and looked at me. I could see her fillin' up like Back Cove during a southeaster, but the words wouldn't come out. So I done the only thing left for me. One thing for sure – Skipper Joe will never get a taste of that bakeapple jam. I'll get *that* much satisfaction.

TAKIN' ADVANTAGE
OF KINDNESS

I'VE HEARD IT SAID THAT THE longer you live the more you learn. And that's certainly true if you happen to live anywhere alongside a man like Grampa Walcott.

Yesterday evenin', just gettin' on towards duckish,* I was just finished clearin' up some firewood when Grampa walked along, and seein' me there he opened the gate and come in. He sat on the woodhorse, so I upended the choppin' block and made myself comfortable while we got to talkin' about one thing and another.

Next thing I knew a couple of young fellows about six or seven years old come into the yard, and one of 'em said, "Uncle Mose, would you like for us to full up your woodbox?" I said, "No thank you boys, I can full it up my own self." That's all the attention I paid to 'em. I didn't look at 'em close enough to notice who they were, although I fancied one of 'em must have been Lukey Bartle's young fellow, 'cause he got foxy hair, and takes after his mother Emma Jane, who's the only foxy-headed woman in Pigeon Inlet.

Well, after I'd said "No thank you" to 'em, they said, "What about your woodbox, Grampa?" and Grampa said,

"Sure, boys, go right ahead, and save my poor old arms the trouble." Then off they went as happy as larks, callin' out, "Thank you, Grampa." Grampa just waved his hand to 'em.

"Mose," said Grampa after they were gone, "I never had you figgered as bein' a selfish man."

"Selfish?" said I. "What in the world have I done now to make you think I'm selfish?"

"Why wouldn't you let the boys full up your woodbox?" said he.

"I didn't want 'em to," said I. "I'd rather do it myself."

"You didn't want 'em to," said he, "but they wanted to do it. Of course, you had the final say. So it ended up the way you wanted. Kinda selfish, I thought."

Now, 'tis not easy to get huffy with Grampa, but for a minute I almost give him a saucy answer. Instead, I just said real quiet-like, "All right," said I. "What good would I have done 'em to let 'em full up my woodbox?"

"Oh, I don't know," said he. "They'd know that. Perhaps they've got nothin' else to occupy theirselves with, and bein' active young fellers they've got to be doin' somethin'. Or perhaps," said he, "they're tryin' to do a good deed every day and they've just remembered they're a few days behind on their quota. What odds about that," he said. "The main thing is they wanted to do it. Why not let 'em?"

"But," said I, "'twould only be takin' advantage of their kindness."

"What else is there to do with kindness," said he, "only to take advantage of it?"

"I dunno," said I. "I'd never thought of it in that light."

"There's not too much kindness in the world," said he,

"and if we don't take advantage of it when 'tis offerin', the only other thing is to douse it by throwin' cold water over it."

I was beginnin' to feel ashamed of myself, but Grampa wasn't finished yet. Perhaps he wanted to cheer me up a bit. "Of course," said Grampa, "there's such a thing as reason and moderation in all things, and I've known people go too far in acceptin' offers of kindness just as I've known people go too far the other way. The saddest case I ever knew about," said Grampa, "was poor old Uncle Matty Rumble. He was one of these fellows, somethin' like yourself, who didn't want to take advantage of anyone's kindness – always afraid he might be puttin' someone out. Why, I've known him to come down here from Rumbly Cove on a bit of business and be around here all day without a bite to eat, just because when we'd invite him in for a cup of tea he'd say no thank you, 'twas very kind but he didn't want to be a trouble to us.

"I remember one time," said Grampa, "it must've been thirty or forty years ago, I was carryin' the mail, and this winter's day I was on my way from Pigeon Inlet to Rumbly Cove with my team of dogs and the mailbag tied onto the komatik. It wasn't a heavy load because that was long before Confederation and we didn't have any of these big catalogues like we do nowadays.

"Well, I was makin' good time along the trail to Rumbly Cove when I spied Uncle Matty Rumble ahead of me. He was on his way home with a bag of hard bread on his back that he'd just bought from Josiah Bartle's shop. He was bent down double with the weight of the bag of hard bread, and he still had three or four miles to go. So I stopped the dogs and told him to get aboard. He said no thank you, Uncle Ben, he didn't want to be a burden to me – but 'twas more than kind for me to make the offer.

"Well," said Grampa, "I couldn't leave him on the trail like that, so I bawled at him and made him get aboard. After hummin' and hawin' a bit, he got in the stern of the komatik, I got up in front, and we carried on. I was so busy bawlin' at the dogs that I paid no heed to Uncle Matty until we neared Rumbly Cove. I spoke to him but he didn't answer. I looked back, and there he was sittin' in the rear end of the sled with that bag of hard bread still on his back and his eyes nearly poppin' out of his head with the strain. I told him to put down the bag but he said no, that 'twas bad enough I had to carry him – without carryin' his bag of hard bread too. And he kept that on his back till I put him off at his own back door."

* duckish: dusk, twilight

MULDOON'S COVE

NEXT TIME YOU OPEN UP your map of Newfoundland, take your pencil and strike out the name of Muldoon's Cove.

Muldoon's Cove is gone. Oh, the Cove is still there, with its kelp-covered rocks stickin' out of the water at low tide, with the mussel beds almost barrin' off the entrance to it. And the beach is still there where the water was so shoal that stageheads* had to reach out nigh a hundred feet to find depth enough to tie on a punt. And the cleared land is there, land cleared with back-breakin' work a hundred years ago and tilled by four generations of Muldoons, Shannahans, and Cassidys. And the ruins of their houses are still there and of the little school chapel where they worshipped as late as twenty years ago.

And Uncle Paddy Muldoon's house still stands there as staunch and sound as when his father, old Danny Muldoon, built it eighty years ago – and every piece of board in it sawn in the saw pit. And a lot of happy remembrances hang around there for all those of us who ever had the pleasure of stoppin' there for an hour or so while passin' through. But, as far as the world is concerned, Muldoon's Cove is finished – done with – and if you can find it on your map, why, just cross it off. As far as Muldoon's Cove, the settlement, is concerned we buried it last Thursday, the day we buried its last livyer, Uncle Paddy Muldoon. Like Grampa Walcott said to me last Wednesday when we were gettin' ready to go down to Uncle Paddy's wake, "Mose," he said, "'tis not just a man we're wakin' tonight. 'Tis a place, Muldoon's Cove, and a fine place it was, too."

I've heard tell how there's about 1,300 little places scattered around the coast of Newfoundland, and I've heard these same people say how we'd be better off if we didn't have so many of these little places, but that people should get together in fewer but bigger communities. I suppose the people who talk that way'll be kind of glad to hear that Muldoon's Cove is gone and, instead of havin' 1,300 places, we've only got 1,299, since we buried Uncle Pad.

Oh well, maybe they're right. Maybe this centralization or whatever they call it is a good thing, but that makes no difference to us people who used to know Muldoon's Cove when there were folks livin' there – real, live folks, friendly, hospitable.

Muldoon's Cove was a sort of halfway place between Pigeon Inlet and Hartley's Harbour. It wasn't actually halfway as it was nearer Hartley's Harbour, about two miles from it, whereas 'twas about four miles from Pigeon Inlet. Many a time people goin' back or forth overland in wintertime spent the night there when a blizzard was on, and even in fine weather, many a traveller stopped at Uncle Pad's for a spell and a warm-up. I remember stoppin' there once myself with Skipper Joe Irwin when we were on our way home from a Lodge meetin' in Hartley's Harbour.

Uncle Pad, of course, didn't belong to our Lodge, but that

made no difference. He and Aunt Bridget made us welcome. He had a piece of kindlin' wood for a handle on his back storm door with the long end stickin' towards the outside. Somethin', he said, for visitors to get a good grip on.

Anyway, like I said, he made us welcome, like he did everybody that come his way. He played us tunes on his fiddle, tunes he'd learned from his grandfather who'd brought them with him from Ireland a hundred years ago. And, before we left, he made us sample what he called his drop of "Oh, be joyful." Skipper Joe and I didn't ask any questions but we figgered that, even if Uncle Pad had give up keepin' pigs, he still could make good use of his potato skin. Anyway, after samplin' the "Oh, be joyful" three or four times, me and Skipper Joe covered the four miles to Pigeon Inlet like we had springs in the bottoms of our feet. I thought about it last Wednesday night at the wake and I thought to myself, "With a supply of that stuff always in his reach, no wonder Uncle Pad stayed young right up till the time he died."

Well, we waked him in his own house in Muldoon's Cove – 'twas his dyin' wish. We buried him next day in the little cemetery which hadn't been opened since old Fergus Shannahan was buried in it twenty years ago. Yes, ever since then, Uncle Pad and Aunt Bridget have lived there, the only two livyers in the place. Now they're closin' up the house and Aunt Bridget'll be goin' down the shore to live with her daughter. She only agreed to go when they promised to bring her back later on and lay her to rest alongside of Uncle Pad. And, so, for all intents and purposes, that's the end of Muldoon's Cove.

How did people ever come to live in a out-of-the-way

place like that? Well, Grampa Walcott explains it this way. He got it from his grandfather that these people, the Cassidys, the Shannahans, and Muldoons were not seafarin' people at all. They'd been used to the land and so, when they crossed the ocean, they steered clear of the barren cliffs like Hartley's Harbour and picked a spot where there was some land to cultivate. There wasn't much land there to clear, but they made good use of what there was. Grandpa says he saw a old receipt one time dated 1867 showin' that Uncle Mike Muldoon had turned in to his merchant three carcasses of pork and sixteen bushels of potatoes, and had took out in exchange, among other things, a gallon of rum and a barrel of flour.

So that proves Muldoon's Cove was well settled as far back as 1867. But not anymore.

* stagehead: end of fishing flake (extended over water) where fish was landed

ROBINSON CRUSOE

THERE'S NO DOUBT ABOUT IT, if Grampa Walcott had a few years' schoolin' when he was a boy, he'd have likely ended up a Senator or a Royal Commissioner or somethin'. But he didn't. The way he tells it, and there's no one livin' old enough to contradict him, his schoolin' was finished before it ever got started.

He tells how one mornin' when he was six or seven years old his poor old mother fitted him out and sent him off to school for the first and only time. He had a slate, a Primer, and a slate pencil, which was standard equipment in those days. But what ruined it all was that she made him take a little bottle of soapy water and a slate rag to clean his slate with. An all right outfit for a girl, but the boys in those days had a simpler way of cleanin' their slates, not what we'd nowadays call sanitary, and a bit hard on the elbows of your jacket, but still there it was. Grampa knowed the other boys'd torment the life out of him if they seen his bottle and slate rag.

So, halfway through that mornin', his mother went up to the schoolhouse door to ask the teacher how he was gettin' on, and the teacher said he hadn't turned up to school at all. Later that mornin' they found him where he'd crawled right up in under the nor'west corner of the school, where the sills come flush with the ground, and it took Grampa's father and the schoolmaster all they could do with a flake longer* each to prise him out of it. Next mornin' his father took him fishin', which he's been at off and on ever since.

But ten years ago, when that adult teacher was here holdin' night school, Grampa went. He didn't learn how to write, exceptin' his own name, but he learned how to read, especially print, and can read out the words now almost as fast as his forefinger can move across the page. Last spring he started to read his first book. He started just after Easter and finished it last week. Grandma didn't approve. In the first place she said 'twas only a old novel, whereas a man his age should be readin' the Blessed Scripture. And besides, it kept him hangin' around the house under her feet like a broody fowl. Besides, he missed two Lodge sessions and a meetin' of the Fishermen's Local. He'd have missed church too, once or twice, but that Grandma wouldn't stand for.

Anyway, he finished it, and last Sunday evenin' after prayers he told me about it.

"Mose," he said, "did you ever read any books?"

"One or two," I said.

"Boy," he said, "you ought to read the one about Robinson Crusoe."

Well now, I have read *Robinson Crusoe*, but I didn't want to spoil the conversation by sayin' so, so I asked Grampa what the book was about.

"'Tis not so much what the book is about," said Grampa, "although to give him his due, Robinson Crusoe would've made a first-rate Pigeon Inletter. But a book like that," said Grampa, "broadens a man's mind and gives him a bigger outlook. Take my own case," he said. "Until I read that book, I used to think that the man with the biggest appetite in the world was Uncle Sol Noddy. Uncle Sol was our cook on the Labrador one summer, and one night he was cookin' a feed of birds for our supper. We found out afterwards that, while he was waitin' to call us down into the fo'c'sle,** he eat two turrs and a white-winged diver and then had the gall to sit in with the rest of us and eat his regular supper.

"But Uncle Sol," said Grampa, "was a sparer compared to these cannibals that Robinson Crusoe tells about. One day while Robinson was on this island by himself, he spotted a trap skiff full of these cannibals chasin' this other poor fellow in his rodney, and they chased him ashore right into the next cove to the one where Robinson was livin'. Robinson couldn't understand what they were bawlin' about, but he figgered they must be awful mad with this fellow about somethin'.

"The book didn't explain what they were mad with him about," said Grampa, "but it must have been somethin' terrible. Perhaps he was a politician and he threatened to cut off their family allowances or keep back their unemployment money. Anyway, whatever it was, they was goin' to make sure he'd never do it again.

"From where Robinson was hidin' in his cove, he could hear a wonderful hullabaloo from the beach in the next cove, so he went into his cave and got his old swilin' gun down off the rack. He crouchied down on his hands and knees and worked his way along to the bill of the point between the two coves and peeped over. Sure enough, they had this poor fellow caught, and what do you think they was gettin' ready to do to him?"

"What?" said I.

"They was gettin' ready to scoff*** 'un," said Grampa. "Friday and all as it was. And I thought to myself," said Grampa, "here's where even Uncle Sol Noddy would have had to take back water."

"And did they scoff 'un sure enough?" said I.

"They would've," said Grampa, "only just then Robinson let go with about seven fingers out of his old swilin' gun, and these cannibals jumped aboard their trap skiff and made off, no doubt to catch theirselves a Friday fish dinner like they should've had in the first place. And that's what I mean," said Grampa, "about books broadenin' a man's mind. I think next winter I'll read another one."

* flake longer: a long pole used to form elevated surface of platform for drying fish

** fo'c'sle: forecastle, forward part of ship

*** scoff: (v) to eat; (n) a cooked meal

PADDY MULDOON

A WHILE AGO I TOLD YOU about how we buried Uncle
Pad Muldoon, the last livyer in Muldoon's Cove, and how
Aunt Bridget, his widow, had gone down the shore to live with
her daughter. There's no one at all left in Muldoon's Cove
now, and I can tell you it's a sad-lookin' sight now whenever
we pass along there on our way overland to Hartley's
Harbour. There's the old house where travellers were always
welcome. It's nailed up now, with boards over the windows
and across the back door. And there's the piles of rocks that
they made when they were clearin' the land years back.
Grampa Walcott says some people might say these rock piles
are ugly, but he says they're beautiful. He says they're monuments to hard, honest work and he says if he had the learnin'
he'd write a piece about 'em and send it to the papers.
Anyway, enough about that. I'm goin' to talk about somethin'
more pleasant – Uncle Paddy. Even though he's dead and
gone, he left a lot of pleasant things to tell about.

Uncle Pad was the tallest man in these parts and the
thinnest. Of course, I only knew him for the last five or six
years and never saw him when he was properly straightened
up, but those who remember him in his prime say he must've
been nigh seven feet. And no fat on him either. The bedlamer

boys* in Hartley's Harbour used to call him "spare ribs," but not to his face. Ah no. Pleasant and good-natured as he was, one look at him could give you an idea of what he'd be like if ever he lost his temper. He did lose it once – but that's another story.

And those long fingers of his. Nobody in these parts ever did find out how much strength there was in 'em. They tell a story in Hartley's Harbour about how a steel drum of Acto gas had been left lyin' on Elijah Grimes's wharf out in the weather all the winter, and the nuts on the drum got rusty. They tried every size wrench in Hartley's Harbour but couldn't loosen 'em.

Later that day, Uncle Pad, not knowin' about this, come to Hartley's Harbour and Lige Grimes, the merchant, for a bit of a joke asked him to slacken the nut. Uncle Pad took a hold to it with his fingers and twisted. No, he didn't slacken it. 'Twas too rusty. But he broke it off!

The first time I ever laid eyes on him was the day he was here in Pigeon Inlet and lookin' for a passage to Hartley's Harbour, which was nearer his home. The Mountie come in about that time on his patrol down Hartley's Harbour way and asked a question or two, but, of course, on a subject like makin' moonshine, every man in Pigeon Inlet minds his own business.

Then Uncle Pad come along and offered to tell the Mountie who made the moonshine in Hartley's Harbour, provided the Mountie'd take him down there. We heard afterwards what happened. They landed on Grimes's wharf in Hartley's Harbour and the Mountie said, "Now, then, sir, who makes the moonshine in Hartley's Harbour?"

Uncle Pad removed his cap with his left hand, and with a forefinger the size of a banana, he pointed his right hand straight up towards the sky. Then he said, as reverent as if he was in church, "My son," he said to the Mountie, "a young man with your learnin' ought to know it's the same Being makes the moonshine in Hartley's Harbour as makes the sunshine in Pigeon Inlet." Uncle Pad went on about his business then, but not forgettin' to thank the Mountie for the trip down. And all that without crackin' a smile, and the Mountie watched him go and never said a word.

If I'm goin' to tell you much about Uncle Pad, I'll have to work backwards, because 'twas only in his last years that I knew him personally and I'd like to tell what I know from first-hand before repeatin' what I've got from hearsay. The first yarn I want to tell is about somethin' that happened to him – strange enough – after he died. 'Twas this way.

Uncle Pad took sick about six months ago and they got him away to the hospital. 'Twas some trouble in his insides. We never found out the rights of it first or last, but the doctors must have thought they could cure him or they'd have sent him home.

Anyway, for six months we used to hear about him every night over the radio in the local news. The News Bulletin used to say, "Mr. Patrick Muldoon of Muldoon's Cove doing as well as can be expected."

Well, after listenin' to this for over five months, Aunt Bridget wrote a letter in to the News Bulletin. She said there wasn't much news in what they were givin' about Uncle Pad and couldn't they make it a bit plainer. The News Bulletin must have got her letter, but, in the meantime, Uncle Pad had gone to his reward and the radio people must've forgot to check with the hospital about him. Here's what happened.

It was the night of Uncle Paddy's wake. There was a houseful of us there, and Uncle Pad was lyin' so peaceful in the longest coffin we'd ever seen. Someone thought about the News Bulletin and turned on the radio, just in time to hear the fellow say, "Mr. Patrick Muldoon of Muldoon's Cove – resting comfortable."

Aunt Bridget looked down at him and said, "Bless him! He got it right this time. How in the world did he ever find out the news so quick?"

* bedlamer boy: youth approaching manhood (from "bedlamer," young seal)

BRAVERY

LAST SUMMER AMONG THE visitors we had from St. John's was Sam Bartle's niece. Sam's sister is married up there in St. John's and she sent her little girl down with her Uncle Sam for the summer, to get her away from the smoke and the dust and the fumes from the motor cars, and to send her where she could get some fresh air and plenty of good, solid grub. She was a delicate-lookin' little thing about eight or nine years old, but you'd hardly know her by the time she had to go back. But to get back to what I was goin' to say.

She brought one of these bicycle things down with her and 'tis no mistake she could certainly handle it. Our roads are not fit for walkin', let alone bike-ridin', but she didn't seem to mind. She'd come down the lane past my house like a shot out of a gun, and you'd swear that when she struck the lower road she'd go right out over into the landwash and break her neck. But no, she could handle that thing like she was a part of it. We got to thinkin' that she didn't know what fear was.

Then one mornin' I heard awful screeches comin' up from the landwash and I said to myself, "She've done it this time, broke her neck for sure." So I hurried down, and what do you think had happened? This youngster and a few others had been playin' aboard my punt where she was tied on to my stagehead. The others, for devilment, like youngsters will, had climbed out, untied the punt, and pushed her off with this little girl left by herself. And there she was, frightened half to death and bawlin' her head off. It never occurred to her that she was ten times as safe there as aboard her bicycle comin' down the hill.

Now a thing like that sets a fellow thinkin' and brings back to his mind a lot of old stories. As far as I can figger out, what made that little girl so brave one minute and so cowardly the next was that she was used to bicycles, but she wasn't used to punts. She wasn't a bit afraid when she was dealin' with somethin' she was used to, but 'twas a horse of another colour when she got in a spot she wasn't used to.

And it struck me that we're all much about the same, and that a lot of this talk about some people bein' brave and others bein' cowardly is a pack of nonsense. We're all inclined to be a little bit scared of things we're not used to.

First of all, take my own case. Comin' as I did from the Sou'west Coast, I'd been used for thirty-four years to fishin' out of a dory, and when I settled down here in Pigeon Inlet six years ago, it took me a long spell to get used to a rodney. 'Tis all right now, but for a summer or two I was like a cat on hot bricks every time I got aboard a punt. I mentioned to a few of the boys that I had a mind to build a dory for myself, but they talked me out of it. They were just as scared of a dory as I was of a punt and they said if I had a dory the youngsters would be gettin' down aboard of her, like youngsters will, and half of 'em would get drowned. I tried to tell Grampa Walcott that a dory was just as safe as the *Kyle,* but

Grampa said he'd just as soon go afloat in Grandma's washin' tub as go out in a dory, or anything else that had no keel.

So there it is! Whatever you're used to. So rather than cause trouble, I got myself used to my old rodney. Though I must say, she'll never take the place of a dory.

Take Uncle Paddy Muldoon. He had the name while he was alive of bein' afraid of nothin'. But that wasn't the case. He was afraid of somethin'. He was afraid of fairies, although Uncle Paddy used to call them lippery-cons. He said the lippery-cons lived in the woods back of Muldoon's Cove. They were in there by the thousands. They were little men, he said, only a few inches tall although he'd never caught a glimpse of any of 'em except one mornin' early when he went in the woods after celebratin' St. Patrick's Day the day before. I asked once how the lippery-cons got there, and he said that, accordin' to his grandfather, old Shamus Muldoon, there were plenty of 'em back in Old County Galway and a few of 'em must have stowed away aboard the ship that brought the Muldoons, Cassidys, and Shannahans out from Ireland to Muldoon's Cove. They'd multiplied until now the woods up in Shannahan's Droke were full of 'em.

I asked Uncle Paddy what there was about 'em to be feared of and he said nothin', only they were mischievious little devils, and when they were so minded they'd play tricks on a man, make him lose his way and have him wanderin' round in the woods for hours on end. He said there was only one way to outwit them, and that was, first of all, to get a rock that had been boiled by mistake in with a pot of potatoes and keep that rock in your pocket whenever you went in the woods. Then the second thing to do, to be on the safe side, was to turn your cap inside out. That'd fool 'em.

"Uncle Paddy," said I to him that day, "is that the only thing you're afraid of?"

"Yes, me son," said Uncle Paddy.

"But," said I, "what about dyin'? Aren't you afraid of that?"

"No, me son," said Uncle Paddy. "But come to think of it, I'd like to know where I'm goin' to die."

"Why," said I, "what good would that do?"

"Because," said Uncle Paddy, "if I knew where I was goin' to die, I'd never go near the miserable place."

STEALIN' THE HOLES

IN ALL THE YEARS THAT Skipper Bob Killick was magistrate along this shore, the shrewdest piece of court work he had to handle was the time Uncle Sol Noddy stole the two holes from Skipper Lige Bartle.

What good, you might say, is two holes? Not much nowadays, since most people give up keepin' dogs, but years ago – well, how else can a man set a herrin' net under the ice? You cut two holes eight or ten foot apart, tie a rope to one end of a flake longer, poke it down through one hole, and hook it up through the other with a hand gaff. Oh yes, if you want to set a bigger net, you cut three holes or even four.

But two holes was enough to serve Skipper Lige Bartle's purpose that evenin' he was comin' home down the Arm on dog team from his rabbit slips. He chopped his two holes, then hurried home to get his net and a flake longer so as to have it set and home again afore night overtook him. He didn't even stop for a bite to eat, just grabbed a pair of dry cuffs* and was off again. A spry man.

But spry as he was, Uncle Sol Noddy was spryer. Uncle Sol was already there and had just finished settin' his net in Lige's holes. Lige ordered Sol to take that net out of *his* holes. Sol said they was his 'cause he found 'em. Lige said they was his 'cause he'd chopped 'em. Sol said, be that as it might, he owned 'em now 'cause possession was nine pints of the law.

Skipper Lige was a younger man than Uncle Sol and a bigger man, and if he hadn't been a churchgoin' man besides, he said after as how he'd have tied Uncle Sol to his own rope and reeved him down one hole and up t'other. As it was, he went home and wired Skipper Bob Killick, the magistrate, to come immediately or a bit quicker than that if at all possible. Skipper Bob wired back that he'd come and have court work in May when navigation opened. Public opinion was one-sided because Skipper Lige was a respectable man, whereas Uncle Sol was the worst miserable hangashore on the coast. To make matters worse, Sol was doin' real well with the her-rin' and even offered Skipper Lige a meal for Good Friday dinner. I can't repeat Skipper Lige's answer, but it made him feel so low that he missed church on Easter Sunday.

Pigeon Inlet school was packed for court work when Skipper Bob Killick come on his rounds in May and read out the charge how Uncle Sol had stolen the property of Skipper Lige – namely and to wit, two holes. Then Uncle Sol, instead of havin' the decency to confess to what he had done and take what was comin', had the impudence to look the magistrate right square in the face and say he didn't know whether he was guilty or not, and that what he would like to know was "What was the law concernin' holes?" Skipper Bob was took right aback and said he allowed the law concernin' holes was like the law concernin' anything else: you mustn't steal 'em. Then Uncle Sol, brazener than ever, asked how could you steal a hole. Skipper Bob said what did he mean, how could you steal a hole, and Uncle Sol said 'cause a hole – well, a hole was nothin' anyway, only a hole.

All this time poor Skipper Lige was there sayin' nothin', but swellin' up like a gurnet,** ready to bust. Then he said as how a hole might be nothin' to the hangashore that stole it, but 'twas somethin' to the man that had to chop it. But Skipper Bob called him to order, so Lige kept quiet, but he swelled bigger, if that was possible, until Skipper Bob ruled that on this first point Uncle Sol had lost out. A hole *was* somethin'.

"All right then," said Uncle Sol, "I only borrowed the use of his holes, never intendin' to keep 'em, and now he can have 'em back." Skipper Lige said the holes was drove out the bay when the ice went out, but Uncle Sol maintained that holes was only fresh air and water, and they was still up in the Arm and Lige could have 'em and a thousand welcomes. Skipper Bob had to call a fifteen-minute recess then, but after 'twas over he come back and ruled as how Uncle Sol was wrong on account of how, in what he called the Common Law, a hole couldn't be a hole unless there was an edge around it.

Then Uncle Sol tried his last dodge. He said as how a man couldn't steal anything without shiftin' it from where he found it, and he hadn't shifted them holes an inch. Skipper Lige said no, Sol hadn't shifted 'em, not 'cause he wouldn't but 'cause he couldn't. If he could've, he'd have slung the two holes over his back quick enough and gone off with 'em. Uncle Sol said, be that as it might, the fact was he *hadn't* shifted 'em. And on that point Skipper Bob Killick had to agree with him.

He give his verdict that, although Uncle Sol hadn't actually stole the holes, he'd trespassed on 'em, and he asked Uncle Sol what he had to say before sentence was passed. Uncle Sol said right cheerful-like that if all he'd done was to trespass agen Skipper Lige, no doubt Skipper Lige, as a churchgoin' man, would be only too ready to forgive those (includin' Uncle Sol) who'd trespassed agen him. And Skipper Lige bust out then for sure, and said he'd forgive Uncle Sol when Uncle Sol give him back his holes, edges and all. And with that, Skipper Bob Killick delivered his judgment. He ordered Uncle Sol to cut two holes the followin' winter in the same place, for Lige to set his nets in, and that was the end of it as far as the law was concerned. Of course Uncle Sol got the best of it in the long run, but that's another story, and like Skipper Bob his own self said the followin' summer when he heard the outcome, he doubted if even the Supreme Count could do much to cure a hangashore like Uncle Sol Noddy. He was one miserable hangashore if ever there was one.

* cuffs: heavy mittens, usually fingerless

** gurnet: gannet – large fish-eating seabird

MY BROTHER KI

KI IS TWO YEARS YOUNGER than me and we both give up school the same year. I was in number 4 book and Ki in number 3. When he was in school, you'd never think he was goin' to end up as one of the biggest building contractors in New Brumsick, but after all, I suppose hundreds of other Newfoundland boys have gone to the mainland and done even better than Ki.

The best time Ki ever had in school, I remember, was one stormy winter's day when Ki went home dinnertime and told Father and Mother the wonderful news that he was second from the top in his class. Mother almost fainted with surprise and Father was so happy about it that I can see him now untyin' his goatskin purse to give Ki a cent for his wonderful progress. I suppose I should have told on Ki and explained to Father and Mother that the reason why Ki was so high as second in his class was that he and Joby Stuckley were the only two there that day. All the rest, mostly girls, were kept home on account of the snowstorm. Anyway, I didn't tell, but I made Ki give me one of the peppermint knobs he bought for his cent.

Well, after leavin' school, Ki took his place in the bow of a Banking dory for four or five years. Then one fall, instead of comin' back to Fortune Bay, he headed west.

For years after that we used to hear from him every six months or so. One time he'd be in the lumber woods up around Millinocket or Bangor, another time he'd be out in the harvest fields. One time he even had a spell oyster fishin', but he soon gave that up. He said he got tired of it because one oyster looked too much like every other oyster. Restless, he was.

Then, by and by, he struck this big place, Toronto, and thought he'd stay awhile. He found out that most of the work was carpenter work and that carpenters were in big demand and gettin' good pay. So Ki figgered out he'd be a carpenter. He couldn't drive a nail straight or saw off an end of board, but he figgered as how anything a Toronto man could do, a Newfoundlander could learn.

So next mornin' bright and early, Ki told a foreman he was a first-class carpenter and went to work. He kept that job until the foreman come around about an hour later and fired him on account of how he was tryin' to saw off an end of board. Ki figgers that that winter he was fired oftener than Father's old muzzleloader. In fact, he was fired off almost every carpenter job in Toronto.

Ki didn't mind bein' fired because he kept his mind made up on two things. First, he'd never get fired twice for the same mistake, and second, that he'd hold each job a little longer than he did the last one. Only once he didn't like bein' fired. That was once when a foreman watched Ki tryin' to fit two ends of moulding in a corner. He fired Ki of course, but not satisfied with that, he called Ki a hard name. Ki laid down the two pieces of moulding and said to the foreman real quiet like: "Mr. Foreman," said he. "You fired me. All right. I've been fired before. Any man that hires me got a right to fire me. But that don't give you the right to call me bad names. So for firin' me, I give you my best respects. But for callin' me bad names, I'm goin' to give you *this*." So he hauled off and let him have it, just once.

He made sure the foreman was only stunned before he picked up his tools and left the place. Next day he learned how to fit two ends of moulding in a corner.

It wasn't till the next winter that Ki learned how to read blueprints, and two or three years before he could draw blueprints of his own, and almost fifteen years before he ended up one of the biggest building contractors in New Brumsick. This was the brother Ki I left to see last month.

He met me as soon as I got off the train in Moncton. I'd never have known him from Adam but he spotted me right away. He said he knew me by my pipe, though I can't see how that helped him because I hadn't had that pipe more than ten years and I hadn't seen Ki for over thirty.

He had a car there right by the station – the longest and lowest car I'd ever seen. I thought she'd be too long to turn the corners, but Ki manoeuvred her around just as well as Skipper Joe manoeuvres his skiff comin' through the Shag Rocks. He took me all the way out to his house, a real mansion. I didn't think much of his missus at first. She was a mainland woman, but she wasn't so bad after I got to know her. One thing I could never understand about that woman was that she'd always get as far away as she could whenever I'd light my pipe. She even offered to buy me a new one, but I thanked her and said, "No, no, my old one is as sweet as a nut, especially with Beaver tobacco in it."

After two weeks, Ki brought me in his car right to North Sydney. He offered to bring the car across the Gulf and take me right to Pigeon Inlet until I explained to him about roads.

So, I've had two weeks on the mainland, and if from now on you hear me criticizin' it once in a while, you'll agree that I know what I'm talkin' about. I've been there.

OLD-FASHIONED GAMES

ONE DAY WHEN GRAMPA and I were talkin' about young people today, I asked him about games. "What kind of games," I said, "did you have here in Pigeon Inlet away back say forty, fifty, sixty years ago?"

"We had lots of 'em, Mose," he said. "I don't know what's come over the younger generation. It seems to me they don't have half as much fun as we used to have. Of course," he said, "they have more of other things to occupy their time than we had in our day. We didn't have any radios to sit down and listen to, we didn't have any comics to read, and we didn't spend our evenin's down to Levi Bartle's drinkin' pop. In the first place, Levi and Josiah, his father, didn't have any pop and, if they'd had any, we didn't have any money to buy it. So," said Grampa, "we had to do somethin' to pass away our spare time. So we had games – lots of 'em. Games that didn't cost any money. The only game that put us to what you might call an expense was bazzin' buttons."

"Doin' what?" said I.

"Bazzin' buttons," said he.

"I can understand the buttons part," said I. "But what was it you said you did with 'em?"

"We used to baz 'em," said Grampa. "Surely you know what 'baz' means."

"I'm afraid I don't," said I. "How did you baz a button?"

"Why," said Grampa, "you'd just bounce it off the corner post of a store out into the road, and the next fellow'd baz his button and try to make it land close to yours. If he could put it so close that he could span the distance with his thumb and finger, he kept the button and you had to find another one to baz with. Sometime," said Grampa, "there'd be eight or ten of us playin' at one time and a fellow who'd win one button could keep right on and try to sweep the board. 'Twas a bit of expense to the fellows who lost, but in those days you could buy a dozen buttons for a cent – when you had the cent."

"But," said I, "what would a fellow do when he lost his buttons and didn't have a cent to buy any more?"

"He'd cut 'em off his trousers," said Grampa. "Why, I remember Paddy Muldoon used to come all the way up here from Muldoon's Cove on purpose to baz buttons. Uncle Paddy figgered he ought to win, seein' as how he had the longest fingers and could span furthest. But 'twas a skilful game and we fellows were too good for him. Uncle Paddy used to walk back home regular as clockwork with his trousers tied up with fishin' line. But he'd be back again a few days afterwards with another stock of buttons – wherever he'd get 'em."

"Grampa," said I, "did you ever try to figger out who started some of these old games?"

"No," said Grampa, "because as far as I can figger out, they were started years and years before I was born. You take another game we had, we used to call it 'Old Cat.' That was a team game and we'd divide ourselves up into two sides, 'Clip and call,' as we used to say. Well, one day a crowd of us were playin' 'Old Cat' when we saw the clergyman comin' along the road. Of course we stopped, half ashamed like, and straightened up so as we could touch our caps to him as he went past us. But he didn't go past us."

"He didn't?" said I.

"No," said Grampa. "He stopped right there in the middle of the road and told us to go on with our game. He wanted to watch us play. And then he told us a funny thing. He said 'twas the first game of' 'Old Cat' he'd seen since he come out from England."

"Oh," said I, "he'd seen it in England?"

"Yes," said Grampa. "He said they used to play it often in the little village where he was brought up. He said that Easter time especially they'd have a real big game out on the green, and just about everybody in the village used to take part in it. This clergyman, he figgered that people who come out to Pigeon Inlet in the first place must have come from around the same part of England that he come from and must have brought out 'Old Cat' with them. He said the same thing about puckin' keels."

"About what?" said I.

"About puckin' keels," said Grampa. "The day that clergyman saw us puckin' keels, he was overjoyed. In fact, he took off his clergyman's jacket, hung it on the fence, rolled up his sleeves, and joined in the game. He was good at it too," said Grampa, "and he showed us things about puckin' keels that we'd never heard about before. And he could knock the middle man out of the pack while standin' almost half a gun-shot away."

"But – puckin' keels?" said I.

"Don't tell me you never pucked keels," said Grampa.

"Never heard of it," said I, "until now."

"Ah, Mose, Mose," said Grampa, "you got a lot to learn."

AUNT SOPHY'S RETURN

AUNT SOPHY IS BACK HOME in Pigeon Inlet after spendin' the winter in Corner Brook with her daughter, Soos, who's married there and got a youngster of her own. Here's a funny thing. Here I've been all the winter missin' Aunt Sophy more than I'd care to let on, and wishin' she was back home, and sometimes even goin' so far as to write her a letter. Very good. But no sooner is she home than I'm in to her black books. Or to put it another way, she's on the outs with me again.

The day the steamer was due, Grandma and Grampa Walcott had Soph's house all opened up and a rousin' fire in to kill the damp and take off the chill. Then when the steamer anchored, I was off with Grampa in his boat to bring her ashore. And as soon as I spotted her on the deck I noticed somethin' funny about her, and of course, havin' no better sense, I had to make a remark about it. Better if I'd kept my big mouth shut, but 'tis too late to talk about that now.

I don't remember that I've ever tried to describe to you what Aunt Sophy looks like and I don't intend to try now. In the first place I'm not at my best when I'm talkin' about women, and in the second place, I figger that how a woman looks is a woman's own business. But I will say this about

Aunt Sophy. She's not one of these women that you can see how to shoot gulls through. She's what you might call a comfortable armful, or to put it in good fishermen's language, she's medium merchantable, or at least that's what she looked like last fall when she left here to go to Corner Brook and that's what I naturally expected her to look like when she came back. But when I saw her comin' towards us on the deck of the steamer, I almost got the fright of my life. She looked as big as the hinder end of Grampa's trap skiff.

"My, Uncle Mose," said she. "You're lookin' well."

"So are you Aunt Sophy," said I. "So are you. You've put on a great lot of weight," said I.

And right away her nose went up in the air and I could see I'd said the wrong thing. But how could I help it? A man must say what he thinks, mustn't he, what he sees with his own eyes? Or perhaps he mustn't when it concerns women. Anyway, she acted kinda cool from then on, so when we all got up by her house and Grampa said, "Comin' in, Mose?" I noticed Sophy didn't back him up. So I said, "No, thank you," and went back down the lane.

'Twas about an hour afterwards before I got a chance to have a word with Grampa Walcott down on his stagehead. We had the place to ourselves because most everybody else was up waitin' for the mail to be sorted.

"What's Sophy mad about?" said I.

"On account," said Grampa, "of what you said about her puttin' on so much weight."

"But she have," said I.

"Mose," said Grampa. "Even if she had, that's not the kind of thing women want to be told. In my day," said

Grampa, "the more weight a woman put on, the prouder she was."

"Oh," said I.

"Besides," said Grampa, "she haven't put on any weight at all."

"But," said I, "I saw her with my own eyes."

"Mose, me son," said Grampa, "when it comes to women, appearances can be awful deceivin'."

"But," said I, "if 'tis not weight she've put on, what is it?"

Grampa went to the stage door to make sure no one was listenin'. Then he come back and whispered. "Crinoline," said Grampa.

"What-aline?" said I.

"Crinoline," said he. "'Tis crinoline that makes her look so big. 'Tis the latest style."

"What's crinoline?" said I.

"Well," said Grampa, "'Tis stuff they wear. You can't see it. You're not supposed to see it. But the idea of it is to make 'em look more spread out."

"But Grampa," said I. "What do they want to look more spread out for?"

"I dunno," said Grampa. "Only 'tis the latest style."

"But," said I, "if they wear this crin-whatever it is, to make themselves look more spread out, why is it that they get mad about it when someone thinks they've put on more weight?"

"Don't ask me," said Grampa. "A fellow'd have to understand women to answer a question like that. I've been married to one for over sixty years and I understand less about her now than first time I laid eyes on her. To tell the truth," said Grampa, "I'm kind of in the dog's house myself."

"Who with?" said I.

"With both Grandma and Sophy," said he.

"How come?" said I.

"Well," said he, "they were admirin' the beautiful effect of this crinoline stuff when I made a remark in the way of no harm. And now they're both mad with me about it."

"What did you say, Grampa?" said I.

"All I said, Mose," said Grampa, "was that instead of usin' this crinoline stuff to make 'em spread out they ought to use birch hoops, and help the cooperage business back on its feet and give a poor man a chance to make a few dollars out of these new styles."

"They didn't take to the idea?" said I.

"No," said Grampa. "It appears to me that these women got no interest in Economic Development."

POTATOES

UNCLE PADDY MULDOON WAS as modest a man as you'd meet in a day's walk. He'd never brag about himself or about anything that belonged to him. Not only that, but he didn't like to hear other people's braggin' and boastin'. He used to say that there were only two men in the world he had no use for and that any man that bragged was both of 'em. And you know how it is when a crowd of fellows get together yarnin'. There's always bound to be one or two among 'em who'll be inclined to brag a bit – you know – about how their cod trap is a few more fathoms on the round than anybody else's or that their motorboat is the fastest one in the harbour. Stuff like that.

Well, Uncle Paddy couldn't bear to listen to that kind of talk, especially the last few years before he died. He used to say it made him sick – used to give him the heartburn or somethin'. And so sometimes he'd just glower at the fellow that was braggin' and get up and walk away. More times, he'd try another remedy. He'd just tell one so much bigger than the other fellow was tellin' that the other fellow'd know he was havin' his leg pulled and would stop braggin' for shame's sake.

Like, for example, the day when a crowd of us were loungin' around in Levi Bartle's store and these two fellows from

Hartley's Harbour were there and the talk got around to potatoes. These Hartley's Harbour fellows started braggin' about the wonderful big potatoes they used to grow down there – a lot bigger, they said, than anything we'd ever grown in Pigeon Inlet. Grampa Walcott tried contradictin' 'em, but that only made 'em worse. One of 'em said he'd dug up a potato last fall as big as his own head. Grampa said it might have been as big on the round, but he'd bet it wasn't as thick through. But even that didn't shut him up.

Out of the corner of my eye I was watchin' Uncle Paddy Muldoon. He'd come up that day from Muldoon's Cove to do a bit of shoppin' and I could see him glowerin' at this Hartley's Harbour fellow from under his eyebrows. He was just gettin' up to go out in disgust, when I figgered that here might be a chance to get a real yarn, so I chimed in and I said, "I bet, boys," said I, "that they can grow bigger potatoes in Muldoon's Cove than in either Hartley's Harbour or Pigeon Inlet." Well, with that, two or three others joined in tryin' to get Uncle Paddy to take part in the argument, but he didn't open his mouth, only glower until this Hartley's Harbour fellow said, "Uncle Paddy never growed anything in Muldoon's Cove as big as the one I dug last fall." That was enough. And so Uncle Paddy finished the argument by tellin' this one.

'Twas in the fall of '22, said Uncle Paddy, or maybe '23, that he was comin' home off the Labrador with his schooner, two cod traps, and five sharemen. They were late gettin' home and the night before there'd been a touch of frost in the air – so he was worried about the potatoes – hopin' that Aunt Biddy had been able to get 'em dug up and in the cellar before the frost could get at 'em. Well, late this evenin' they got home, moored up the schooner, and Uncle Paddy and the crew went ashore. The first question he asked Biddy was about the potatoes.

"Did you get 'em all dug up?" said he.

"Yes, Paddy," said she, "every blessed one of 'em, exceptin' one."

"Oh?" said he.

"Yes," said she, "one of 'em was a bit too big for me to muckle. So I left it bide for you and the crew to handle – after you've had somethin' to eat."

So, after they'd had a mug-up, Uncle Paddy and the crew took a flake longer each and went up the side of the hill to where this potato was lyin'. They surveyed the situation, and four of them pried it out with longers while the other two went off aboard the schooner for a quile* of rope.

Well, by this time, the two Hartley's Harbour fellows were tryin' to sneak towards the door, but a bunch of us leaned up against it, so they had to stay and listen. Uncle Paddy went on with his yarn.

It didn't take long, accordin' to Uncle Paddy, to pry the potato out with the longers. Then they got the rope around it and eased it down the hill towards the cellar door. Of course, when they got it down to the door, they could see he'd never go in through. So they left it there. Like he told Biddy – the crew'd be around with us for three or four days and, if she kept cuttin' pieces off it every day for dinner, they'd make a good dent in it before the crew was finished takin' out the fish.

Well, said Uncle Paddy, they eat off that potato for two or three days, and, sure enough, you could almost notice the difference in the size of it. Then one night there was this heavy rainstorm. Next mornin', Aunt Biddy went off as usual with her knife and her pan to the potato. A few minutes later, back she come bawlin' like she'd gone crazy.

"Paddy," she bawled, "the pig is drowned."

"Where, where?" Uncle Paddy said. "Did he fall over the stagehead?"

"No, Paddy," she said. "Somehow or other he must have managed to climb up on top of the potato, lost his footin', and drowned in the potato's eye."

"A heavy loss," said Uncle Paddy. "That pig would've dressed two hundred pounds by Christmas."

Well, that was the end of Uncle Paddy's story, and you can be sure those Hartley's Harbour fellows never did any more braggin' about their potatoes – not when Uncle Paddy was around, anyway.

* quile: coil

FOOTBALL

WATCHIN' OUR PIGEON INLET football team givin' the crowd from Hartley's Harbour such a lickin' every twenty-fourth of May, 'tis hard to believe that only fifty years ago such a thing as football had never been seen or heard tell of in Pigeon Inlet. As a matter of fact, I wouldn't believe it myself only Grampa Walcott tells the story, and everyone knows he's a truthful man.

'Twas forty-three years ago last week, accordin' to Grampa, that Uncle Solomon Noddy was rowin' in from fishin' when he spotted this thing driftin' along just ahead of him. First he thought it was the head of a swile. But just then a flaw of wind lifted it right out of the water, so like he said after, he knowed it wasn't a swile's head cause there was nar swile under it. Nor was it the head of a drowned man for the same reason. He rowed up closer and figgered that, unless it happened to be a German bombshell, it'd come in handy for a trawl bobber. So he said a short prayer and picked it up. 'Twas laced up just like a boot, although he'd never seen any-one with a foot *that* shape. He shook it, but it seemed all hollow inside, so he figgered 'twas a trawl bobber sure enough, and he brought it in.

He carried it up to his house, showed it to Aunt Paish, his

missus, and told her not to let young Jethro fool with it 'cause he wasn't sure yet but what it might be a bombshell after all. He laid it on a kitchen chair while he went back to put away his bit of fish. Young Jethro, says Grampa, was just a little nipper then, about six or seven year old with a nasty temper and a dirty habit of kickin' at everything that didn't please him. Well, he come in from wherever he'd been out around the backyard – probably kickin' the cat – and spotted this thing on the kitchen chair. Aunt Paish was busy gettin' Uncle Sol's dinner ready and didn't notice anything until she heard him say, "Look, ma, it pops," and when she slewed round from where she'd been bendin' over the stove, there was Jethro bouncin' this thing on the floor. Well it popped sure enough, right up agen young Jethro's nose, and before Aunt Paish could scravel* over to stop him, he'd up foot and let this thing have it. Aunt Paish, says Grampa, never could describe exactly what happened for the next few minutes after that, but it could be pieced together by examinin' the wreckage later on.

It appears that this thing left young Jethro's boot and headed straight across the front of Aunt Paish's dresser where, like a tidy housekeeper, she had all her best jugs and cups hung on little hooks on the outside, with the lower-grade stuff in back on the shelves. Well, it swept the top row on the way over, bounced off the kitchen wall, and took the other row on the way back. It smashed everything, includin' Uncle Sol's moustache cup with "Love the Giver" on it, that'd been in the Noddy family for three generations. The lifter was stickin' up out of the cover of the stove. It hit *that* and sent it flyin' end on right through the half-gallon brown teapot that had just been set to brew on the back of the stove. So, from then on, the steam was so thick that Aunt Paish wasn't prepared to swear what it was that smashed the lamp and the motto with "God Bless our Happy Home" on it.

Anyway, in the middle of it all, in come Uncle Sol lookin' for his dinner like a man would, and seen the mess. The fog was lightened just enough for him to see young Jethro and Aunt Paish pointin' to this thingamajig lyin' on the floor, as harmless-lookin' a thing as you'd care to see. 'Twas then Uncle Sol showed where it was young Jethro got his temper from. "Gimme the axe," he bawled, "and I'll fix it."

So out he darted into the backyard and come back with an axe, and a good job it was, said Grampa, that it wasn't a double-bitter. 'Cause Uncle Sol bended over that thing where 'twas lyin' on the floor, swung the axe over his head, and brought it down as hard as he could. We'll never know, says Grampa, whether 'twas the axe or the other thing that bounced back and struck Uncle Sol right between the two eyes. Anyway, Aunt Paish dragged him outside into the fresh air where she thought he'd have a better chance of comin' to. Then she went back into the kitchen with her mind set on endin' this foolishness once and for all.

The thing was still lyin' there peaceful on the floor, so she grabbed it up, opened the end of the Waterloo stove, poked it in, and closed the door on it. Well, sir, says Grampa, the Hartley's Harbour people come hurryin' in off the fishin' grounds. They thought 'twas the smoke of the old *Glencoe*.** And of course all the neighbours in Pigeon Inlet come runnin'.

That night, after Uncle Sol had come to and the women

had helped Aunt Paish clean up the mess, 'twas the general opinion it must have been a bombshell after all. And those of us, says Grampa, who liked to look at the brighter side of things couldn't help remarkin' how it had cured young Jethro of his habit of kickin' at things, besides givin' the Noddy's chimney the first cleanin' out it had in years.

And it wasn't until two or three years afterwards that Aunt Paish was thumbin' through a catalogue up at Grandma Walcott's one night, and what should she spy but a picture of the very thing that'd caused all the trouble. And now, says Grampa, not fifty years later, to think that our fellows trim the socks off the Hartley's Harbour crowd at football every twenty-fourth of May – reg'lar as clockwork.

* scravel: move in a hurry

** *Glencoe*: an older steamer put into the coastal service early in the twentieth century

John Cabot

WE'VE BEEN TRYIN' FOR YEARS down here in Pigeon Inlet to make a Canadian out of Pete Briggs, and Pete bein' the kind of man he is, 'tis not an easy job. But we've been makin' progress, and that night last fall when the Women's Association had their concert, and we were all doin' our best with that song, the one that starts off "O Canada," I was standin' right behind Pete and I can swear his lips moved. Skipper Joe swears that no words came out, but that's not the important thing. 'Tis not likely that Pete knows the words. Anyway, the important thing is that his lips moved – a sure sign we were makin' progress. And then, to spoil it all, there had to come this unfortunate business about John Cabot.

Now, with all respect to Pete, some of the arguments he used to use against bein' a Canadian didn't carry much weight. Like sayin' he was born a Newfoundlander and that every man should bide wherever he was born. Grandma Walcott answered that one. She said yes, she could remember the very night Pete was born. He was born a Newfoundlander all right, but he was a awful scrawny one, and he should be thankful he didn't bide like that. I think 'twas fishermen's insurance that started to convert him, 'cause Pete knows you need hundreds of thousands in a scheme like that to make it work. We had it in our Lodge once, and it went all right, till Skipper Lige Bartle broke his leg in caplin scull,* and ate up all the savings we'd been seven years tryin' to scrape together.

But to get back to John Cabot. Personally, I can't get worked up about John Cabot the way Pete gets. What I mean is – he either discovered Newfoundland or else he didn't. Perhaps the mainland people are right. Perhaps when John Cabot got to Newfoundland he said, "Well, there's Newfoundland. I've got half a mind to discover it, but on second thoughts, I s'pose I'd better sail round it and try to discover somethin' big while I'm at it." What I mean to say is, 'twas his own business, and we can't do much about it at this late date. Then again, of course, 'tis possible he come right along by us and didn't discover us at all, but like Skipper Joe says, if John Cabot was as stupid as that, the mainland can have him and welcome.

Jethro Noddy says that, perhaps if they want John Cabot on the mainland bad enough, they might be willin' to pay us a little somethin' for him. But I told him 'tis too late to talk about that now. Besides, when I mentioned such a thing to Pete Briggs, he was fit to be tied. He'll neither sell John Cabot nor give him away. We haven't got much left, he says, but if we happen to lose John Cabot, we'll have nothin'. But I'm way ahead of my story.

What happened to make Pete so mad in the first place was that, in her Christmas history exam, his little girl said, naturally enough, that John Cabot discovered Newfoundland in 1497, and the teacher put a question mark by it. 'Twas the girl teacher, a little thing just out of University up in St. John's and fair burstin' with book learnin'. When Pete went up to the school the next day to ask her what did she mean by questionin' somethin' every Newfoundlander knowed as well as his own name, she tried to brazen it out by sayin' as how the history experts had figgered out nowadays that it wasn't Newfoundland that John Cabot discovered but some place up on the mainland. Pete asked her how stunned did they think John Cabot was, to pass right along by Newfoundland and not discover it. Or did they think somebody lifted Newfoundland up out of the water long enough for John Cabot to sail under it – and then put it back again? He'd have said more if he hadn't choked up. So he come home. But he said that, family allowance or no family allowance, he wasn't goin' to send his youngsters to *that* teacher again to be corrupted.

But somehow down deep, I had a suspicion that Pete must have some special reason for gettin' so worked up over John Cabot. I watched my chance till I got him, just the two of us. Then I said to him, "Pete, what odds about John Cabot?"

"What do you mean," he said, "what odds about John Cabot?"

"Why," said I, "I mean, if they want him up on the mainland, let 'em have him. After all, there's more of them than us, so if they're that anxious to have him, we can't save him."

He looked around to make sure there was nobody else within earshot. "Uncle Mose," he said, "when I went to school, I didn't learn much. But one thing I did learn was that John Cabot discovered Newfoundland in 1497. Now if I've go to lose that, it'll mean I made a complete waterhaul. And that's a hard thing for a man to swallow."

And he's still findin' it hard. Only last night at the school concert when that "O Canada" came up again, I took special notice of Pete's lips.

Not a bivver in 'em!

It looks like, in tryin' to make a Canadian out of him, we've got to start all over again.

* caplin scull: period during June and July when caplin come ashore to spawn

ARGUMENTS

WHEN YOU COME TO THINK of it, there's an awful lot of time wasted in this world tryin' to make people own up that they're in the wrong. I've seen men like Skipper Joe and Sam Prior get Pete Briggs into a corner after Pete had got the worst of an argument. They'd say to him, "Now Pete, you know you're wrong, why don't you be a man and own up to it," forgettin' that it's just because Pete is a man that he won't own up to it, even when he knows down deep inside him that he is wrong. And Skipper Joe and Sam and the rest of 'em'd be just as pigheaded as Pete if the shoe happened to be on the other foot.

Mind you, a man that's wrong should own up to it. Like the sayin' goes, "Confession is good for the soul," and no doubt there's a time and a place for that sort of thing, but what I'm tryin' to say is – that the place for it is not on the net loft nor yet in the fo'c'sle of a schooner. In places like that 'tis only a waste of time expectin' a man to own up he was wrong. He won't do it.

Like the time early last winter we were havin' an argument on Skipper Joe's net loft about the hunter and the squirrel. You know – the one where the hunter is tryin' to get a shot at the squirrel, but the squirrel is perched up on the big burl on a tree and he always manages to keep the tree between himself and the hunter. The hunter makes a big circle around the tree, but the squirrel keeps shiftin' his position so that he's always on the wrong side of the tree and the hunter never gets a shot at 'un first or last. Well, as you know the question is – did the hunter walk around the squirrel? Everyone knows he went around the tree, but then, so did the squirrel. And the squirrel managed to keep his face towards the hunter all the time he was doin' it – which leaves us with the question "Did the hunter walk around the squirrel?"

Well, all of us figgered out the right answer except Pete. I won't say exactly what we figgered out because there might be other people listenin' just like Pete, and I don't want to start another argument. Anyhow, Pete took the contrary view as usual and he wouldn't give in first or last. Not even when Skipper Joe went and got his muzzleloader and Jethro Noddy acted out the part of the squirrel – usin' the post in the middle of the net loft for the tree. And he went off home still sayin' he was right and the rest of us didn't know what we was talkin' about.

Even next day when Skipper Joe tried to bring up the subject again, hopin' that Pete might admit he was wrong. All Pete would say was that 'twas all a pack of foolishness and he was sick of it. Which in my opinion is as close as you can reasonably expect a man to come to ownin' up he was in the wrong. 'Cause after all, even if a man is in the wrong and knows it, he still got his self-respect to look after.

Like the time years ago that Grampa Walcott tells about when Uncle Sol Noddy insulted Skipper Lige Bartle up in the waitin' room of the Post Office. Uncle Sol told Skipper Lige right to his face that he was uglier-lookin' than an old dog hood.* Naturally, Skipper Lige threatened to have the law on Uncle Sol if he didn't take it back. Sure enough a few nights after when the Lodge was havin' a time,** Uncle Sol walked right over to Skipper Lige and said right in the presence of a lot of witnesses. "Skipper Lige," he said, "I'll take that back about you bein' uglier than an old dog hood, 'cause now that I'm gettin' a closer look, I'm willin' to admit, you're not just a bit uglier."

Well now, for some reason or other, that made Skipper Lige madder than ever. He said that was no fit apology, but Grampa Walcott finally cooled him down. Grampa put it this way: "Uncle Sol had said part of an apology and kept back the other part." The part he'd said was just enough to save Skipper Lige's face while the part he'd kept back was just enough to save his own. And even though most people might figger that Uncle Sol's face was hardly worth savin', yet after all, 'twas the only one he had, and you had to look at it from his point of view.

So Grampa advised Skipper Lige to accept Uncle Sol's apology – such as it was – and by doin' so, he'd be meetin' Uncle Sol halfway, which was the right and proper Christian thing to do. Like the character in the Bible who didn't wait for his Prodigal Son to come all the way back by hisself, but actually run out to meet him.

I wonder how many of the arguments goin' on today could end peaceable instead of breedin' bad feelin', if only each side'd be willin' to let the other save a bit of face – if we didn't insist that the other fellow had to come all the way and own up that he's in the wrong, and we're right. Sometimes I think that we handle these things better on Skipper Joe's net loft than they do in lots of higher places.

  * dog hood: mature male seal

  ** time: community social event

GEESE

NOW, I CAN'T PERSONALLY vouch for the truth of all Grampa Walcott's stories, on account of how most of 'em happened before my time. All I can say is that Grampa is as truthful a man as you'll find in Pigeon Inlet.

'Twas one fall's day about sixty years ago, says Grampa, that he took his muzzleloader and went in on the barrens hopin' to get a goose before they all left for the south'ard. He didn't see a thing till, all at once, he spotted this big black cloud risin' in the nor'west and headin' straight for him. Thundercloud? No, 'twas geese sure enough, but about two gunshots over his head. Anyway, he up gun, hopin' to get a cripple or two, and fired.

For the next few minutes, he said, there was a shower of geese fallin' on all sides of him. They were only stunned, and the best he could do was to secure as many of 'em as he could before they come to.

He had a ball of fishin' line and he cut it into lengths and tied one end of each length to a goose's neck and the other end to his belt, intendin' to finish 'em off when he got around to it. But he was greedy. He had twenty-five of 'em fastened that way when they come to, and next thing Grampa knew they were liftin' him off the ground and flyin' away with him.

In the excitement he'd dropped his knife, so he couldn't cut himself loose, and in less time than it takes to tell it there he was up off the ground with twenty-five tow ropes stretched out ahead of him – headed for Florida, or Jamaica, or wherever it is geese go to spend their winters.

Now, Grampa says he personally got nuthin' against Florida, but with forty quintals of fish in his stage at the time needin' a few more hours' sun, he just couldn't afford the trip. So he started to figger a way to get down out of there. After all, a man who could handle his own schooner ought to be able to steer a flock of geese. Grampa decided to take his bearin's.

He was flyin' face down, stretched out as comfortable as on a feather bed, and Red Indian Lake was just comin' up in the skyline. So Grampa decided to try somethin'. There was one big gander with a longer tow rope than the others, so Grampa found the tight string and give it a little jerk to starboard. Sure enough, the gander slowed and the others followed suit. A minute later Grampa was headed north straight for Pigeon Inlet. 'Twas only then, he says, that it dawned on him he was the first man to fly an airplane, and if he could somehow turn it into a helicopter he might come through all right.

He looked right down at his own house as he passed over Pigeon Inlet and there was Liz (Grandma she is now, but they'd only been married a year or two then), and Liz was lookin' up at him makin' some kind of motions with her hands. He was sure Liz was givin' him some kind of signal, if only he could make out what it was. Well, by this time he was almost down off Belle Isle, so he twigged his gander hard a-port and headed back toward Pigeon Inlet again.

By this time, he'd got the hang of his steerin' gear, so he circled around a few times watchin' Liz until he made out her signal. She was makin' motions like wringin' necks.

That was it! Why hadn't he thought of it before! So he hauled in one of the geese by his painter and wrung his neck. Then two more. Now there were only twenty-two tow ropes out ahead, while he and the three dead ones were strung behind.

Sure enough, he was slowin' down a bit and droppin' lower. He kept circlin' round and looked down at Liz again. Now he could make out a patch of somethin' white on the ground by her, and he figgered she had it there to guide him in makin' a landin'. So he wrung more necks and kept circlin' lower and lower.

At last, said Grampa, he manoeuvred until he was right fair over his house, then he wrung all the necks except three. And there they hung. That old gander – what a bird! He and his two helpers were pointed straight up by this time and barely holdin' up the weight of all the rest of 'em. Accordin' to Grampa, he had one bad minute when Lige Bartle, seein' this strange thing in the sky, started to come with his swilin' gun. But Liz told him who it was.

Finally, Grampa looked down again. The white patch was right below him. So he wrung the other two necks and him and that gander fluttered down so gentle that he wouldn't crack a egg if there'd been one on that white patch where his feet landed. There he stood, chock to his waist in dead geese, and glad to be back home again.

"Liz," said Grampa, "bless your heart for savin' me."

"Ben," says she, "take your dirty muddy boots off my clean tablecloth."

"But Liz," said he, "you did save me, you know, by advisin' me to wring their necks."

"Ben," said she, "I was only tellin' you what I'd like to be doin' to *your* neck, up there playin' with a lot of foolish geese. But seein' as now you're home, wring that other one's neck and let's start pickin' them."

Well, said Grampa, he untied the twenty-four geese from his belt and was just about to wring the gander's neck too, when somethin' in that old bird's expression made him change his mind. To hurt that bird – why, 'twould be like hurtin' an old shipmate. So he untied him and let him go. He circled a few times then took off for Florida, or Jamaica, or wherever it is that geese go to spend their winters.

That was, said Grampa, his one and only helicopter ride. He was tempted to try it again, when that old gander used to pitch in front of his door every fall with a length of string in his bill. But after eight or ten falls he give up and Grampa never saw him again. But, said Grampa, he was a wonderful knowin' bird.

EDUCATION

GRAMPA WALCOTT ADVISES me not to talk about education because, he says, havin' so little of it myself, I'm bound to make a show of myself talkin' about a thing I know nothin' about. But, bein' as how the public of Newfoundland (and that includes me and Grampa) are spendin' millions of dollars a year on education, well that kind of makes it our business, with all due respect to Grampa and everybody else who thinks like him.

Still, Grampa is right in one way. I probably don't know what I'm talkin' about, and in case any educated people happen to be listenin', I hope they'll forgive me, and understand that I'm not educated myself. I'm only one of the ones that's helpin' pay for it. And bein' educated, I'm sure they'll understand.

Sometimes when I listen to experts on the subject talkin' over the radio or read what they write in the papers, it makes me wonder if in some ways we're not goin' backwards instead of ahead. The big object of education, to judge by what they say, is to get a good job and make more money than the next fellow. And so you've got to have Grade XI* or you'll be lost. In fact, they're beginnin' to figger that in this modern world of push buttons and automation, where more things'll be produced and fewer men'll be needed to produce 'em, that even Grade XI'll soon be not enough. And then they're talkin' about streamin' all the youngsters in school when they get up around Grade VIII or IX. One stream'll flow on towards the University where they'll wash ashore somewhere as doctors, lawyers, teachers, clergymen – all the learned professions. Another stream'll flow towards business where they'll become merchants or general managers or learn how to push the button that'll keep the office accounts. The last stream'll flow towards the technical schools where they'll be trained as highly skilled mechanics, electricians, bricklayers, and the like. And that, as far as I can judge, is the purpose of education nowadays, which is why I can't help wonderin' if we're not goin' backwards in spite of all the fine schools we're gettin' and all the money we're spendin' on 'em.

Mind you, there's nothin' wrong with educatin' people to the professions, or to business, or to the skilled trades. The Blessed Lord put so many people in the world with the special talents to do these jobs, and it's only right they should get the chance to get 'em. But anyone who listens to the news nowadays can't help but see that everybody is not goin' to get a job pushin' a button, or runnin' a diesel, or pullin' teeth. What about all the rest of us?

My poor old father, Skipper Obe Mitchell he was called – though he never was a skipper of anything, 'twas just a title of respect – was a believer in education. He kept me to school until I was old enough to go in the bow of a dory with him on the Grand Banks – which wasn't very old. I learned to read, and write, and figger out his account. It never occurred to him that I'd get a big job through it, but he used to say,

"Mose, boy, a bit of book learnin' is no burden to carry around, not even in a fishin' boat."

'Twas a good job he didn't try to keep me in school till I got Grade XI. I'd have been there yet and the economy of this country'd been the worse off by a good many quintals of codfish. So what did I learn? Well, I learned the two most important things anybody can learn in school; and judgin' by what they're turnin' out of school nowadays, a lot of Grade XI's are not learnin' 'em today. I learned to read, for one thing, and I learned how to want to learn more. I didn't get an education, but I got what you might call the foundation of an education, and what I built on that foundation afterwards was more or less up to myself. My brother Ki got the same, and he went on to make a small fortune as a buildin' contractor on the mainland. I've ended up down here in Pigeon Inlet – with nothin', you might say. But I'm independent and just as happy as Ki.

What I'm afraid we're in danger of forgettin' about education is that it's a good thing in itself, apart altogether from what kind of a livin' it'll help us make. I didn't have many school books when I went to school, but I remember one of 'em, a Hygiene Book, I think it was, that said we were all made up of three things – a body, a mind and a soul. And we should keep all three of 'em healthy. You kept your body healthy by obeyin' the rules of health, your soul by religion, and your mind by education.

And so, I hope our education experts won't get all excited and flustered over this automation business. There's a lot of people that need a bit of education just so as they can have healthy minds. It might never be the means of turnin' 'em in an extra dollar, but sure it'll help 'em to live with their eyes open to what's goin' on around 'em, and with the ability to judge for theirselves between sense and foolishness, to be more enlightened citizens of whatever place they live in, big or small. In fact, I can't put it any better than my father Skipper Obe put it to me when he said, "Mose boy, a bit of book learnin' is no burden to carry around, not even in a fishin' boat."

* Grade XI: the final year of high school until the introduction of Grade XII in the early 1980s

Traffic in Pigeon Inlet

I WAS READIN' A PIECE IN A newspaper the other day that was written by a fellow who was tryin' to prove that the place he lived in was better than another place, and he seemed kind of half mad because somebody had said it wasn't. Skipper Joe was with me at the time, so I read it out loud to him and asked him what he thought about it. Skipper Joe laughed and said it reminded him of what Pete Briggs said one time to Lukey Bartle – when they were talkin' about Lukey's wife, Emma Jane.

"What was that?" said I. So Skipper Joe told me. As you know, before poor Lukey married Emma Jane, she was a Grimes from Hartley's Harbour, and when Lukey married her, he thought for sure he had a prize. And to tell the truth, said Skipper Joe, she did look a bit better than some of the other women around here who worked harder, but her looks were the best part of her, and everybody sized her up pretty quick – except Lukey, of course. Still and all, like Skipper Joe said, that was Luke's own business, so nobody said anything. Until he started braggin' about her and then he got under our skins, and one day Pete Briggs couldn't stand any more of it. Luke said to a crowd of us, "Boys," he said, "'tis a good thing everybody is not of the one mind. For instance," he said, "if everybody was of my mind, everybody'd want Emma Jane." So Pete said, "Yes Lukey, boy, you're right. And if everybody was of my mind, nobody'd want her."

Well, as Skipper Joe said, he supposed 'twas the same way about people and the places they lived in and 'twas only natural for people to think their own place is the best. Perhaps that's why me and Skipper Joe and the rest of us down here – fair-minded men – agree that the best place of all is Pigeon Inlet.

Now, don't misunderstand me. We people down here are firm believers in this idea of shiftin' people out of the little isolated places and gettin' them into bigger ones. You take a place like Rumble Cove – only six or seven families and half the time with no teacher. They ought to be encouraged to move to Pigeon Inlet. There's plenty of room for 'em here and they'd be a help to us instead of an hindrance, because, for one thing, their fifteen or twenty youngsters'd be the means of us gettin' a fourth room built onto our school. The way it is now, we've got almost too many youngsters for three rooms and not enough for four. Oh yes, we're all in favour of movin' people, from places like Rumble Cove to bigger and better places like Pigeon Inlet.

What have we got in Pigeon Inlet to make it such a fine place? Well, first of all, let me mention some of the things we haven't got – things we're better off without.

Accordin' to the radio and the newspapers, one of the worst things today in a good many places is traffic accidents. Now, we don't have any traffic accidents. And you might say, "Oh yes. No wonder! You don't have any traffic." But we do have traffic, only like Grampa Walcott says, in all his eighty-odd years livin' in Pigeon Inlet, he's got yet to hear tell of any-body gettin' run over by a wheelbarrow or of two wheelbar-rows havin' a head-on collision. But here's a funny thing I'm goin' to say. I've watched the way people behave in places where they've got motor cars, and if we behaved the same with our wheelbarrows as they do with their cars, we'd have plenty of accidents. But we don't.

Last time I was in St. John's, Skipper Bobby Blagdown from Fortune Bay – he's livin' in St. John's now – took me out for a drive in his motor car, and bein' always wantin' to learn, I asked him a lot of questions about her. Accordin' to him, you can steer these things whatever way you want 'em to go; you can slow 'em down or even stop 'em altogether if you want to, and besides, everyone got to know how to drive 'em before they can get a licence. So then I asked Skipper Bobby, if all that was so, what was the cause of all the accidents. "Uncle Mose," he said, "'tis just as well to face it. The cause of most of the accidents is bad manners, just plain old-fash-ioned rudeness. They got schools," he said, "where they can teach people how to drive these cars, but all that's no use unless they teach them some good manners at the same time."

And I'm convinced Uncle Bobby is right and that's why we've got no traffic accidents down here. Not that we haven't got the traffic, but we've got common sense enough and good manners enough to handle it proper. 'Cause if I was fool enough and ignorant enough to run down the road as fast as I could pushin' a wheelbarrow, the chances are I'd break somebody's leg before I got down to Levi Bartle's store. And perhaps break my own foolish neck in the bargain. And while

I was in St. John's, I saw fellows in cars do things – well, if we behaved like that when two or three of us are down on Levi Bartle's wharf wheelin' salt from Levi's shed out to the salt shute, why we'd knock one another over the wharf, wheelbarrows, salt, and all. But like I said, we got more sense than that, and better manners.

Now, I'm not sayin' we got perfect manners down here. Why sometimes, myself, I forget to touch my cap to the member or even the clergyman and lots of times I've let Aunt Sophy open a door her own self. But good manners is more than that. It's showin' a respect for other people's feelin's and other people's rights. Sometimes I've seen a bit of bad manners, possibly when some youngster tries to push other people aside to get up near the wicket when the mail is bein' give out, but some elder person'll always explain the difference to him and even pick him up and put him back in the line where he belongs. That way he grows to learn good manners too, and in later life takes care not to run over people with his wheelbarrow.

Santa Claus

WITH CHRISTMAS GETTIN' closer every day, there's one thing I think I ought to mention. It's this argument we hear sometimes over the radio about whether Christmas nowadays is what it used to be. Some people think it's turned into a money-makin' affair, what they call bein' "commercialized." Others don't agree. Naturally the newspapers and radio stations that make money off advertisin', and the merchants with a lot of Christmas goods to sell, and the companies that want to lend people money to buy 'em with, they don't see anything wrong with the way things are goin'. But other people seem to think it's a bad thing, and that Christmas is not what it used to be years ago.

Of course it's all away over our heads down here in Pigeon Inlet and, to tell the truth, up till lately, we figgered 'twas none of our business. What other people did with their Christmas in places like St. John's or Toronto, well, there wasn't much we could do to stop 'em, and in any case, it couldn't affect how we regarded our Christmas in Pigeon Inlet. That's what we used to think. Now I'm not so sure. Look what happened to me about four weeks ago.

Little Judy Briggs is Pete Briggs's youngest. She can't be more than four or five years old. She come to my door this day to bring me back a screwdriver I'd loaned Pete the day before. So I asked her to come in while I hunted around to see if I could find her a candy, and my radio was turned on and she happened to hear what was on it. 'Twas all about this big Santa Claus parade somewhere up on the mainland, and this only the early part of November. After I found the candy, I almost had to wake her up to give it to her, she was so much interested in the radio. She looked so sad, I thought she was goin' to cry.

"Uncle Mose," she said, "is that really Santa Claus up there in that place on the radio?"

What are you goin' to tell a youngster that age? So I said to her, "Well Judy," said I, "what do you think?"

"Oh, I think it must be," said she, "'cause they say it is. And they wouldn't tell lies like that over the radio, would they, Uncle Mose?"

And again, what could I say? There's a lot she's got to learn, but five years old is perhaps a poor time to learn it. But then she said, "Is he comin' here this year?"

So I said, "Yes, he never failed to come to Pigeon Inlet yet and he'll be here again, just wait and see."

But she wasn't satisfied. If he was comin' Christmas, what was he doin' visitin' other places almost two months before Christmas? Did that mean he was goin' to visit these places twice and Pigeon Inlet only once, or worse still, did it mean that he'd give up Christmas and was visitin' these big places now while navigation was open and perhaps wouldn't come here at all? Anyhow, if he was up there in Toronto now, and he must be, the radio said so, how could he be up at the North Pole where he was supposed to be, gettin' ready for his Christmas Eve visit to places like Pigeon Inlet?

Now what could I tell her? I'd like to have told the radio somethin'. How if they wanted to pretend that Christmas came in October or November instead of in December, the least they could do was keep it to theirselves instead of blarin' their nonsense all over the world where little people like Judy could get upset by it. And I couldn't tell her the radio was tellin' lies. But I had to tell her somethin'. So I scratched my head a bit and done the best I could.

"Judy," said I, "you know when Santa's birthday is?"

"Yes," she said, "Christmas Day, isn't it?"

"Right," said I, "and Christmas Day is a special day with Santa on account of it bein' his birthday. Now," I said, "Judy, take your own birthday. That's a special day with you, isn't it?"

"Oh yes," she said.

"And what do you do on your birthday?" said I. "Do you go away to places like Rumble Cove or Hartley's Harbour?"

"Oh no," she said, "'cause it's my birthday. I stay home with mommy and daddy and have my really best friends in with me for a party. But," she said, "I go one place on my birthday. I always go up and visit Grandma every birthday."

"Why?" said I.

"Oh, because," she said, "now that Grandma is not able to get out of doors anymore and come down to see me like she used to, I've promised her I'll come and see her every year on my birthday. I love Grandma."

"But," said I, "you do go to Rumble Cove sometimes?"

"Oh, yes," she said, "but not on my birthday. Birthday is for bein' home with mommy and daddy and my friends, and visitin' Grandma."

"And Judy," said I, "that's just how it is with Santa Claus on his birthday. That's the day he visits the people he loves, like you visitin' your Grandma. Other days of the year you mustn't mind him visitin' other places like on the radio. If you hear of him bein' in these places in October or November or even June or July – the way things are goin' – don't get upset or worried about it. Santa's got a birthday and he's savin' that special day for a special purpose, to visit the people he loves."

And do you know, that cheered her up. Only she said she felt a bit sorry for the places that Santa had to visit on other days besides his own special day. And come to think of it, I can't help feelin' a bit sorry for them too.

KING DAVID'S
WINTER OUTFIT

I SUPPOSE WHAT JETHRO Noddy is doin' and sayin' these days is crazy, but for the life of me I just can't spot what exactly is crazy about it. No doubt after the present holiday season is over and we get down to more or less normal thinkin', we'll all be able to see the faults in Jethro's present line of reasonin', but in the meantime, let me tell you about it and you can judge for yourself. Jethro calls it his Christmas present to all of Canada and he wants to donate his idea especially to this new Productivity Council that the authorities are settin' up, 'cause for sure they're the proper ones to make the best use of it.

It should turn out to be a big new industry for Canada – winterizin' goats. 'Tis not surprisin', 'cause as everyone knows, fish-eatin' gives brains, and so naturally enough a place that consumes as much fish as Pigeon Inlet ought to be able to come up with a bright idea once in a while, and no doubt as time goes on the rest of Canada will be lookin' to us people more and more for their ideas. Anyway, gettin' back to this idea of winterizin' goats. Jethro says Canada can have it for nothin', he won't charge a cent for thinkin' it up – he's not money-minded – all he wants is enough money to spend whenever he wants it. But he says he wants it to be remembered in Canadian history books in years to come (after the industry is all set up) that the first Canadian goat ever to be winterized was King David.

The big idea came to Jethro one night just before Christmas when his missus, Soos, and he were sittin' in the kitchen one night after the youngsters were all in bed. He'd been just listenin' to all this gloomy talk over the radio about the terrible unemployment problem we got in Canada, when he noticed Soos with a darnin' needle in her hand and a ball of yarn and asked her what she was goin' to do with these two old-fashioned things. She reminded him that he had two guernseys – a blue one and a grey one – and they was both more holey than righteous, so she was goin' to get the darnin' needle and brail* 'em up somehow so that Jethro wouldn't make a show of hisself whenever he wore one of 'em. 'Twas then Jethro says the idea begun to dawn on him. He told Soos that if she was a patriotic Canadian and listened to the radio more she'd know that 'twas people like her, brailin' things up with darnin' needles, that was causin' all this unemployment and had Canada into the mess 'twas in. 'Twas her duty to buy a new one and help keep a factory open somewhere up on the mainland. And when Soos said what would she do with these two guernseys he had, he said as how they could make a wonderful outfit for King David. The blue one – with the buttons – would need very little alteration to fit over his forward end while the grey one for the hinder end'd be a bit more trouble 'cause naturally the turtleneck'd have to plunge a bit. But with that done and the two waists stitched together to fit around King David's midship room, there he'd be with as fine a two-toned outfit as you'd see anywhere in a catalogue. Although next year no doubt the catalogues'll be full of 'em.

Well, for a while Soos thought Jethro was cracked. But 'tis natural for a woman to think that. The schoolteacher says Shakespeare's missus was the same way. She told Jethro who ever heard of a goat dressed up, but Jethro said Soos was old-fashioned, livin' in the past. She had to realize that King David wasn't a Newfoundland goat anymore – he was a Canadian goat and entitled to be both comfortable and stylish. Then she asked Jethro how long did he think 'twould be before King David had it wore out. Jethro said a question like that proved Soos was old-fashioned. The quicker King David wore it out the quicker he'd want another one, just like the last pair of snow pants they'd bought for young Sol didn't last a fortnight. That's what kept factories goin' and people employed. So they set to work.

Jethro said afterwards they'd liked to have had time to have dyed the outfit green and red to give it a Christmasy touch, but they had to be contented with runnin' ribbons through it to add the right colours.

Anyway, two or three days before Christmas they had it ready and King David modelled it all up and down the road in Pigeon Inlet. He was admired by one and all. As he was headin' south'ard we noticed where a few improvements might be needed around his nor'ard end, but all in all – 'twas a wonderful success. Every youngster in the place is makin' a rosette or a bunch of ribbons to pin on him for Christmas Day. And the other goats shiverin' in the cold look like they envy him – which no doubt they got good reason to – he bein' winterized, and they not.

Anyway, two or three other goat owners here are watchin' the situation careful-like, and if their goats got to spend the winter shiverin' in the lee of goat's houses while King David struts up and down the roads gettin' his exercise regular – there's likely to be a brisk demand for these outfits quicker than you might think.

* brail: rough, careless darning

AUNT SOPHY ON THE OUTS

MANY TIMES I HAVE TOLD you about what a nuisance King David is to anybody who's tryin' to grow a few vegetables. Today I must tell you the worst of all – how he got me into a row with Aunt Sophy Watkinson. A bad row, too. Although it's two months since it happened, Aunt Sophy is still on the outs with me and the way she looks at me sometimes you'd think I was no better than a sculpin* or a dogfish, and all on account of King David. I've mentioned my cabbage garden before, and when I call it a cabbage garden, that's exactly what I mean. Not a kitchen garden like most of the people have got, but a cabbage garden. I grow nothin' else in it except cabbage.

It's the smallest garden in Pigeon Inlet and I've got to put every inch of it to best use. I've noticed that nearly everybody here grows enough potatoes, carrots, turnips, and beet for their own use, but cabbage is a very scarce article, especially around Christmastime and from then on. So I figger I can always barter a few good heads of cabbage for the other few vegetables I want, and then later in the winter I can even change some cabbage for a brace of rabbits or a turr or even a flipper in the spring. Besides, I'm awful fond of cabbage myself and I'm proud of the way I can grow it and keep it over winter.

Well, this day a few weeks ago, Sunday mornin', it was just after I had come back from New Brumsick, I was gettin' spruced up to go to church. The first bell had just stopped, which made it about a quarter past ten. I had the salt meat and the peas duff** simmerin' away in the pot on the back of the stove and the vegetables all peeled and ready to put in the pot as soon as I got back from church, all except the cabbage. *That* was still out in the garden, so I took my enamel pan and my knife and went out to get a head for my dinner.

The gate to my cabbage garden is about two steps from my back door and I can swear there wasn't a living thing in sight as I untied the gate. I went into the garden, picked out the best head I could see, and cut it off. Then I came out, laid the pan with the head of cabbage in it (and the knife), and turned round to tie the gate again. I had to make sure it was well tied so that King David would not get in.

When I was finished I turned round and picked up the pan and was almost in through my back door when I noticed I had the pan all right and the knife, but no cabbage. I looked around on the ground by the back door, but no cabbage. Then I went, still with knife and pan in hand, and peeped around the corner of my picket fence. There was the goat hightailin' it up the lane with my best head of cabbage in his mouth. Of course I took chase after him.

Now, I know I was shoutin' somethin' while I was chasin' him, but I'll never remember what it was. Anyhow, I'd have caught him if I hadn't slipped in a puddle just as I was passin'

Aunt Sophy's house. That probably made me shout all the more, but when I got up and saw I had no chance now of catchin' up, I flung the knife and then the enamel pan after him. The knife struck a rock and broke off short to the handle while the pan struck another rock and knocked a big hole in the bottom. The last I saw of King David, he was on top of the big boulder behind Aunt Sophy's house. He had the cabbage laid down between his feet and his mouth was movin' as if he was sayin' grace. I bawled a few more things at him, brushed some of the muck off my Sunday trousers, and turned to go down the lane. And there was Aunt Sophy on her doorstep, ready for church. She plays the organ in church, you know, and always leaves a bit early to put up the hymns. Anyway, she had seen and heard it all.

"Aunt Sophy," said I. "Did you see what that goat did?"

"No, Mr. Mitchell," she said, "but I saw what you did and heard what you said, and I'm shocked. On a blessed Sunday mornin', too."

And she pointed her nose straight up in the air and walked by me without another word. From that day to this she's never even bid me the time of day. I've tried everything. I even tried to get her father, Grampa Walcott, to intercede for me. Only last night, Grampa said, "'Tis no use, Mose. Soph is a grown woman and Soph's mind is Soph's own to use. She's shocked. She says she never saw a man in such a vicious temper, and bein' Sunday mornin' made it all the worse. And Mose," said Grampa, "you must have used some awful cuss words."

"Grampa," said I. "I don't remember what I used."

"They must've been pretty bad," said Grampa, "because

Soph says she never heard anything approachin' them in all her life. And Mose," said he, "she's heard me use some pretty strong ones myself over that same goat, years ago before I got short-winded."

So that's how things stand now between me and Aunt Sophy.

* sculpin: a scavenger fish

** duff: pudding boiled in a bag

New Year's
Resolutions

WITH NEW YEAR SO CLOSE, I got to thinkin' just now about the resolution I made last New Year's Eve, and tryin' to figger how well I got on with keepin' it. So as I could decide whether I'd have the pluck to make another one this year. The one I made last year was to keep out of arguments, because arguments never settled anything, not since Adam and Eve got into the argument over who give which the apple.

Now, come to think of it, I didn't do too well about keepin' that resolution, and two or three times during the year I found myself into arguments, mostly with Jethro Noddy and Pete Briggs. Jethro especially, he'd try the patience of a saint. I had a mind one time to give up the resolution altogether and say 'twas just as well to be hung for a sheep as a lamb, but Grampa Walcott give me good advice. He said as how a man should stick to his resolution even if he breaks it a time or two. Why, he said, forty-odd years ago he made a New Year's resolution not to say a certain little bad word that he used to say every time he lost a codfish off his hook – and he's stuck to that same resolution ever since. Of course, he said, he breaks it once in a while, but even so, he's made a lot of progress, and only says that word now when he loses a real big one.

When I told Grampa the resolution I have in mind for the year, he give me a pat on the shoulder. "Well done, Mose," he said, "that's a great idea." You see, my New Year's resolution this year is to keep my temper (as best I can, of course). Grampa thinks that every man ought to try to control his temper, not so much for his own sake as for the sake of the people around him. Says Grampa, "A man loses his temper and gets off a lot of old nonsense. 'Tis all right for him, because his mind is so fixed on what he's sayin' that he don't even hear it. But what about other people? The ones that got to listen to the trash? 'Tis not fair to them," says Grampa. "A man has got no more right to a dirty temper than he's got to a dirty face."

That last expression might sound odd, but wait till I tell you the story behind it. It concerns Jethro Noddy. Jethro is not exactly the tidiest fellow in the world. Ordinary times, I should say that Jethro remembers to shave once every week – Saturdays – but oftentimes it slips his memory. To explain to you how serious that is, I'd better explain what Jethro's face looks like with a two- or three-weeks' whisker on it. If he'd grow a decent whisker, 'twould be all right.

The only thing I can compare it to is the nor'west corner of the Gull Mash, just after you've crossed over the barren part and you're gettin' near to the foothills where we go for firewood. Well, that section of the Mash is all spotted – mostly bare spots with here and there a clump of ground juniper or a small patch of alders, or a few blueberry bushes or a old gnarled stump – stuff like that. I don't know if I'm makin it clear, but I hope that'll give you some idea of what Jethro's jowls look like with a two-weeks' whisker on 'em.

To make matters worse, he's not the cleanest fellow in the world neither. He's got an awful size of a mouth and he told someone one time he was glad 'twas so big because he opened it as wide as he could whenever he went to wash his face, and that meant a great savin' on soap, because with his mouth wide open, there wasn't much face left to wash.

Well, one day last summer he looked so untidy that Grampa hit him up about it and told him for goodness' sake to go home and shave and wash up. Jethro said he allowed his face was his own and that he supposed he could do what he liked with it. But Grampa said that's where he was wrong. A man's face wasn't his own. It belonged to the neighbours that had to look at it, and about all a man owned in his own face was the responsibility to keep it lookin' shipshape.

Jethro got contrary and didn't shave for another two or three weeks, till his wife got after him 'cause he was scarin' the baby, and he's been better ever since.

So perhaps Grampa is right and a man's temper is like his face – somethin' he's responsible for keepin' shipshape for the sake of his neighbours. But I've got another reason besides that for tryin' to keep my temper and I'll tell you about it some other time. Right now I'm overhaulin' my old duds pickin' out somethin' to wear tonight mummerin'* – somethin' people are not likely to recognize. Yes, I'm goin' mummerin', playin' the fool like everybody else and havin' a good time for myself.

I've heard people say there's a law against mummerin', but there's not. I asked the Ranger years ago and he said you could dress up however you liked provided you didn't have your face covered up in public. So what we people do in Pigeon Inlet is wear lace or scrim** over our faces and keep it up till we've knocked on someone's door and they're just about to open it.

You might think I oughtn't go mummerin' at my age. But then, who do you think is goin' with me? That's right. Grampa Walcott.

* mummering: visiting houses in disguise during the Christmas season

** scrim: gauze material that allows one to see in one direction but not in the other

Grampa and the
Hockey Game

I'M SURE I'VE TOLD YOU over and over again about what
a wonderful man Grampa Walcott is and how much we fellows here in Pigeon Inlet respect his opinion. Now, that don't
mean to say that Grampa Walcott is right all the time. On
local matters, yes. On things like fish-makin' or keepin' our
fishin' stages in proper order, he knows it all. Then again, on
Pigeon Inlet history he's an authority. But when it comes to
things outside Pigeon Inlet, he's not so good. Sometimes he
makes mistakes and we've got to laugh at him – behind his
back, of course, so as not to hurt his feelin's.

Take, for example, the things he hears about over the
radio. Perhaps 'tis because his hearin' is not quite as good as
it used to be or perhaps it's because the things he hears about
are strange to him, but whatever the reason, he gets tangled
up sometimes and hears things over his radio that the rest of
us never hear over ours.

There was that time last fall when the talk was goin'
around about polio and some people was sayin' we ought to
close up the schools to keep it from spreadin' – though what
good that'd do we couldn't see. Well, one night Grampa

frightened us nearly to death. He said accordin' to what he heard over the radio that day, polio was spreadin' somethin' terrible and by all accounts we'd soon all be havin' it. He said he'd been listenin' over the radio to about fifty or sixty thousand people, all bawlin' and screechin' like mad and they all had polio and were all fenced in into a place by themselves, over fifty thousand of 'em. He said the place they were barred up in had a special name – the polio grounds.

Well, it wasn't until next day that we found out what Grampa had been listenin to was a baseball game somewhere up in New York and it wasn't the polio grounds at all, although it sounded somethin' like it. Polo,* it was – I think.

Then again, take what happened on Sunday afternoon not long ago. Skipper Joe dropped in to see me and we were sittin' there, the two of us, cuffin' the yarn when I turned on the radio and it sounded like a crowd playin' hockey – Sunday and all, as it was. We listened to it for a minute and then we got right interested. One crowd was Russians and the others were from Canada – out somewhere in British Columbia. Well, British Columbia is just about as far from Pigeon Inlet as Russia is, but after all, it was Canada and not Russia that we went into Confederation with six years ago, so we got hopin' the Canada team'd win and, sure enough, that's what happened. They seemed to be a lot better than the other fellows, and Skipper Joe said this was one of the times when a fellow could feel proud he was a Canadian. Besides, they seemed more like our own on account of their names. The Russians had all odd names like Boboff, Catchemoff, names like that, while the Canadians' names were common ones. Why, there was one Canadian fellow – he seemed the spryest of the lot – his name was Bill Warwick and Skipper Joe said he bet if you could trace it back far enough, you'd find he was related to Skipper Tom Warrick from Pummelly Cove who was pretty spry himself when he was younger.

Well, that was that. But a few minutes later, in come Grampa Walcott all excited to ask us if we'd heard about the ructions that'd been goin' on just now between the Roosians and the Canadians. We said yes – and Grampa said the Roosians certainly got the best of it. He said 'twas the first time he'd ever listened to a hockey match, but you couldn't fool him on who was best. We tried to tell him 'twas the other way round, but 'twas no good. Then we told him the Canadians got five and the Russians got neither one, but he said that made no difference – he said the Roosians were the best. We told him the best fellow in the game was a fellow Warrick who was probably related to Skipper Tom up in Pummelly Cove. He said that might be right enough. Skipper Tom Warrick had two or three brothers that'd gone out West years ago, but that there was a better fellow there than Warrick – a Roosian fellow – he was the best fellow in the game.

"Why," said Grampa, "this Roosian fellow was all over the place, and besides that, he was tougher than the others. They used to get tired and take a spell sometimes, but he was right in the thick of it all the time."

"Are you sure he was a Russian?" said I.

"Of course I'm sure," said Grampa. "I'm sure on account of his name. He had a Roosian name."

"What was it?" said I. "Was it Pushemov?"

"No," said Grampa, "not him.

"What about Shovemoff?" I tried.

"No. Oh now I remember. It was Faceoff," said Grampa. "And what a fellow this Faceoff was to be sure – why, one minute you'd hear about Faceoff bein' up at one end and next minute there'd be Faceoff down at the other end, and sometimes Faceoff'd be right out in the middle. Ah," said Grampa "'that fellow Faceoff must be some man."

Well, what could Skipper Joe and myself do only agree with Grampa, that if the Russians had a few more fellows like Faceoff on their team, the Canadians wouldn't have had a chance in the world.

* Polo (Grounds): baseball park, home of the New York Giants during the 1950s

DRESSMAKIN'

WHEN A WOMAN KEEPS A man under her thumb the way Emma Jane Bartle keeps poor Lukey, she ought to know that if ever he gets a chance he's likely to go to wing.

Like the night last fall. We were aboard Skipper Joe's schooner in St. John's. Our fish was all out, our freight was aboard, and we were leavin' for Pigeon Inlet at daylight. Now here 'twas twelve o'clock, and one of our crew still ashore – Lukey Bartle. He'd gone ashore to do some shoppin', he said, and that was nine hours before. Well, about half past twelve, two policemen came down on the wharf. They had Luke with them, and they told us, if we owned him, to take him and keep him out of further trouble. All they could get out of him, they said, was that he was a Pigeon Inletter, and not to tell Emma Jane. So we hove him into his bunk and he didn't stir till next mornin' when we were halfway across to Baccalieu Tickle. 'Twas then we heard just how big a mess he was in.

It seems that Emma Jane had only let him come in with Skipper Joe on condition that he'd buy her a dress in St. John's, so she'd have it in time for Christmas. She saved up $20.00 of the money she earns helpin' the Post Office and had given it to Luke.

Well, now Luke remembers that he hadn't bought the dress. The thought of goin' back to Pigeon Inlet and facin'

Emma Jane frightened all of us, so Skipper Joe offered to turn back to St. John's. But then we heard the real bad news. Luke had spent all the money. All he had left was thirty-one cents, and 'twas a wonder he had that much. Between us all we didn't have enough to buy a dress. So, Luke crawled back into his bunk, wishin' he was dead, and I went up on deck to relieve Jethro Noddy at the wheel.

Skipper Joe come up a few minutes later, lookin' as miserable as a man can look. "Uncle Mose," he said, "what in the world are we goin' to do?"

Well, I told him, in a time like that, the only hope was to figger out the things you couldn't do, and see what you had left. One thing for sure we couldn't do was face Emma Jane without a dress. She'd blame us just as much as Luke. And we couldn't sail around the ocean forever like that *Flyin' Dutchman* fellow. Skipper Joe thought perhaps we might run ashore on Baccalieu and tell Emma Jane the parcel was lost in the wreck. But finally he changed his mind about that. So what was left? "Only one thing, Skipper Joe," I said. "We got to do some dressmakin' right aboard this yer schooner."

For a spell he thought I was crazy, but what else was there? So he called Jethro back to the wheel, while he and I went below to rummage for dress material. Sail canvas was too heavy, and potato sack was too coarse grain. A sheet or tablecloth might have served the purpose, but we had nar one.

'Twas then, lookin' at Luke groanin' in his bunk, I got the idea. I told Luke he'd have to lie on the bare boards the rest of the trip, 'cause I had to have his mattress. 'Twas actually an old sack, stuffed with shavin's and hay and goodness knows what else. So we emptied it and examined it. It had been white years ago, but was what you'd call baccy-juice brown. I thought the colour'd just suit Emma Jane. The problem was how to make it fit her.

The most Luke could tell us about Emma Jane's dimensions was that she was about the same build as Jethro Noddy, with allowances of course, for here and there. So Lukey relieved Jethro at the wheel, 'cause I had to have Jethro for my model.

I made a hole in the closed end, slipped it over his head, cut two armholes, and sliced the other end off just below his knees. 'Twas twice too wide, but that could be fixed. And as for the way it hung, well, I could see where I had to make a belt and Emma Jane could belay it tight or pay it out to suit herself.

Well, for the rest of the trip, I was relieved of all seamen's duties, and I want right here and now to thank the other fellows for what the sports writers call a real team effort – Skipper Joe for always carryin' a sewin' needle on board, Lukey Bartle for keepin' my pocket knife sharpened, Fred Prior for unravellin' his shirt to keep me supplied with sewin' cotton, and Jethro Noddy for the way he stood up for his fittin's and the true Christian spirit he showed one time when I stuck a bastin' pin into his starboard quarter. The hardest job of all was makin' the belt, but finally 'twas done, and Jethro modelled it all for us, just as we were turnin' in towards Pigeon Inlet. We parcelled it up, give it to Lukey, and hoped for the best.

'Twas long after dark that night when Skipper Joe come over to my house. He was worried, just like I was, because there hadn't been a sound from Lukey Bartle since he went home with the parcel. Perhaps she'd killed him! Anyway, we had to know, so over we went.

We could hear Emma Jane singin' like a twillick,* so that

encouraged me to peep in under the kitchen blind. And what do you think? There she was with the dress on, admirin' herself in the lookin' glass, and every once in a while runnin' over to kiss Luke where he was lyin' down on the settle.**

So we went and knocked on the door, and she almost dragged us in to see the beautiful dress Lukey had brought her from St. John's. The very latest thing in the catalogue, she said, and when she wore it to church on Sunday, Aunt Sophy and the other women'd bust themselves with jealousy. She even told Skipper Joe she bet he hadn't thought of his wife like Lukey had thought of her. I could see Skipper Joe was beginnin' to full up, so I got him out of there quick.

Lookin' back at it now, there's only two things I'm sorry for. One is the trouble I went to to make that belt. 'Cause Emma Jane never wears it. No more do the other women who ordered dresses from the catalogue as soon as they saw Emma Jane's. Emma Jane says 'tis even stylisher without the belt.

Another thing I'm sorry for is that I didn't use up all the material in that mattress sack. There was plenty left over to make another dress, and I ought to have made one for Aunt Sophy. After all, why should Emma Jane be the best-dressed woman in Pigeon Inlet?

* twillick: long-legged bird that frequents seashore and streams

** settle: wooden bench or couch without upholstery

AUNT JEMIMA
AND THE UNITED BUS

AUNT JEMIMA BRIGGS, that's Pete's mother, poor old
Uncle Jonathan Briggs's widow, had a very unfortunate experience the Sunday before last, and she was in to see me yesterday to know if I'd write a letter for her to the Premier
about it, 'cause like she said, 'tis not good enough and somethin' got to be done about it.

Her misfortune? Oh yes, she missed church the Sunday
before last, the first Sunday she's missed church since her
youngest child was born, thirty-five years ago last January.

About a fortnight ago, the doctor was here on his rounds
and he advised Aunt Jemima to go into St. John's to the hospital for an examination. So that Monday mornin', after bein'
to church as usual on Sunday, she went into St. John's, and
by Thursday she was in the hospital. They kept her there for
two days and let her out Saturday. Aunt Jemima's niece,
that's Pete's first cousin, is married to a fellow that lives just
a few miles out the road from St. John's, and she heard tell
over the radio about her aunt bein' in the hospital and come
to visit her. Furthermore, she invited Aunt Jemima to come
out and spend the weekend and that her husband on his way

home from work Saturday evenin' would call at the hospital to pick her up and bring her home.

And sure enough, he did. But like Aunt Jemima said to me last night, if she'd a knowed the way, she'd a walked there faster than he took her in his truck. Not that he didn't drive fast; too fast to her liking when he did drive. 'Twas the number of places he had to stop at on the way out the road, on business, he said, though he didn't explain to her what business. But she kept her eyes open, and she noticed that, whatever the business was, it was the kind where you wiped your mouth with the back of your hand after doin' it. Anyway, she said, she was good and dunch* from sittin' up in the truck before they finally got home.

They certainly treated her kind, though, Aunt Jemima says, and everything went well until she mentioned that the next day, bein' the blessed Sunday, they'd all be goin' to church, 'cause in that case she'd go with them. They hummed and hawed a bit over that, and finally her niece said that they wasn't much for churchgoin' and generally took it easy on Sunday mornin'. But if Aunt Jemima was real anxious to go, no doubt the husband would get up next mornin' special and drive her there in his truck. Aunt Jemima said no, she didn't want to put anybody out, and she'd go her own self if they'd tell her how to get there. Besides, she had it figgered that, with all the little business calls her niece's husband had made that evenin', he wouldn't be in much of a mood for church or anywhere else next mornin'. After all, she hadn't lived with Skipper Jonathan Briggs for forty years for nothin'.

So they told her that the church was too far for her to walk, but if she'd go out by the side of the road next mornin', a bus would pick her up, take her right by the church, and bring her back. And she said that's what she'd do. She'd never been on a bus before, but there was a first time for everything.

Well, after supper the husband went off in his truck, no doubt to make a few more business calls, and the niece showed Aunt Jemima her lovely furniture. Aunt Jemima made so bold as to ask if it cost much, and her niece didn't know what the actual cost of any of it was, 'cause she said that nowadays you didn't buy things in that old-fashioned way of payin' for them. You just made a small down payment and they brought the stuff right to your door. Well, Aunt Jemima told me that she had it in the back of her mind to buy a stove while she was in St. John's, but if that was the way you had to buy it, she said she would rather save up steel wool and knit one rather than buy it and go into debt perhaps for the rest of her life.

Anyway, the next mornin' she got up without wakin' the rest of the house and went out to the place they told her at the side of the road and waited – and waited – and waited – until she knowed that church must be in and out again. Then she went back to her niece's. They never asked her and she never told them what happened. But now here she was tellin' me so as I'd write a letter to the Premier and get him to fix it.

"But, Aunt Jemima," I said, "didn't you go to church that mornin'?"

"No, Uncle Mose," she said, "I didn't. I couldn't."

"But didn't the bus come along?" said I.

"Yes," she said, "there was one every few minutes and it used to slow down to know if I wanted to get aboard. But I didn't."

"Why not?" said I.

"Because it was always the wrong bus goin' to the wrong church. Every one of them had 'United' marked on them plain enough. And what would I be doin'," she said, "a hypocrite under false pretences getting' into one of them buses to go to *my* church. What I want you to do," she said, "is to write a letter to the Premier askin' him to put an Anglican bus on that road on Sunday mornin's. Otherwise I won't be caught in there again of a blessed Sunday with no way of gettin' to my church."

* dunch: cramped or numbed from sitting in one position

AUNT SOPHY'S PREDICAMENT

PERHAPS I SHOULD BE married. Perhaps I've been neglectin' a man's duty all these years. I dunno. All I do know is that, in the thirty-odd years I fished the Grand Banks out of Fortune Bay, I was only ashore from November to February, and 'twas a mystery to me how any Bank fisherman ever found time to get to know a woman well enough to ask her to marry him.

And now, since I've come to live in Pigeon Inlet, I've passed into what you might call "the ungainly age." What I mean is, if they're young, they call me "sir" or, more often, "uncle" – whereas if they're not, I can't somehow keep myself from callin' them "Ma'am" or "Auntie." It makes me think that young Bill Rumble had a point. His father, Uncle Matty Rumble, was pesterin' him to get married. And Bill said, "'Tis all right for you, father, you married Mother. But if I get married, I've got to marry a strange woman."

Of course, there's Aunt Sophy, not long back from Corner Brook, all titivated up, crinolines and everything, from where she'd been visitin' her own daughter Soos that's married there. But every time we seem to be gettin' to the point where

I might work up a bit of courage, somethin' happens to put her on the outs with me again.

Like that Sunday mornin' just after she'd got back from Corner Brook. The clergyman'd got here Saturday, and that meant early service. So Sunday mornin' I was up just about sunrise, with my good suit and everything, on my way to church. And some sight it was that met my eyes out in the lane.

The lane runs out to the main road where you turn up towards the church, and it's got seven or eight houses along it, includin' mine and Aunt Sophy's. Jethro Noddy's fishin' punt lay right across the lane where some skylarkin' bedlamer boys must have hauled her the night before. The punt made a perfect fit from fence to fence, leavin' no room to squeeze around either stem nor stern. But that wasn't the worst. She wasn't restin' on an even keel. The starboard side, the one towards me, was tipped up. So it wasn't till I hove up along-side that I spotted Aunt Sophy. I can't describe her position. 'Twas about halfway between a squat and a crouchie. 'Twas hard to say exactly where she was sittin' – on the ground, the port gunnel,* or the risin's, because the place was overflowin' with crinolines. And to make matters worse, those mischie-vous boys hadn't even bothered to bail out the punt.

Well, I rested my chin on the starboard gunnel and looked down at her – puzzled like – and she looked up at me, I can't describe what like. I should've sized up what'd happened. Tryin' to get to church, she'd got into the punt all right, but must've got tangled up tryin' to get out again. So perhaps I shouldn't have said what I did. But in a time like that a fel-low got to say somethin'.

"Aunt Sophy" said I, "what in the world are you doin' there?"

"Come here," said she, "you foolish gommil,** and help me."

So with that, what else could I do, but start to climb over the starboard gunnel. My weight brought my side down and hers up, and 'tis a wonder the screech she let out didn't wake up all the rest of Pigeon Inlet. I figgered right there and then that she must be fouled up in the thole-pin,*** but 'twas too late to turn back, so over I went.

"Here, Aunt Sophy," said I, like talkin' to a child, "let me unhitch you." All I could tell from her look was that a human face can be purple and red at the same time. She couldn't get words out, but she waved to me to go away.

"But," said I, "I can't leave you like this. What'll I do?"

Then she spoke. "Get a woman, you hangashore," she said. "Get Emma Jane Bartle."

Well, Luke Bartle's house is next one out the lane, but Luke and Emma Jane are not good churchgoers in early mornin', so it took me a spell to wake 'em, get 'em downstairs, and explain how Aunt Sophy was hitched up in the thole-pin of Jethro Noddy's punt. But finally Emma Jane looked out the window and saw for herself. Then she put on somethin' and went out, givin' me and Luke strict orders to bide out of sight.

Ten minutes later by Luke's clock, he was still too afraid of Emma Jane to peep. But I did. They hadn't made any progress. "Luke," said I, "we've got to do somethin'."

"Uncle Mose," said he, "can't you sort of lift her off?"

"Who? Her?" said I. And he agreed no, I couldn't.

"But," said he, "what about tippin' the punt all the way over. Then she'd sort of drop off."

"I thought of that," said I, "but the port side is restin' on a big boulder."

"Oh," he said.

"Luke," said I, "there's only one cure for this."

"What?" said he

"Gimme your handsaw," said I.

He brought it from the porch and asked, "What're you goin' to do?"

"I'm goin'," said I, "to saw off that thole-pin – flush to the gunnel – together with whatever crinolines happen to get in the way." And off I went, to do what I thought was right, like any man should in an emergency. When she spied the handsaw, her screech *did* wake up the neighbourhood, but I paid no heed and had her free before people could gather.

Did she say thank you? No. What did she say? Nothin' from that day to this. Except once about a week after, when I called on her and offered some sort of compensation for the clothin' I'd damaged with the handsaw. What she said then would've been better left unsaid. After all, how was I supposed to know that a good firm birch hoop off a five-quintal fish cask wouldn't make a reasonable substitute for those crinolines?

* gunnel (gunwale): upper edge of a boat's side

** gommil: stupid person

*** thole-pin: wooden peg used on a boat as fulcrum for an oar

VITAMINS

THERE'S NO DOUBT ABOUT IT, there's an awful lot of kind-hearted people in this world, people who are well off and got nothin' to worry about on their own account, so that gives them time to worry about other people. And one thing that seems to be worryin' them more than anything else is the kind of grub that we folks down in Pigeon Inlet eat.

It wasn't so bad until about a few years ago when they found out about these things called "vitamins," but now 'tis terrible. 'Cause by all accounts, we're not gettin' enough vitamins in our grub and when we do get hold of somethin' with vitamins in it, we cook it too much so that we kill all the vitamins or boil them away to nothin' – which is just as bad.

Grampa Walcott says 'tis an awful thing when you come to think of it. Take a man like, say, Uncle Matty Rumble. Now, he died when he was 104. He lived all that spell thinkin' he was hale and hearty, strong enough to tear the tail out of a bull. And all the time, without knowin' it, he was pinin' away – no vitamins. Likely he never eat a vitamin in his life, unless 'twas a dead one in vegetables his missus had cooked too long. Poor old fellow! He didn't even know there was a vitamin. If he had known, and found out he wasn't gettin' any, he'd likely have been so discouraged that he'd have given it up for a bad job and died years before he did. But 'twasn't his fault, 'cause nobody told him the difference, and so he lived and died thinkin' that the only thing wrong with his grub was that in poor times he didn't get enough of it.

Nowadays it's different. Anybody that don't know all about vitamins, it's their own fault. We first heard tell of them a few years ago when this woman came here to visit us. A "nutrition expert," she called herself. And she knowed so much about vitamins that you'd think she was related to them. She was doin' a survey and she was especially interested in tryin' to figger out how we people managed to live at all on the kind of nourishment we were gettin', or not gettin'. She used to get the women together and explain to them about how their menfolk were not gettin' their proper vitamins. And naturally, the women got interested in that and wanted to do somethin' about it.

Well, accordin' to her, there were two things wrong with the grub they were feedin' us. The first thing was there were not enough vitamins in it. It was the same things over and over, week after week. It was a wonder we didn't starve to death for want of variety.

Anyway, Aunt Sooz Prior took it to heart and, one day, just by way of variety, she cooked a pot of pea soup for Bill on a Wednesday instead of a Saturday, like she and everybody else always did. It would have been all right if Uncle Bill hadn't been sexton of the church at the time and, next mornin', Thursday, he woke up the whole place ringin' the church bell. Now most of us jumped out of bed and hurried to church thinkin' the clergyman must have made a surprise visit, and we had the work of the world persuadin' Uncle Bill that it was Thursday. 'Cause he was sure and certain it was Sunday on account of how he had had pea soup for dinner the day before. Fortunately the rest of us hadn't had pea soup like he had, so we knew the difference.

Well, another thing wrong with our grub, accordin' to this expert, was that it was cooked too much. Especially the vegetables. Like cabbage. It appears that cabbage is chock full of these little vitamins, all dancin' and jumpin' around, just waitin' to get inside a man and make him all full of pep and vigour. But after you boil it for ten or fifteen minutes, the vitamins all leave it and go out into the pot liquor and get drowned.

Even Grandma Walcott got interested in that, and poor Grampa told me that for weeks afterwards he suffered somethin' awful, tryin' to eat half-cooked cabbage. He said he used to feel his forehead to see if there was any horns comin' through, and finally he up and told Grandma that if he was goin' to have to eat goat's grub, he might just as well go out in the goat house to sleep, and make a complete job of it.

Only once in his life, said Grampa, did he ever see food cooked too much to please him, and that was one time early in his married life when Grandma went down the shore to visit her people and Grampa cooked his own dinner, the first one he'd ever cooked in his life. Pork and doughboys, it was.

Grampa, as he tells it, mixed up the flour and water and made two goodish-sized doughboys and put them on to boil. Then, after they'd been boilin' for a spell, he put in the pork, figgerin' that when the pork was ready the doughboys ought to be done too. Well, he had his dinner all right – pork. I asked him what happened to the doughboys.

"Uncle Mose," he said, "them doughboys, was a problem. I couldn't bury them 'cause 'twould give Pigeon Inlet a bad name if future generations dug them up and thought 'twas cannonballs. So I lugged them down to the stagehead, when nobody was lookin', and I hove them overboard, one at a time. A gull dived after the first one, and he must have got it. Anyway, he never come up no more. T'other one I dropped just over the stagehead and thought no more about it, till two or three days afterwards I saw somethin' stirrin' on the bottom. When I looked closer, I made out 'twas a flatfish tryin' to work his way free from somethin' that was on his back and had him penned down onto the bottom. So," says Grampa, "I reached down with the boathook and after a spell I managed to roll that doughboy off the flatfish's back and released him. He was the happiest-lookin' flatfish you ever hoped to see."

CONTRARINESS

I'VE SEEN CONTRARY MEN IN my day, but Pete Briggs takes the cake. Here, for years now, Pete has been just as loud as any of us in his demand for unemployment insurance for fishermen, and now that we've been guaranteed that we'll get it, Pete is tryin' his best to pick holes in it. The first thing he found to grumble about was that we ought to be sure we were gettin' it from the right government. That 'twas the one in Ottawa ought to give it to us instead of the one in St. John's. "Now, what odds what government gives it to us so long as we get it?" I say, and everyone else agrees with me, let's get it and let the governments figger it out afterwards among themselves who should foot the bill. Jethro Noddy says he don't care if it's the Pigeon Inlet Community Council that pays for it so long as he gets it, and although the rest of us don't go quite so far as Jethro, we agree he's got the right idea.

Yes, Pete is one contrary man. Another thing he's grumblin' about. He says we wouldn't get it at all only an election is comin'. Perhaps that's true and perhaps 'tis not. But what's the odds? That's what comes of livin' in a democracy where poor people's votes count. Elections, and the right to vote in 'em, is what gives people like us a chance to have our needs attended to. Pete tried to say 'twas a promise that might never be kept, but even Pete knows the difference of that. Whoever gets in will know that this is a promise they got to keep.

I asked Grampa Walcott last night, "Grampa," I said. "What makes Pete Briggs so contrary? He's a good, level-headed man in lots of ways. But contrary! Why?"

"Well, Mose," said Grampa, "Pete can't help his contrariness. What's bred in his bones got to come out in his flesh." Then Grampa went on to tell me that, contrary as Pete was, he was nothin' compared to what his father Jonathan Briggs was, and Jonathan was nothin' compared to his father, old Simeon Briggs. "Now Simeon Briggs," said Grampa, "there was a contrary man. Right up to the time he died, twenty-odd years ago. He was in his nineties and last few years of his life the only way they could get him to go to bed was to tell him not to go."

"I remember as well as if 'twas yesterday," said Grampa, "the year we started havin' John Anderson's time* down here in Pigeon Inlet. That spring we all put our clocks on an hour, and by and by that fall we had to put 'em back an hour to make up for it. Somebody made the mistake of tellin' Uncle Sim Briggs to be sure and put his clock back and, of course, contrary as he was, he insisted that 'twas not back he had to put it but ahead. Well," said Grampa, "the upshot was that, all that winter, he had his clock two hours faster than anybody else's. He must've knowed he was wrong, but he wouldn't give in. Goin' to church Sunday mornin' was all right, because they'd have their dinner finished before 'twas time for eleven o'clock service to start. Uncle Sim went so far as to say he liked afternoon service instead of havin' it in the mornin' – although he thought 'twas a blasphemous time to be readin' mornin' prayer.

"The worst of all was on Lodge nights. With all his faults and contrariness Uncle Sim was a faithful old Lodge member, and that winter it must have hurt him awful bad to have to miss meetin's. But of course he had to miss 'em or else give in that he was wrong about his clock, because accordin' to his clock 'twas about half past ten in the night before Lodge started and he said that was time for all decent people to be goin' to bed instead of goin' to Lodge. He threatened to complain to the Grand Lodge about how we were violatin' our Constitution by startin' our meetin's so late in the nights."

"Did he complain to the Grand Lodge?" said I.

"No," said Grampa. "He couldn't write his own self, and of course he was too contrary to ask anyone to do it for him. There was one good thing come out of it though," said Grampa. "His youngsters were the best-behaved ones in school all that winter. You see, the teacher's favourite punishment in these days was to keep youngsters in recess time, and that's when the Briggs youngsters used to have to dart home to get their dinners."

"How did it end up?" said I.

"Well," said Grampa, "the followin' spring, when the rest of us put our clocks on an hour, he was still contrary and said they should be put back, so that brought him right again. That fall his wife saved the situation by startin' to put the clock ahead again, but he caught her doin' it, so he put it back and we had no trouble with him after."

"A contrary man is an awful torment," said I.

"Well now," said Grampa. "In one way Uncle Sim Brigg's contrariness come in handy."

"How?" said I.

"Election times," said Grampa. "'Twas said, and I can well believe it, that Uncle Sim voted in every election since Newfoundland got Responsible Government – and lost every vote. The way it was," said Grampa, "for pure cussedness and contrariness he'd sort of figger out how the majority was goin' to vote and of course he'd go agen 'em. It got so that the member when he come round to see us (that'd be once every four years, just before election time), he always ask us how was Uncle Sim Briggs feelin' about the political situation, and when we'd tell him that Uncle Sim was dead against him, he'd know everything was all right. One time when he come he got a awful fright because that particular year Uncle Sim was blood and fire in his favour. But the member fixed it. He met Uncle Sim in Josiah Bartle's shop and slapped him on the shoulder. He told Uncle Sim he'd rather have his vote than any other man's in Pigeon Inlet. Uncle Sim replied that he wouldn't give him a vote if he had fifty. So our member got in again.

"Yes," said Grampa, "while Uncle Sim was alive you could always bet your bottom dollar on the election out-come."

* John Anderson's time: Daylight Savings Time, named after the Newfoundland legislator who introduced it in 1917

BABYSITTIN'

OF ALL THE JOBS I'VE EVER done in this world, the one I never want to do again is babysittin'. Yes, I had a good dory-mate, Grampa Walcott, and we come through safe and sound, but when I think of it – never again!

Grampa was stuck that night, good and proper. Grandma and her daughter Aunt Sophy, and *her* daughter Soos, who was visitin' from Corner Brook with her six-months-old baby, had all been invited out to this special party the Women's Association was givin' on account of three generations of members bein' here all at the one time.

Of course, they could've got Liz Noddy, Jethro's daughter, to babysit, but Liz would have chewed bubble gum all night and brought along her grammyphone records (the ones Grampa can't stand). He said a night like that would've drove him cracked. So, that evenin', he asked me if I'd take a berth with him babysittin', and I signed on. Well, from now on, whatever babysittin' there is in Pigeon Inlet can be done by Liz Noddy, with her bubble gum, All Shook Up, Jailhouse Rock, and all the rest of it.

The women had gone when I got there. The baby was sound asleep upstairs and Grampa had the cribbage board all set upon the kitchen table. I asked him did he have any instructions what to do if the baby woke. He said no, Soos had made some funny remark about a formula bein' somewhere, but bein' as how the only formula he knew about was the one for findin' the number of cords in a pile of pulpwood, we figgered *that* had no connection with the baby. So we started our game of cribbage.

The women had said they'd be home before ten, but bein' women, there was no sign of 'em at half past, when the baby started to bawl. We waited to see if the squall'd die down, but it got so bad 'twas likely to frighten all the neighbours, so Grampa went up and brought him down.

When that baby grows up, it won't cost him much in soap to wash his face. All he'll have to do is open his mouth and there'll be no face left to wash. Grampa had him wrong end up when he brought him down, but even after he upended him right, he bawled harder than ever. I made signs to Grampa (there was no sense tryin' to talk), that there must be a pin stickin' in him somewhere. Grampa held him up sort of by the crosstrees,* while I examined among his riggin'.** Next thing I knew, the whole outfit tumbled to the kitchen floor, and there he was in his bare poles, bawlin', if 'twas possible harder than ever.

Grampa screeched out somethin' to me about gettin' the canvas back on him quick, but like I told him, anybody with one eye or, for that matter, nar eye at all, could tell we weren't supposed to put *that* back on him. We agreed that the only thing to do was poke it into the kitchen stove and look in the sail locker for a new outfit. We located the sail locker on top of the sewin' machine and, after an argument as to whether we should put a jib on him or a foresail, we put both of 'em on. Like Grampa said, 'twas best to play safe. The trouble was it only made him bawl more than ever. "There's only one salvation," said Grampa. "Grub. 'Twould have been better," said he, "if Soos had told us what to feed him instead of talkin' about cords of pulpwood."

But what could we feed a young fellow that age? There was cold moose meat in the pantry, but like Grampa said, the rough edges might choke him. Somethin' smooth we wanted, but what? There was only one thing – made to order, you might say. Fat pork. So I took him, while Grampa headed for the pork barrel in the back room and come back with a lovely little chunk, 'bout a half-inch each way.

But I had misgivin's. There was no question as to smoothness, or even nourishment. But with no teeth to chew it, supposin' it gave him indigestion? Grampa had the answer to that. Tie a string to it. Then after he'd gone to sleep on it, if it hurt him, we had the wherewithal to get it back.

And that's what we did. He swallered that hunk of salt pork like a real north-shoreman, and before Grampa had him halfway up the stairs he was half asleep, and quiet as a mouse.

'Twas then this horrible thought struck me. Supposin' he swallowed the string too. But when Grampa got downstairs he said as how he'd thought of that very danger, and had belayed the other end of the string to the baby's big toe.

"But," said I, "when you laid him down didn't he stick up his legs and slacken the string?"

"Yes," said Grampa, "he did, and then I tied a sheepshank*** on it to tighten it again. Then when he dozes off and straightens his legs, up 'twill come, easy as anything."

Five minutes later by Grampa's clock, he creeped up again, and there was the youngster, sound asleep, with his legs straightened out. Grampa untied the string from his toe, picked up the other end off the pillow, and we had both that string and the fat pork in the kitchen stove on top of that other thing, just as we heard the women comin' back from the party.

* crosstrees: two horizontal bars of wood near top of a ship's mast

** riggin': ropes and chains used to support masts and sails

*** sheepshank: a knot made on a rope to shorten it temporarily

BLOOD PRESSURE

I WAS READIN' A PIECE IN A newspaper the other day, and no doubt a lot more people – especially fishermen – noticed it too. 'Twas all about the need for eatin' more fish and less meat – that is, if we wanted to stay alive to eat anything. Accordin' to this article, and it appeared to come from the United States Government, which is about as high up as anything can come from in this world, meat-eatin' got a lot to do with high blood pressure, whereas fish-eatin' serves the same bodily purpose as meat, but don't make the blood pressure go up at all. This interested me, naturally, first of all because, bein' a fisherman, I'm glad to hear that every time I catch a fish I'm helpin' to keep down the world's blood pressure, and besides that, it helps to explain a lot of things that's always puzzled me.

This blood pressure is a funny thing. Personally, I don't understand it, but those that do, or say they do, tell me that this heart we've all got inside us got the job of pumpin' blood all over our bodies to keep us alive, and it pumps it along through these pipes called arteries. Now, like any other pump, a fellow's heart'll only last so long before 'twill wear out, and how long 'twill last depends to a great extent on whether you overwork it or not. It works twenty-four hours a day in any case, but that makes no difference so long as it doesn't have to work any harder than it ought. And to give it a fair chance, all it asks for is that these pipes should be kept free of sludge and muck, just like the pump on my motor engine don't want to get anything like slob ice or kelp sucked into the intake to choke it.

Another thing about these arteries, they're soft and pliable and need to stretch a little bit as the blood is pumped through 'em. If they do that, the heart don't have to work as hard and will last that much longer. But if these pipes get hardened or partly clogged up, then comes this extra strain on the heart which results in all kinds of things called hardenin' of the arteries, high blood pressure, heart trouble, arteriosclerosis, and a lot of other names that I couldn't pronounce even if I knowed 'em. But the main thing is that they're all bad.

Now, accordin' to this article, got out, as I said, by the American Government, people who eat too much meat are more likely to get their arteries stogged up and get hardened arteries than people who don't. Meat, so they say, forms a substance that gets in the blood and is inclined to stick onto the walls of these arteries, thereby makin' the passage smaller and harder for the blood to get through, whereas on the other hand, fish, so they say, don't form that substance at all. And if that's so, it's a good reason for everybody eatin' a little less meat and a little more fish.

But is it so? Personally, in these days of propaganda of one kind or another, 'tis hard for us people to know what to believe, but I'm inclined to believe that there's somethin' to this. In the first place, look where it comes from – the United States. If they were a big fish-exportin' country, you might be tempted to think they were sayin' it to increase their business. But the United States – thank goodness – imports fish, so it can't be that. 'Cause if this report got to be believed, 'twould mean they'd have to import more – a lot more. So, even if 'tis not true, I hope they believe it anyway.

I'm inclined to think it is true, for another reason. If it's true, it explains a lot of things that have puzzled me, and a good many more, for years. Take that thing I was talkin' about once before. Vitamins. Accordin' to the authorities we people here in Pigeon Inlet don't get enough of 'em in our grub. A woman in St. John's that heard me wrote me a very nice letter on the same subject. She said she'd been to a meetin' one night the week before and heard a doctor say how the children growin' up in the cities were bigger and stronger than the ones their own age in the outports. He put that down to the extra vitamins they were gettin' in their grub. But this same doctor went on to say a peculiar thing. He said that these same outport children are likely to grow up and live years and years longer than the stronger and healthier ones in the city. And his reason was that a good many of these strong youngsters would probably die of heart trouble, or high blood pressure in their forties or fifties, whereas the outport youngsters, even without their vitamins, would be more likely to live to be eighty. Or ninety.

Well, maybe Pigeon Inlet is a little short of vitamins. And maybe not. I wouldn't know. But this I'm sure of. Pigeon Inlet must have about the lowest blood pressure and the softest arteries in the world. And if you'd seen Grampa Walcott out on the floor step-dancin' the night of the Women's Association sale, you'd agree with me.

Pete Briggs says he understands now why they want to centralize us. It's so as we'll get high blood pressure like the rest of 'em. But Grampa Walcott says that can't be it. Because even if they did manage to centralize him – which they won't – they'd have to shift him to a place where he could get plenty of fish to eat or else he'd die of starvation before blood pressure could get at him.

Yes, it must be the fish that's doin' it. Apparently all human bein's got to have somethin' in their grub called "proteins" and the commonest ways of gettin' it are in fish and meat. We eat fish.

We've knowed all along that eatin' fish gives a man brains. Now it looks as if 'twill not only give him the brains but 'twill help him stay alive longer to use 'em.

COLD WEATHER

THE NEIGHBOURS DOWN HERE in Pigeon Inlet often tease me in a good-natured way because up till eight years ago I was a Fortune Bayman, and I can't seem to get used to the winters down here. As far as I'm concerned, they're some cold – each one colder than the last. But I don't get any sympathy. Not even from Grandma Walcott. Grandma is losin' hope that me and her daughter Aunt Sophy'll make a match, and she said one time how some men were so slow-blooded 'tis a wonder they didn't get scrammed* with the cold in August.

Skipper Joe tells a yarn that he heard one time (or he says he heard) about how there's so little snow up around Fortune Bay wintertime that they don't wear rackets – and how one time when a Green Bay man lost his way and walked along in on the back with a pair of rackets on, every Fortune Bayman that saw his tracks in the woods next day got frightened to death thinkin' 'twas the footings of a turbot.

We got into an argument down on Skipper Joe's net loft the other day, when Grampa Walcott remarked on how even in Pigeon Inlet – where, unlike Fortune Bay, they did have winters – they were nothin' compared to the winters they used to have years ago. I know now I should've left well enough alone, but even though I'm no longer a Fortune Bayman, a man got to stand up for a place where he lived most of his life. So I spoke up and said I'd seen winters up there just as cold as Grampa'd ever seen it in Pigeon Inlet. Grampa said, no doubt, if that was so I'd be glad to give him an example, so I racked my brains for a second or two and then told 'em the one about the clergyman's photograph in my Aunt Becky's parlour.

Aunt Becky used to always board the clergyman when he'd come on his rounds. She kept this parlour specially for him, with the keyhole stogged up all the rest of the year to keep out the flies, with the fire laid in the little stove but never lighted until the day the clergyman was due. He was the same clergyman that give Aunt Cassie Tacker the big teapot cozy for a weddin' present that she wore on her head to early service in church next mornin'. 'Twas after that that he give out photographs of himself instead and Aunt Becky had one of 'em hung on the parlour wall right over the mantelpiece and Queen Victoria shifted over to the opposite side. Well, this bitter cold winter's mornin' Aunt Becky got a message the clergyman was comin', so Uncle Bill unstogged the keyhole and opened up the parlour and put a match to the fire he'd laid three months before. Then he straightened up, looked around, and got the surprise of his life. The clergyman's hands in the photograph, instead of bein' folded across his weskit** like they'd always been, was up over his ears – and they bided there till after that stove'd been blood red for a good ten minutes. Even then, Uncle Bill always figgered he'd have kept 'em there longer only for the look Queen Victoria was givin' him from the opposite wall.

Well, Grampa looked took aback for a minute after I'd finishcd, and hc had to agree that was kind of nippy sure enough. But he said that was only what we'd call a cold snap down here in Pigeon Inlet years ago – and there's a lot of difference between a cold snap and a winter. Like the winter we had down here in 1914 – the winter Uncle Joby Noddy stole the molasses from Old Josiah Bartle. There was bad times that winter besides the frost, but everybody had his winter's grub in except poor Uncle Joby, who run out of molasses in January and Josiah wouldn't let him have any more. Cut him right off, and he with a puncheon partly full that he kept locked away in his outside store.

Accordin' to Grampa, Uncle Joby was desperate, so one dark night with his auger and a water bucket he groped his way in the landwash among the ballicaders*** under Josiah's store and bored a hole right up through the floor, puncheon and all. Then he stood to the side and put the bucket on the ice under the hole. Nothin' happened and he figgered he'd have to bore again, when he looked up and seen this thing like a eel squirmin' down towards him. He tried to quile it into the bucket, but that was too slow so he grabbed bucket and auger in one hand and the end of the long thing in the other and made for home – all the way across the harbour ice to his own stagehead. Then he hauled it in hand over hand and piled it up in his net loft.

And all that winter, said Grampa, Uncle Joby lived like a lord, and when he wanted molasses he'd take his hatchet and go down to his net loft and chop off a fathom. And when there was visitors in his net loft, as sometimes is bound to happen, they noticed that Uncle Joby had a favourite seat on this special pile of rope. And he'd never have been found out if I hadn't happened to have been there with him the day the spring thaw come, and I had to help him up and get him down off his net loft and into his house out of sight.

And I wouldn't have told it now, said Grampa, only he's gone to his reward, poor fellow, and I know he'd sooner have it told than have anyone come around tryin' to pretend they have colder winters in Fortune Bay than here in Pigeon Inlet.

* scrammed: paralyzed

** weskit: waistcoat

*** ballicader: layer of ice

DICTIONARIES

WE PIGEON INLETTERS HAVE been tryin' hard to make ourselves into good Canadians, but I'm afraid we're makin' only slow headway. We're makin' progress all right, but we can't seem to catch up.

You take last spring, on a simple thing like figgerin' the best way out of a depression – whether you should do it by cuttin' down taxes, or by startin' to build a lot of public works. Everybody else in Canada, why, they found it easy, but accordin' to reports we went wrong again.

Grampa Walcott says he's goin' to give up tryin'. He allows he'll die like he lived, a Newfoundlander. He's got a suspicion (he's wrong, of course) that to be a good Canadian he's just got to be like everybody else – talk like 'em, think like 'em, vote like 'em. He admits it might be a wonderful thing, or then again it mightn't. You'd think, if the Blessed Lord had wanted us to have been all alike, he'd have made us that way, and saved all the teachers and politicians the trouble they're goin' to. But Grampa figgers the Lord intended us to be different and to bide different. Like he says, Jack Spratt and his wife. If they hadn't been different, 'twould have been a awful waste of good grub.

The hardest thing for us is the business of bein' like everybody else. Up in the Mainland they got that fixed up nice. When there's a holiday comin' up, the authorities can tell beforehand exactly how many of 'em are goin' to break their necks in motor cars, and how many of 'em are goin' to go out in boats and capsize and drown theirselves. It must be a great satisfaction to the authorities after the holiday is over to see just how the people behaved in the way they was expected to.

But down here in Pigeon Inlet it's not like that. Not with people. Caplin, yes. I'm able to predict that every year about the middle of June the caplin'll strike in to spawn on Bartle's Beach. And the squid – no. To give the squid their due, they seem to have minds of their own, and you go predictin' the squids'll strike in at such and such a time, and chances are they won't come in at all. Still, generally, they do come in like well-behaved folk ought to do.

But people! Well, let me predict that Jethro Noddy'll tumble off his stagehead tomorrow mornin', and Jethro will just take extra care to prove me wrong.

And we're even supposed to talk alike. Why, they've even got books, dictionaries they call 'em, but perhaps I can best bring out my point by tellin' you about Pete Briggs. Pete's boy, Jimmy, about nine years old, was goin' to school last winter. One day the teacher asked him to write a sentence with the word "father" in it. Jimmy, naturally enough, wrote down "Father shot a swile," and the teacher marked it wrong, the last word, that is.

Pete didn't feel too pleased about it and went straight up and asked the teacher what was wrong with it, and she (that's the same one that said John Cabot didn't discover Newfoundland) told him it ought to be spelled "seal" instead of "swile." Pete said maybe so. She was the teacher and she ought to know, but to him "seal" was an awful foolish way to spell "swile." The teacher met Grampa that same day, and asked him how did *he* spell "swile," and he said he didn't spell 'em at all. He towed 'em in like everybody else.

But to get back to what I was sayin' about the dictionary. Grampa says it's the most undemocratic book in the world, tryin' to make everybody talk alike. Personally, I disagree with him. I think the cookbook is worse, but that's another story.

Anyway, as I was sayin', one day after I'd told over the radio the story about some goin's-on up there on Gull Mash, Grampa dropped in to see me.

"Uncle Mose," he said, "I hope you'll excuse me, but you got part of the story wrong."

I asked him what part and he said that part about Gull Mish. Well, where I come from in Newfoundland we always called it "Mash" and, ill-mannered like, I hadn't noticed that down here in Pigeon Inlet everyone calls it "Mish." So I argued the point with Grampa. We couldn't agree, and we figgered the schoolteacher ought to be able to settle it for once and for all. We told her our trouble and asked her was it Mash or Mish.

Instead of helpin', she only hindered. 'Cause, she said, 'twas nar one of it, 'twas "Marsh." Grampa asked her where she got that from and she said there was no doubt about it. "Marsh" was right, because that's how it was in the dictionary.

Grampa laughed at her. "How long," said Grampa, "have these dictionary things been on the go?"

"Oh," said the schoolmaster, "two or three hundred years."

"And what," said Grampa, "did they call it before they had dictionaries? Do you think," said Grampa, "that generations of people lived for thousands of years alongside a mish, and even tumblin' into the mish, and pickin' berries off the mish, and then had to wait until two or three hundred years ago for some fellow to write a dictionary to tell 'em what to call it?"

And the cookbooks! But like I said, that's another story.

TOUTENS

I'VE GOT TO CONFESS THAT bein' a bachelor is a wonderful thing, but it's got a few shortcomin's. One of 'em is this business of cookery. Another one of 'em of course is... But never mind that one – let's get back to cookery.

Now I'm not goin' to start any argument over whether men can cook better than women. All I'm goin' to say is that I could cook if I had to. I remember, thirty-odd years ago when I was in a Banker out of Mose Ambrose in Fortune Bay, that our cook was laid up for a week and, well, I didn't poison anybody, and apart from one fellow from Bay de L'eau, I didn't get cussed on – much. But it's a lot easier cookin' for a crew of twenty-two men than it is cookin' just for yourself, and I'll confess that if you ever come to my house dinnertime to take potluck, there's lots of times you'd find the pot empty.

If there's one thing I mortally hate more than anything else in this world, it's tryin' to make my own bread. I remember the time I made a batch for the crew on the Banker while the cook was laid up. It wasn't too bad, because then a man had a mixin' pan of dough big enough to give vent to his feelin's on. But tryin' to make bread for just one. Well, either the ball of dough is too small to get a proper hold on, or else you bake so much bread that most of it dries up before you get a chance to eat it. So in later years, I've got away gradually from makin' bread at all and to depend more and more on toutens. Right this minute if you was to drop in for a visit, I'd be hard put to offer you a slice of bread, but I could pass around a plateful of toutens that'd make you come back for more. Not only that, but if you did come back a month later for what was left out of the same plateful, you'd find 'em as fresh as ever.

I'll give you my recipe for makin' toutens. But whatever you do, don't copy it out. You can't make 'em any sense if you go by a recipe, and thank goodness you can't find anything about 'em in the cookbooks. In my opinion cookbooks are not democratic. Imagine a man or a woman writin' a cook-book and tellin' me I must only put one cupful of molasses to every three cups of flour, or one spoonful of sugar to every cupful of butter. No thank you. I'll make my toutens to suit my own taste and I'll advise you to do the same. So here's my recipe to bachelors for makin' 'em.

First of all you need flour. How much flour? I don't know. That's up to you. It depends, I s'pose, on how big a batch of toutens you figger on makin'. So the first item is flour – any amount. Suit yourself.

Next comes molasses. How much? I don't know. It depends first of all on how much flour you got and second on how sweet you want to make 'em. And for one man to try to dictate to another man how sweet he ought to make his toutens – well, there's too much of that kind of thing goin' on in the world already.

Then comes the fat pork. It's got to be chopped up in lit-tle snags about a quarter-inch each way, or smaller. How much fat pork? Well, that's your own business, providin' of course you don't have more fat pork than flour. A lot depends on how long you want 'em to keep from dryin' up – and, of course, how fond you are of fat pork.

Well, if you've got flour, molasses, and fat pork you can go ahead. There's two other things that's nice to have around, in case you decide to use 'em – water and bakin' powder. Whether you'll need water depends on how much molasses you use, and as for bakin' powder and how much of it, well, how fluffy do you want 'em anyway? Personally I never touch the stuff, but that's no reason why you shouldn't use bakin' powder if you feel like it.

As for how long to bake it or how hot an oven to have, I don't know. There's no thermometer on the oven of my old Waterloo, so the only advice I can give you is to bake 'em until they're baked and then give 'em a minute or two extra to make sure. Then, after you've tasted one, you'll find out that men are not so helpless in this world as the women try to make out.

And speakin' of women, I'll never forget the look on Aunt Sophy's face that day last winter when I was laid up with a bit of a cold, and she and Grandma come down to my house to do what they call "lookin' out for me and straightenin' my place up a bit." 'Twas lucky I spied 'em comin', just in time to lock my bedroom door and put the key in my pocket, because sure enough, Grandma tried the door, but when she found it locked, she just give Aunt Sophy a signal and they said no more about it. But they give the rest of the house a goin' over – sweepin' and dustin', even polishin' my stove, talkin' all the time about poor dear helpless Uncle Mose.

Then Aunt Sophy opened my kitchen cupboard and spotted a platter full of toutens. She broke off one and tasted it. Then she turned to Grandma and said, "My, mother, that's the best toutens you ever made. But you didn't tell me you sent any down to Uncle Mose." Grandma looked puzzled.

Then she tasted one and she said, "It's lovely, all right, but I didn't give 'em to Uncle Mose. It must've been Aunt Mary Bartle."

"Go away, mother," said Aunt Sophy, "Aunt Mary can't make 'em as good as that."

"Who *did* make 'em, Uncle Mose?" asked Aunt Sophy.

"I made 'em myself," said I, "that's who." And poor Aunt Sophy's chin dropped down onto her blouse. That was bad enough, but then I said somethin' I shouldn't have said – only I was kinda riled on account of how they'd just been callin' me "poor helpless Uncle Mose." So I said to 'em, "I'm awful sorry you caught me with such a poor batch. I don't know what could've happened unless I lost the heat out of my oven just at the critical moment. But," said I, "next batch I make I'll be more careful and I'll send a few up to you."

Well – poor Aunt Sophy. She finished sweepin' up my kitchen, but the pep was gone right out of her and she and Grandma slipped away the first chance they got.

THE VALUE OF
KING DAVID

GRAMPA WALCOTT THINKS that, bein' as how King David is not likely to get any official recognition while he's alive, the very least he ought to get is some kind of a monument to him after he dies. And when anyone speaks against the idea, Grampa just snorts and says he's heard tell of monuments bein' built for lots less deservin' cases. Take, for instance, says Grampa, the thousands and thousands of dollars that King David saved Pigeon Inlet by weather forecastin' alone, a thing that every fair-minded man'll admit is above and beyond the call of a billy goat's duty.

Now, weather forecastin', as every fisherman knows, is a thing that's gone to the dogs in late years. Instead of the radio tellin' us whether we're goin' to have southeast wind and fog, or strong nor'west wind and snow, or light sou'west wind and sunshine, what 'tis more likely to tell us is a lot about regions of high pressure and regions of low pressure and goodness knows what. Jethro Noddy says 'tis all the fault of the army. He figgers they took it over during the last war – fellows like General Synopsis and Major Disturbance – and naturally they use big words like isybars and precipitation, and others like 'em. Jethro says that isybars no doubt is as cold as it sounds, while, as for this precipitation, he's willin' to bet that even old General Synopsis hisself don't know what *that* means.

And that's why, says Grampa, King David – Jethro Noddy's billy goat – was the one and only reliable forecaster we ever had, more reliable even than Lige Bartle's rheumatism. And since King David done what you might call "retired from active service," there's no trouble to see the effects of it.

Ah, says Grampa, 'twas a sight to behold years ago, when King David was in his prime. Instead of lyin' around under the fences like nowadays, you'd see him every summer day organizin' all the goats in the place and leadin' 'em in over the hills to the grazin' grounds. And leadin' 'em back home in the evenin's. He come out first to the edge of that big hill in full view of every livyer in Pigeon Inlet, and not a single goat'd dare to start comin' down the hill until King David had looked back and made sure they was all lined up in proper fashion. Then down they'd come!

But 'twas when rain threatened that he showed his true value, scurryin' for home when rain was comin'. But nowadays 'tis not till the rain is fallin' on their heads. King David'd have 'em all out to the brow of the hill long before the rain started and many's the day, with the sun up splittin' the rocks, Grandma had looked out her kitchen window and seen his horns showin' over the hill. And before the rain did come, every quintal of fish on every flake in Pigeon Inlet'd be faggoted* up and safe. Thousands of dollars he saved us, says Grampa, and nar a cent put by even to build him a monument after he's gone. Not only that, but there two years ago we almost sold him, after all he's done for us.

And Grampa is right. Year afore last we come nigh losin' him, sure enough. How it happened was that Jethro Noddy, while eatin' his breakfast, happened to read the piece of the St. John's newspaper that Soos was usin' for a tablecloth and he spied this ad in the paper that made him all excited. 'Twas stained with molasses but he could still make out enough to read where somebody up around Dildo where they've got all the mink farms was wantin' to buy up all the goats he could get for mink feed and was offerin' $2.12 a pound. Soos remarked how it sounded like a high price even for goat, and Jethro said like he'd heard over the radio this mink business must be payin' awful well and no doubt $2.12 was only a fly bite to 'em. Jethro said at that price King David's horns alone'd fetch a barrel of pork and, although Soos screeched and bawled and the youngsters likewise, Jethro stuck to his guns and went out to hunt up some board to build a crate to ship him off in on the next steamer.

Pigeon Inlet was horrified when the news got around, but 'twas no use pleadin' with Jethro. He was gone fair money-mad. Grampa couldn't hardly believe the price was right, but by that time some more molasses had been spilled over the paper and Soos had burned it. So Jethro went ahead mea-surin' King David for his crate. We appealed to him usin' every argument we could think of. We said as how sendin' King David away would be like upsettin' the whole economy of Pigeon Inlet, but Jethro said 'twas no good expectin' him to carry the whole economy of the place on his back, and if Pigeon Inlet wanted to keep King David let them subsidize him or nationalize him if they wanted to – at $2.12 a pound – and he went ahead makin' the crate.

Then Grampa asked him did he think 'twas honest and fair to the mink industry to ship King David among 'em as food. For one thing, how could the mink chew him, when Joe Prior's dogs couldn't. But Jethro said that'd be the minks' own hard luck. Once he got his $2.12 a pound, the mink industry could look out to itself as best it could.

He'd have shipped King David off, too, only the mornin' before the steamer was due, I was takin' a scrap of old newspaper out of my woodbox to light the fire when it caught my eye. The same ad, but it was 2½ cents, not 2.12. So Jethro didn't ship King David after all. And Pigeon Inlet is better off that he didn't. So, too, are the mink. For puttin' King David in a pen of mink would be like puttin' a lion in a den of Daniels.

* faggoted: placed in piles

THE SHOW-OFF

ONE DAY NOT LONG AGO A crowd of us, with nothin' better to do at the time, were sittin' around in Grampa Walcott's net loft, and the talk veered around from one thing to another till it got round to strength. And then a bit of an argument started about what made one man stronger than another. All of us agreed that the size of a man or even the size of his muscles didn't have much to do with it, because all of us in our time had seen big muscle-bound fellows get tied up in knots by other fellows half their size.

Skipper Joe Irwin said that what made one man stronger than another was his back, Pete Briggs thought 'twas his legs, someone else said 'twas his arms and shoulders. Then, like we always do, we ended up by askin' Grampa his opinion. And Grampa said, "Boys, what makes one man stronger than another is his mind. And," he said, "to prove my point I'd like to tell you about what happened here forty-odd years ago."

Accordin' to Grampa, the strongest man we've ever had in these parts was then right in his prime. His name was Jonas Tacker. Come up here from Hartley's Harbour and lived here eight or ten years. Jonas was a strong man, no doubt about it. The only trouble was he was a bit of a bully besides, and we fellows figgered that, if Jonas ever was certain sure he was the strongest man in the place, he wouldn't be fit to live with.

The next-strongest man to Jonas, said Grampa, was Zebedee Briggs, Pete's uncle, livin' up in St. John's these last twenty years. Zebedee was as quiet as an old worm and wouldn't hurt anybody, but we figgered, and rightly too, that the way to keep peace and quiet in Pigeon Inlet was to make Jonas Tacker believe he wasn't as strong as Zebedee Briggs. And, said Grampa, that was no easy job, because it looked like everything Zeb could do Jonas could do it too, only a little bit more so. One day a big boulder rolled out into the middle of the road down by Josiah Bartle's shop. None of the rest of us could lift it, but Zebedee picked it up and staggered to the side of the road with it. Jonas picked it up from there, pretended he was doin' a bit of serious thinkin', and then hove it ten or twelve feet out into the landwash.

Another time, accordin' to Grampa, they was sittin' in Elijah Bartle's kitchen and Zeb happened absent-minded-like to pick up the scraper off the stove – quarter-inch iron, it was – and he tied a bowline-eye* in one end of it. Jonas said, "Show me that," and then he said, "Why Zeb, you oughtn't to do that to the man's scraper." So he untied the bowline-eye and straightened it out. That's the way they were goin' on all the time. Then one day it happened. Jonas got put in his place good and proper, and all their worries about strife between him and Zeb come to an end.

"It happened," said Grampa, "one day the followin' spring, when supplies were runnin' a bit short in Pigeon Inlet and a crowd of us planned to go to Hartley's Harbour for a few items to keep us goin'. We went in Lige Bartle's boat 'cause he had the only motorboat here up to that time. There was me, Lige, Zeb Briggs, and Joe Irwin's father went in her and ever so many people give us a list of items to bring back for 'em. Among them, Jonas Tacker asked us to bring him a barrel of flour. Jonas wanted to come with us, but like we said, everybody couldn't go, so Jonas stayed back. Good job he did too, the way it turned out.

"Well, we went to Hartley's Harbour and loaded all the stuff aboard, includin' Jonas Tacker's barrel of flour with his name wrote on the head in blue pencil, and then the last of all, Zeb come down aboard with a empty flour barrel. He'd got it from his sister who was married in Hartley's Harbour and he was goin' to earn a few cents with it, by makin' it into a quintal fish-drum like they used to use in those days for the Brazil market. 'Twas the sight of this empty barrel that put the idea in my head, and as soon as Zeb had it aboard I said to him, 'Zeb,' I said, 'put the head in that flour barrel, so's it'll look like a full one.' He didn't want to first goin' off, but when I explained my idea, the rest helped me persuade Zeb to do it. Then Zeb made sure he was sittin' on his own flour barrel when we tied on by the steps of the wharf here in Pigeon Inlet.

"When everything was out except the two barrels, I said to Zeb, 'Zeb,' I said, 'do you want a hand to get your barrel of flour home?' 'No Ben, thankee all the same,' said Zeb, 'I can manage.' So he grunted a bit while he swung the empty barrel up onto his back, and went up the steps and in across the wharf puffin' like a walrus.

"Well, then, you should've seen Jonas. How he done it we'll never know, but he swung his full barrel up on his back and took to go after Zeb. We watched them goin' up the hill. Zeb a gunshot ahead, just puffin' a bit, and Jonas with his legs bucklin' under him but holdin' his own. And it wasn't until Zeb stopped a minute and Jonas caught up to him, that Jonas give up in despair. He put his barrel down on the ground, waited till the strength got back in his legs, and then bawled for his young fellow to come with the handbarrow.

"We asked Zeb afterwards what it was that made Jonas give up so cowardly and Zeb told us. 'Well,' he said, 'when Jonas caught up to me, I steadied my barrel with one hand and reached out my other hand towards him. I told him if he was gettin tired, I'd take the two barrels for a spell. I allow that finished him.'

"And so it did," said Grampa, "'cause we had no more trouble with Jonas Tacker from that day till two years after, when he went back to Hartley's Harbour where he rightfully belonged."

* bowline-eye: attachment for fastening rope to load of wood on a sled

UNDER THE MISTLETOE

ON CHRISTMAS DAY – of all days in the year – I did an awful brazen thing and I still can't figger out whatever in the world possessed me to do it, especially in someone else's house. Perhaps if I tell about it 'twill help get it off my mind.

You see, I spent Christmas Day with Grampa and Grandma Walcott. They invited me two or three weeks ago and wouldn't take "No" for an answer. Said 'twas a day when no bachelor should be alone. So I was there. Their daughter Aunt Sophy got no boarders now, except a girl teacher, and she was invited out to Fred Prior's. So Aunt Sophy was there too. Just the four of us, spendin' Christmas Day together. Like Grampa called it, a snug crew.

Aunt Sophy's a wonderful woman, young-lookin' too, and there's been jokes and gossip about us ever since I come here. Not a word of truth in 'em, of course. How could there be? Why, she could pick and choose anywhere.

That's why I was uneasy until Grampa talked to me after church Christmas mornin'. He said, "Yes, among the decorations Grandma and Soph have put up, there are two of these wreaths of boughs with dogberries tied on 'em," but he figgered they were just decorations. After all, what else would two grown-up women like Grandma and Soph have 'em up for?

That eased my mind a lot because I've heard tell about what young fellows and girls do Christmastime under those wreaths. Of course I knew Aunt Sophy wouldn't have the like in her mind, but I was afraid I might get under one of 'em unknowst to myself and she might think I was brazen enough to have it in my mind. Then Grampa told me that one of 'em was pinned up over the inside door of the front porch and the other to the parlour ceilin'. "So, Mose" he said, "me boy, there's your chart. Now, steer accordin' to it."

Sure enough, as soon as I opened Grampa's front door I could see for myself that Aunt Sophy had these wreaths up just for decorations, or else she'd forget where she'd hung 'em. Because there she was standin' right under one, invitin' me in. But I wouldn't embarrass her for the world, so I pretended I'd left my pipe home and said I'd be back in a minute. When I did, 'twas go through the back door. There was nothin' in that to make her look disappointed, was there? No. I must have just imagined it.

After dinner, and I hope you've tasted saltwater ducks the way Grandma bakes 'em, we went into the parlour. Sure enough, the other one was hung right from the middle of the ceilin'. So, I tell you, I hugged the shoreline pretty close except when Aunt Sophy was playin' hymns on the organ. But, she must've forgot about that wreath too, because one time she stood right under it and said that, with her high heels, she bet she was just as tall as I was. She's not, of course, but bein' polite I said yes, I allowed she was. What else could I do?

Once Grandma and Grampa stopped under the wreath and Aunt Sophy nudged me and said, "Oh, Uncle Mose. Look at 'em. How Christmasy."

Lucky I was holdin' the snapshot album at the time, so I looked at 'em on page four, and when she said, "No, not there," I looked at 'em again on page ten.

Then Grampa kept hintin' about how 'twas a special occasion and Grandma said, "Oh well, all right," and she sent Aunt Sophy out to the pantry to bring in what she'd find behind the bread tin. Now, perhaps 'twas the fault of her high heels, but even so, she should have brought the bottle back in her hands, not on a tray. Anyway, she stumbled, the tray tipped, and Grampa let out a dismal groan. I got there in time, grabbed the bottle in one hand, while with the other I brought Aunt Sophy up into the wind on an even keel.

She must've misunderstood me, because when I asked her was she hurt, she just looked straight up at the spruce bough and dogberries. "Oh, Uncle Mose," she said, "You've caught me at last." Then it happened. Or I should say it half happened, because all I could do was stand there like a gommil, holdin' the bottle.

Then a funny thing happened. You see, she asked me to come with her to the pantry for the wine glasses in case the top shelf was too high, and I said I would, in a minute. Now, I won't say I hold with what young people do under these wreaths Christmastime, and I won't say I don't. But I will say this. A man got pride in his work and he don't like to half do a thing and have people think that's the best he can do. That's why, as soon as Sophy was gone to the pantry, I asked Grandma if I could take that wreath with me for a minute and pin it up over the pantry door. She said, "yes."

But did I hang it over the pantry door? No, 'cause by that time Sophy had the one brought in from the porch and hung there. She explained that pretty things should be where people could see 'em.

Is she cross with me? No, either she's very forgivin' or else she's forgot all about it. Because afterwards, when I tried to apologize and blame it on Christmas, know what she said? She said she wished 'twas Christmas all the year round.

TEACHERS

WE'VE GOT A LOT OF FINE things here that I'd like to tell you about. Take our school, for instance. Even though I've got no children of my own goin' to it, I'm a bit proud of that school. In fact, I helped to build the new schoolhouse, give two or three weeks' free labour on it, just to help out. Some people said to me, "Uncle Mose," they said, "we don't expect you to chip in on this." But I'm glad I did my bit. It makes me feel that I've got a share in it and a right to be proud of it.

But before I go tellin' you about the schoolhouse, perhaps I ought to express an opinion about education generally. Perhaps I'm a bit contrary, but somehow I can't agree with all these people who say that education and schools and youngsters are goin' to the dogs, and that teachers are not as good now as they used to be years ago. Of course, it's for every man to speak as he finds and that's exactly what I'm goin' to do. Take teachers, for example, and compare the teachers we've got today with the ones we had twenty to forty years ago.

Down in Hartley's Harbour last year a lot of the people were grumblin' because teachers were hard to get. One of their teachers took sick in the middle of the year and had to go home. Somewhere to the southard she lived and they thought 'twas terrible because the one they got to take her place didn't have a grade. She only had what they called a certificate. There were a crowd of people up here in a boat from Hartley's Harbour all day and they were standin' around Levi Bartle's store grumblin' about it, and Aunt Sarah Skimple was grumblin' worst of the lot.

After they were all gone, Levi Bartle turned to me and said, "Uncle Mose, what do you think of 'em?"

"Well, Mr. Bartle," said I, "they seem awful upset because they haven't got a full-graded teacher. Especially Aunt Sarah."

"Do you know somethin'?" said Levi. "Aunt Sarah used to be a teacher herself years ago."

"I suppose," said I, "that's why she's so particular."

"She got no right to be," said Levi. "Wait till I show you somethin'." So he went into his office and came out with a sheet of paper. "Here," he said, "here's a note she sent up to me last week."

I took it and read it. Here's what was on it:

"Dear Mr. Bartle:

Please send me down a sack of potatos.

(Then she crossed out potatos and started again on the same page.)

Please send me down a sack of potatose.

(Then she crossed out potatose and started again – still on the same page.)

Please send me down a potato.

P.S. Please put it in a sack and put enough more in with it to make up a sackful.

Yours truly,

Sarah Skimple"

"She's someone to grumble about teachers nowadays."

Of course, there's one thing we've got to face. Whenever teachers are scarce, we're bound to have to take on a few that are not quite as good as the others, but how do you think it was years ago? A clergyman – he was Chairman of the School Board in the place where I belonged – he said to me one day, "Mose," he said, "I wish you'd have gone in for school teachin' instead of Bank fishin'."

"Why, your Reverence?" said I.

"Because," said he, "I'm findin' it awful hard to get enough teachers this year to fill up all the schools in my parish."

"A poor teacher I'd make," said I. "I hardly know a B from a bull's foot."

"You'd be no worse than some of 'em," said he. "I had a letter from a fellow not long ago. He wrote and told me he'd like to have a berth school teachin'."

"A berth school teachin'?" said I.

"Yes, Mose," said the clergyman, "and I'm so hard up for teachers that I believe I'd have taken him on, only he had 'berth' spelled wrong."

I heard over the radio not long ago that some of the schoolchildren last year didn't know what the United Nations was. Well, that's bad, but it's not as bad as what happened once with my brother Ki.

The School Inspector visited us one day. He was a gruff old fellow and he used to point his finger at each one of us and ask us questions. By and by he pointed his finger at my brother Ki and he barked out, "Who killed Cock-Robin?"

"Please, sir," said Ki, "I didn't do it."

The Inspector turned round to our teacher and said, "What in the world do you think of that?"

The teacher spoke up. "Well, sir," he said, "he might say he didn't do it, but if I were you I wouldn't believe him. He's the worst liar in the school. Besides, he's always throwin' stones."

So like I said, things mightn't be all we'd wish in education, but they're a lot better than they used to be.

THE DRAMA FESTIVAL

ALL LAST WEEK YOU MUST have heard tell about the wonderful doin's up around Grand Falls. The Drama Festival, 'twas called, with crowds there from Corner Brook, Gander, and goodness knows where, to see who could do the best play-actin', and with the winners havin' a chance to go on to the mainland and perhaps end up champions of Canada. And, wouldn't that be somethin'. You heard all about it, I'm sure.

What you *didn't* hear was about the Pigeon Inlet Drama Club and how close we come to bein' in there among 'em. 'Cause like Grampa said, 'twas too good a chance to let slip. Bein' champions of Canada'd put Pigeon Inlet on the map for sure. And Pete Briggs said how 'twould be a wonderful chance for us after we'd won the championship up on the mainland to put in a word for a bait depot. But that shocked Emma Jane Bartle, who said we shouldn't try to get fish tangled up with culture.

Aunt Sophy started our Drama Club during Christmas and we put off our play the week before last. It must have been wonderful to those who could sit back and see it. Aunt Jemima Prior says she can still cry down tears whenever she thinks of it, especially the part where – but I'm gettin' ahead of my story.

Pickin' the right play is half the battle. First goin' off, Aunt Sophy, who was a schoolteacher one time, wanted to do one called *Macbeth* or some such name, but Grandma put her foot down 'cause it had bad words in it. Besides, there was a part in it for everyone in Pigeon Inlet and, if we *all* went to the mainland to this Dominion Festival, who'd bide home to get the salmon gear in the water? Pete Briggs backed her up because, he said, if we went up on the mainland usin' a play with bad words in it, 'twould ruin our chances of gettin' a bait depot or anything else.

So we settled on a better play, one that went by the name of *Rich Old Uncle Sam,* a lovely thing, all about a poor widow – Aunt Sophy took that part – and her daughter, about eighteen years old – young Maisie Bartle just fitted this. She's Levi Bartle's daughter, clerk in his store, and a brazen young thing if ever there was one. Nice-lookin', though. Well, those two were poor off, 'tis no mistake, right down to where they just about had to beat up the flour barrel to boil the kettle. Then there was their next-door neighbours, Skipper Joe and Emma Jane Bartle, who used to come in to help 'em out, but what with Skipper Joe only havin' fourteen stamps in his unemployment book, there wasn't much *he* could do for 'em or Emma Jane neither. There was one other character in the play, this Uncle Sam, but he was up on the mainland somewhere with oodles of money and they was all wishin' he'd come home and save the situation. But they didn't know his address. And nothin'd do Aunt Sophy but that I had to be Uncle Sam.

I had misgivin's right from the start. You see, a year ago I'd been listenin' over the radio to the judge of one of these

Drama Festivals praisin' one couple for the nice job they'd done of kissin' one another in the play and, even though he said there was no fun in doin' it – not in a play that is – they'd pretended they'd been enjoyin' it wonderful. But when I looked through this play we had to do, there was none of that between me and Aunt Sophy, thank goodness, so I agreed to do it. And we started practisin' just after New Year's.

We had trouble right from the start. On the very first page, Emma Jane Bartle, the neighbour, is in tidyin' up the place for the poor widow and her daughter and the first thing she says is, "I must dust the chair, Flick, Flick, this chair is dusted." Aunt Sophy told Emma Jane she had to do "flick, flick" but she mustn't say "flick, flick," and Emma Jane said how Aunt Sophy was just plain jealous and, besides, takin' the longest part for herself, she wanted to cut some of Emma Jane's part besides. Emma Jane said, "flick, flick" was in the book right there in print and she was goin' to say it, and that was that.

Well, as you know probably better than I do, the play goes on all right from there till the point where I'm supposed to come. The poor widow and her daughter are sittin' there thinkin' about rich old Uncle Sam when I walk in and I say, "Good evenin', I'm your Uncle Sam," and young Maisie says, "Oh you dear, kind, rich, old Uncle Sam," and she runs over and, the book says, "flings her arms round his neck." Brazen young thing, but she done that part well, I thought. Aunt Sophy didn't think so. She said that part'd have to be altered. First she said she and Maisie'd change parts, then she thought better of it and said 'twould be more fittin' and proper for the widow to run over and greet Uncle Sam than for the daughter. But Maisie said, no, 'twas her part and she wasn't goin' to be robbed of any of it, especially the best bit. Aunt Sophy finally made the best of it by givin' me and Maisie strict orders just to rest our chins on one another's shoulders and keep side on to the audience. And that's what we done all through rehearsals.

But the night when we put off the play, what do you think happened? Aunt Sophy was fit to be tied over what that brazen young Maisie Bartle done. And she said she wouldn't take that play to Grand Falls or anywhere else, not unless she had that part herself, someone that could be trusted to do it right. As for me, I said nothin'. Only I couldn't help thinkin' to myself about that Drama Festival judge I heard over the radio last year. He might know a lot, but he's astray on one point. It can be fun even on a stage in front of a crowd of people.

Oh yes, Uncle Sam wasn't so rich after all, as it turned out, but he was gettin' his old-age pension. So no doubt they lived happy ever after, though the book don't say for sure. Grampa thinks there must be another book comin' out after this one.

AUNT SOPHY AND
KING DAVID

TODAY I'M GOIN' TO TRY TO tell you about the trouble that
broke out not long ago between Aunt Sophy and King David,
Jethro Noddy's billy goat. First of all, though, I'd like to say that
opinion is divided here in Pigeon Inlet as to which one of them is
in the right. If there could be a vote on it, I wouldn't be surprised
but what King David would go in with a sweepin' majority.

Here's another funny thing. I read or heard somewhere
how a fellow said one time that this life was like a big wheel,
always turnin' over so that what was on top now was sure to
end up on the bottom sometime later on. Well, whoever said
that never spoke a truer word, 'cause look what's happened
now. A while ago, I had cause to abuse King David for stealin'
my cabbages and Aunt Sophy took his part and was on the
outs with me for weeks about it. Now she's mad with King
David and, in all fairness, I had to take his part this time, and
she's on the outs with me again.

Well, here's what happened. Up till a year or two ago,
Aunt Sophy used to keep three or four sheep. Then she give
it up. Like she told me, it was too much trouble for a woman
when there was no man around the place. Ever since then,

she has had a little problem about what to do with her potato scraps. She used to save 'em in a little bucket in her back
porch and every Monday mornin' she'd put 'em out.

King David got to know Monday mornin' just as well as
if he'd had an almanac to go by. I don't know how he figgered
it, but he did. It wasn't by the clothes on the line, 'cause even
on rainy Mondays he'd be there just the same. And when
Aunt Sophy had put the bucket of scraps outside her back
door, he'd just say whatever grace he says and dig in.

Aunt Sophy said afterwards, in tryin' to defend herself,
that she usen't to notice that he was there. All she said she'd
do was to put out the bucket full and take it in empty an hour
or two later. Well, that might be. But one thing for sure – if
she didn't know, King David did. It got so that he used to
look forward to it every Monday mornin'.

Three Sundays ago, comin' home from church, Emma
Jane Bartle happened to tell Aunt Sophy how hard it was to
get food for her three sheep. Aunt Sophy promised to run
across next mornin' with her bucket of potato scraps. So next
mornin', with poor King David all ready to ask whatever
blessin's goats do ask, Aunt Sophy went right by him with the
bucket over to Emma Jane's sheep's house. The only time she
looked back was to admire her wash that she had out on the
line that fine Monday mornin'.

She says she didn't even notice that King David was
there. She noticed him on the way back, though. First thing
she spied was the big gap in her line of clothes where her best
tablecloth had been hangin'. Then she noticed King David
trottin' off down the road towin' the tablecloth along behind
him through the mud and the slush. So Aunt Sophy went

wing-and-wing right after him. I missed that part of it myself, but Sam Prior told me afterwards that, when they passed along by his place, it was somethin' worth seein'. He was lookin' out through his window and he hurried to put on his boots and cap. But when he got there, 'twas too late.

What seems to have happened is this. Aunt Sophy got close enough to tread on the rear end of the tablecloth, and that of course brought King David up into the wind, facin' her. But he didn't let go. She scooped up a mixture of mud in her hand and hove it at him. Now, any schoolboy in Pigeon Inlet could have told her that this was the wrong thing to do. But by this time she'd lost her temper, and then she made the biggest mistake of all.

She looked round for a rock and spied one just behind her. She turned around to pick it up. 'Twas stuck into the ground, so while she was tryin' to pry it loose with her fingers, King David had plenty of time to survey the situation and figger out what he could do to vent his spite on Aunt Sophy for throwin' the mud at him.

Grampa Walcott often says that an older man looks back at the happy days when he was young and wishes he could have the same chances over again. Well, I imagine the same thought was in King David's head when he viewed Aunt Sophy with her back turned, tryin' to pick up that rock. To him it must've looked like his happiest days had come back again and he'd better not miss this golden opportunity.

Accordin' to Sam Prior, who was just too late to save her, King David didn't hit her hard. He just nudged her enough to topple her over so that the crown of her head – pincurls and all – went into the mud. It took Sam all he could do with his brother Joe's help to straighten her up. Aunt Sophy expressed her opinion about King David, about Jethro Noddy, about the Community Council, and a few other things that come into her mind as well.

MORE TROUBLE OVER KING DAVID

AS I TOLD YOU LAST TIME, King David was over by Aunt Sophy's door on Monday a few weeks ago expectin' his weekly ration of potato scraps. When he didn't get 'em he dragged her best tablecloth off the clothesline and ran off with it through the mud and slush. Aunt Sophy got it back, but 'twas in a awful state and she wasn't much better. She went home in a terrible temper and, later on that day, I dropped in to say a few words of comfort. Grampa and Grandma were sittin' down in her kitchen, but Aunt Sophy was standin' up by the dresser. I didn't think about it at the time, but she had good reason for not sittin' down. She wasn't able to, on account of what King David done to her when she turned round to pick up a rock to heave at him.

The three of 'em were lookin' right solemn when I went in, so I thought I'd do the right thing to cheer them up by crackin' a little joke. So I said as how 'twas the best bit of excitement we'd had in Pigeon Inlet since the boys hauled Jethro Noddy's punt across the lane and Aunt Sophy got hitched up in the starboard thole-pin. Then I noticed the glare in Aunt Sophy's eye and decided I'd better get off on another tack.

I said (to no one in particular) how, in sizin' up a thing like what happened that mornin', you had to look at both sides of the story. You had to look at King David's side as well as Aunt Sophy's. I said I'd read in a book somewhere how you should never break a promise to a child. Perhaps, said I, a goat was like a child, even though King David certainly didn't look like one. But he'd got so used to gettin' his Monday mornin' scraps from Aunt Sophy that he'd begun to feel almost as if they were promised to him. Then when Aunt Sophy walked right by him to carry the scraps over to Emma Jane Bartle's sheep, well, perhaps King David's feelin's had been hurt.

I looked at Aunt Sophy when I said this and, if anything, the glare in her eyes was worse than ever. I noticed her hand reach out towards the back of the stove where there was a flatiron, and Grandma, who knows Aunt Sophy better than I do, reached out too and moved the flatiron further away, but all Aunt Sophy said was "King David's feelin's?" and she seemed to have a job sayin' that.

"Yes," I said, "and with his feelin's hurt, he lost his temper and didn't rightly know what he was doin' next."

Well, that wasn't gettin' me very far, so I tried another tack. Besides, said I, I've heard tell as how goats resemble human bein's in some ways. They need starch in their diet, and if they can't get it one way they try to get it in another. Probably what happened was that King David had a cravin' for starch and that's why he was so fond of potato skins. Then, when he was deprived of his starch that day, why, he naturally looked around for the next best place to get his balanced ration of starch, and there was the tablecloth. 'Cause, like I said, everybody that knew anything about Aunt Sophy's tablecloth would know that, for anybody needin' starch, there wasn't a better breakfast food in Pigeon Inlet.

I noticed while I was sayin' this that Grandma moved the flatiron a bit further out of Aunt Sophy's reach, but like a fool I kept on tryin'. I stopped for a minute to see if she agreed with me, but again she seemed to be havin' a job to get her words out and all she said was somethin' like "Balanced ration – my tablecloth – starchy diet – my best tablecloth." What I mean to say, it didn't seem to give me any clue as to whether she was agreein' with me or not. So I kept on. I said as how I'd heard tell of a remedy for curin' dumb animals from eatin' clothes. I told about a cow up in Fortune Bay that used to fatten up on what she'd graze off clotheslines until someone come up with a cure. They set fire to a piece of old clothes, a old tablecloth or skirt or somethin', and while 'twas still smoulderin' they poked it into the cow's mouth. It cured her. She never touched a garment afterwards. Not even one winter when they ran short of hay and tried to make her eat a condemned suit of the old man's underwear. So, I said, I'd be glad to cure King David. If you'll snip off the corner of the tablecloth that he's already been chewin' on, I'll take it over to Jethro Noddy's backyard, set fire to it, and poke it into King David's mouth.

Well, that seemed to make Aunt Sophy madder than ever and she said somethin' I didn't catch, but Grampa told me afterwards that 'twas just as well I didn't, because he wished he hadn't caught it neither. So, since talkin' didn't seem to be doin' any good, I thought I'd try a Christian action. I took Aunt Sophy by the arm, led her over to a chair. "Here my dear, sit down," said I. And I plumped her down in the chair.

Well, she give a dismal screech and come up out of that chair like a poppin' ball and darted across the kitchen, through the door, and into the parlour. Grandma said as how 'twas true enough what was in the book of Job about "miserable comforters are ye'all" and followed her.

Grampa and I were lookin' at one another like two fools, then the door opened and they called Grampa in. He come out a minute afterwards and he said to me, "Mose boy," he said, "you and I'd better be goin'. Grandma says if we're not out of the house by the time Soph works up strength enough to swing a broomstick, she can't guarantee what'll happen."

So, out I got and I haven't been back there since. I suppose I must've said somethin' wrong or done somethin' wrong. But for the life of me I can't imagine what it can be.

ELECTIONS

NOW THAT THE ELECTION IS past and done with, I suppose I can mention it without anybody thinkin' I'm favourin' one side or another. There are two or three remarks I'd like to make about elections without offendin' anyone. Some people think we have too many of 'em, especially since Confederation, now that we have two lots of politics instead of only one. But Grampa Walcott says no. Election time is the one sure time when big important people from outside think about Pigeon Inlet and 'tis good to see the candidates from the different parties come here and tell us about the independent voters of Pigeon Inlet. Not that any of 'em by comin' here ever changed a vote, 'cause Pigeon Inlet, generally speakin', got its mind made up a long ways ahead. But 'tis nice to go to a meetin' even to hear the fellow we're not goin' to vote for, and give him a clap to cheer him up – until the count comes in, that is. 'Cause, like Jethro Noddy says, there's no need of makin' the poor fellow miserable until he got to be.

One thing we can't understand down here is why about half the people in other parts of the island who *can* vote don't vote at all. The way we Pigeon Inletters feel about turnin' out on Pollin' Day can perhaps best be described by Grampa Walcott. Only once in all his long life did he neglect to cast his vote, and even though, as he says, 'twas the means of savin' his life, he never neglected to vote afterwards.

Well, you might wonder how in the world neglectin' to vote saved his life. I wondered too and asked him was it 'cause someone was goin' to kill him if he voted. He just laughed and said no. Election times used to be rough fifty or sixty years ago in Pigeon Inlet, but never that rough especially if you voted on the right side, which he said most people did, just as they still do. No, he said, that particular time, nigh on fifty years ago, he just didn't bother to vote at all. He figgered it didn't make a pin's point of difference to him who got in. And Pollin' Day he was busy muckin' around at this and that until, by and by, the booth was closed and 'twas too late.

"How it saved my life," he said, "was not till years afterwards. One day late in the fall I took the gun and went in over the hills to look for a duck, or a goose or a partridge, or whatever might happen to cross my sights. And I lost my way. Now," he said, "gettin' lost in over the hills is all right if a man knows he's lost, 'cause all he got to do is turn his cap inside out and he'll find his way again. But I didn't know I was lost until comin' on night. I climbed a pinnacle and there I was, miles and miles from anywhere, dead tired, no grub, and too famished to walk another mile. The only hope was to lie down somewhere and get a good night's rest in the hope of feelin' better in the mornin'. But," said Grampa, "'twas a airsome* night threatenin', and besides, I was afraid to go asleep in the open on account of the bears, so what was I to do for shelter? I come down off the pinnacle and looked around till I found the very thing – a big hollow log, with plenty of room for me to crawl in and stretch out in solid comfort.

"Well," said Grampa, "I crawled into that log, kicked the immets** out as best I could, and settled away for the night, half wishin' I had Grandma in there with me. Well, sometime just before daylight I woke up in a awful predicament. 'Twas like somethin' was squeezin' me to death. The log had got a lot smaller, 'cause now I was nipped so tight on all sides that I couldn't move my arms or legs and could just barely breathe.

"Then, lyin' there quiet, I soon found out what was doin' it. Outside I could hear the rain peltin' down harder than I'd ever heard it in my life before. So I knowed what was happenin'. The rain was soakin' through the log and plimmin'*** it, and of course the more it rained the smaller the hollow was gettin', and there I was nipped like a bit of corkin' in a seam.

"Well," said Grampa, "at a time like that, a man thinks about all the sins he's ever committed in his life and it's surprisin' how some of 'em come back to him that he'd forgot about years before. So I thought about mine and I was gettin' nipped tighter and tighter all the time. And then," he said, "I remembered the time I'd neglected to vote on pollin' day. As I thought about it, it made me feel awful small, so I kept on thinkin' about it till it made me feel so small that I stood right up straight inside that log and walked out through the open end and made tracks for home.

"And," said Grampa, "I never failed to cast a vote every election since."

* airsome: fresh, bracing

** immets: ants

*** plim: expand due to absorption of liquid

SETTLIN' AN ARGUMENT

LAST WINTER SKIPPER Jonathan Briggs and Matty Prior had a row over that little job of land we call No Man's Land. 'Twas on both their grants, on account of the surveyor's mistake, and they kept knockin' down each other's fences and threatenin' each other till the magistrate had to come and bind 'em over to the peace for six months. July twenty-second they were bound over and all Pigeon Inlet lived in dread of what would happen on January twenty-second, when the bond run out. Grampa remembers all about it and 'tis he that told me the story.

"Just two days before January twenty-second," said Grampa, "'twas a Monday, and a fine crisp crackly winter's mornin' it was too. Just about every man in the place was up at daylight and off in over the hill to cut firewood. It started in to peck snow just after daylight, and most of us got back home before the storm broke. Well," said Grampa, "what a blizzard – for forty-eight hours. The worst snowstorm in the memory of livin' man. And it wasn't until that night when meself and a few more of the hardiest ones ventured out to the houses nearby, to lend a hand if needed, that we found out Skipper Jonathan and Uncle Matty hadn't got home."

"Did you organize a search party?" said I.

"Search party!" said Grampa. "Why, all that night and all next day, a man couldn't venture out to the well, or the wood-pile, or the goat's house without a lifeline. So all we could do was hope that somehow or other Uncle Matty and Jonathan were weatherin' it as best they could. To make matters worse, Aunt Jane Prior said that Uncle Matty didn't have any grub with him, while Aunt Liz Briggs said Jonathan had plenty of grub but had forgot to take any baccy so, she said, wherever he was, he was havin' a awful time. He was contrary enough the best of times, she said, but with nothin' to smoke!

"We figgered," said Grampa, "that there was a fair chance of findin' one or both of 'em alive after the storm was over, because they might have reached the old halfway camp that the mailman used to use between here and Rumble Cove. It wasn't a palace, but two men if they were so minded could keep alive in it all right. But with two men so bitter against one another as these two, 'twas hard to say.

"Wednesday mornin' the twenty-second," said Grampa, "the storm had died down enough so we could venture off to look for 'em, and we made straight for the old camp because, to tell the truth, if they weren't there, 'twasn't much use lookin' anywhere else till after the snow melted next spring."

"Did you find 'em?" said I.

"No," said Grampa, "they found us. 'Bout halfway in, we met 'em comin' out, chattin' away the best of friends – Jonathan with his pipe goin' full tilt, and Matty chewin' away on a mouthful of hardtack."*

"But Grampa," said I, "Jonathan didn't have any baccy and Matty didn't have any grub."

"No more they didn't," said Grampa, "and it took us days

and days before we got the story from 'em in dribs and drabs. When Uncle Matty stumbled into that old shack Monday night and found Skipper Jonathan there, he had a mind to go out again – so he said. And all that first night they huddled there, one on each side of the stove, without speakin' a word. To make it worse, Matty could hear Jonathan munchin' hardtack, whereas he was so hungry his pipe wasn't givin' him its full benefits. Skipper Jonathan, on the other hand, said afterwards that his vittles tasted like dishrag on account of how he was dyin' for a smoke and the lovely fumes from Matty's pipe were nothin' short of torture. And all the next day it got worse and worse. The same thought was runnin' through both their minds; and if they hadn't been bound over to the peace there's no mistake but what they'd have settled it then and there and winner take all. But their time wasn't up till next day, and they couldn't hold out that long.

"'Twas sometime that second evenin'," said Grampa, "that Skipper Jonathan accidental-like laid a piece of hardtack halfway on the floor between him and Uncle Matty. Then he turned his back for a minute, and when he looked again, the hardtack was gone and there was a snag of baccy there in its place.

"Well, that broke the ice and later that night they got on speakin' terms and even agreed to stand watch all night to keep the fire in and get a few hours' sleep besides.

"Next mornin', they knew, was the day they'd been waitin' for, when the law no longer had 'em bound to the peace, but they were so busy diggin' themselves out that they had no time for foolishness like quarrellin'. So they swapped their last bit of hardtack and baccy and were halfway home when we met 'em."

"And what did they do about No Man's Land?" said I.

"They signed a paper that very day," said Grampa, "and witnessed it and everything – sayin' that neither the Briggses nor the Priors would ever claim it again, but would give it to the public as a commons. And that," said Grampa, "is what it's been ever since.

"And," said Grampa, "whenever I hear over the radio about two big world leaders threatenin' each other, I can't help wishin' they could get caught in the old halfway camp for forty-eight hours – with one of 'em havin' all the baccy and the other with all the hard tack. That'd teach 'em."

* hardtack: hard bread

Skipper Jonas Tacker

A FEW DAYS AGO I WAS down in Hartley's Harbour and Skipper Jonas Tacker invited me inside his gate for a chat. He didn't invite me in, though, until he first of all made sure that I wasn't down in Hartley's Harbour tryin' to breed strife by talkin' Town Councils, and also that I wasn't tryin' to borrow anything.

'Tis no trouble to see that Skipper Jonas is not in favour of Town Councils. In fact, Skipper Jonas don't seem much in favour of anything exceptin' himself and his family – his wife Prudence, his daughter who's married in St. John's, and his two sons, Joey and Bill, who live in Hartley's Harbour but who've been workin' on the bases makin' big money the last three or four summers.

Skipper Jonas is a self-centred man. Grampa Walcott calls him selfish. Grampa says there's only two selfish men on the coast and Skipper Jonas is both of 'em. Obadiah Grimes tells a story (I won't guarantee it's true) about how he walked into Skipper Jonas's kitchen one mornin' during family prayers and Skipper Jonas was sayin': "May blessings fall upon us all Good Christians here below, Meself and Prue, Our daughter Sue, Our two boys - Bill and Joe." Obe Grimes can stretch the truth sometimes, but that'll give you an idea. Thank goodness Skipper Jonas lives in Hartley's Harbour instead of Pigeon Inlet. Well, that was the man that invited me into his garden for a talk.

"Uncle Mose," he said, "come in. I want to show you somethin'." I went in and, sure enough, what he had to show me was well worth lookin' at.

I'd like to explain how Hartley's Harbour is laid out. Everyone's land runs back in narrow strips, right from the waterfront road to a low ridge five or six hundred feet back. Just behind the ridge is a big pond, and all the people got their wells up under the ridge, where the water seeps through from the pond behind it.

Well, what Skipper Jonas showed me was a trench about four feet deep that he had dug right from his house, past his son's house, straight up through his garden to the foot of the ridge – must have been six hundred feet.

"My gracious," said I. "That's some ditch. Who dug it?"

"I did," said he. "Every day and every hour I could spare from fishin' the past spring and summer. I hired two or three men whenever I could," he said, "but mostly, I worked at it myself. Daylight till dark."

"But what's it for?" said I.

"Water," said he. "We're goin' to have runnin' water in our houses," said he. "Mine and my son's house there."

Then he told me the story. It seems that his two sons, Bill and Joe, in their recent knockin' around have got used to better livin' conditions than they were brought up to. Besides, the daughter Sue, married in St. John's, is used to hot and cold runnin' water in the house and says she don't know how people can live without it. So, the upshot is that the boys have told their father, Skipper Jonas, that if he'll do the necessary gettin'-ready job, they'll bring home all the pipes and fittin's when they come home this fall, and connect it all up, inside and out, upstairs and down.

Then I had to follow him all the way up through his garden to the far end of the trench, to where he had a fine concrete well, with a cover made for it and a vent hole down close to the bottom of the trench. "There," he said, pointin' to the vent hole, "there's where the boys'll connect up one end of the pipe. I got it plugged now," said he, "to keep the trench dry. But that well'll give us all the water we'll ever need."

Then he explained to me why the well had to be so far away up the garden. It seems he wants the level of the well to be up as high as the upper floors of their houses.

"Wonderful," said I. "Wonderful. Why," said I, "after you get this workin', you and your sons'll have it just as good as your daughter got it in St. John's."

Skipper Jonas give me a funny look. "Uncle Mose," he said, "you're not as smart as you might be. Why," he said, "we'll have it better than she will."

"How?" said I.

"Because," said he, "she's got to pay taxes for hers, and we're gettin' ours for nothin'."

"Oh," said I.

"Yes," said he, "she told us on a letter this summer that her water tax is fifteen dollars a year. Think of that – fifteen dollars taxes. That's what comes," said he, "of gettin' tangled up with Town Councils. Fifteen dollars a year taxes. And we're gettin' ours for nothin'! Now Uncle Mose," said he, "own up like a man that you're wrong in believin' in Town Councils – and taxes."

"I'll think it over," said I. "But before I go, Skipper Jonas, tell me somethin'. Why don't you and your son have separate wells, and separate trenches, and separate pipes?"

"Ah," said he, "we're too cute for that. Usin' the one well and the one pipe splits up the labour and the expense."

"I see," said I. And then I left him. What was the use of sayin' more to a man like that? He and his boys are doin' a wonderful thing. But he's thinkin' round and round in a circle. He starts off by disagreein' with taxes and he ends up the same place.

I figger that the cost of the labour he's done already, and the wages he's paid out, and the cost of the cement and the pipes and his sons' labour after they come home this fall, would pay their Council taxes for the next thirty or forty years, and by that time they'll have to dig up their pipes and lay new ones.

But, after all, what's the use tryin' to explain *that* to Skipper Jonas? He'd only say I was tryin' to breed strife.

GHOSTS

GRAMPA SAYS, WHAT WITH the radio and movin' pictures and one thing and another, people are gettin' so much knowledge they can do anything. Why, years ago, says Grampa, when a man left this shore for the first time 'twas a big adventure, and to prove his point he told me about the time Uncle Jonathan Briggs – Pete's father – went into St. John's and saw a train for the first time. It took him years to get over it.

'Twas at a place called Badger. Uncle Jonathan had got that far and somebody showed him the way up to the station house, where he had to wait for the train. 'Twas in the night and he couldn't see anything exceptin' this big buildin' with a flat-firm all along the front of it and a crowd of people waitin' like hisself for the train. He couldn't see nar thing that might be a train, but someone told him she'd be comin' in from that direction any minute now, and sure enough he heard a awful noise gettin' louder all the time and the brightest flashlight he'd ever seen in his life comin' toward 'em.

Well, Uncle Jonathan grabbed the fellow that was with him and dragged him back into the lun* of the building while this girt** long thing come right along by the flat-firm and stopped.

Uncle Jonathan got aboard of her all right and went on to St. John's, but it took him an awful long spell to get over his fright. Like he said afterwards, 'twas a lucky thing that train come in end on, 'cause if she had come in sideways, she'd have made a clean sweep of Badger.

But now, says Grampa, we all know too much. There's no adventures left. Take another thing. Ghosts, or give 'em their rightful name – spirits. Years ago a man could hardly walk anywhere nighttime without seein' one. But not now. Where's 'em gone to? No doubt they're just as plentiful as ever but they don't show theirselves. I suppose, says Grampa, if a spirit had it in his mind to show hisself he'd think twice about it. In the first place, he'd be afraid he'd be laughed at for bein' old-fashioned. Worse still, hardly anybody he'd run into'd believe in him. And if he tried to strike up an acquaintance with another spirit, he wouldn't know whether the other one was a genuine spirit or somebody dressed up to look like one. 'Cause there's been too much of that done in these parts, dressin' up like ghosts. Not in recent years though, on account of what happened to Uncle Sol Noddy the time he dressed up, intendin' to frighten the everlastin' daylights out of Jonas Tacker from Hartley's Harbour.

In those days, says Grampa, Jonas used to come up all the six miles from Hartley's Harbour courtin' one of Uncle Sol Noddy's daughters. It had not only Uncle Sol worried but all the rest of us too, because even though she was only a Noddy, we figgered that the worst in Pigeon Inlet was a sight too good for the best in Hartley's Harbour. So we tried to figger out some way to put a stop to it before 'twas too late. One Saturday night, late this particular fall, we got what we thought was our chance. We was havin' a wake for Aunt Jemima Briggs, Pete's grandmother, and we'd finished diggin' the grave that evenin' just before dark. Jonas Tacker had a habit every night when he'd finished courtin' to take the shortcut through the graveyard to connect with the footpath goin' in over the hill towards Hartley's Harbour. So, right there at the wake we naturally got talkin' about spirits and we persuaded Uncle Sol, he bein' the one with most at stake, to dress up like a spirit and be alongside the grave for when Jonas passed along through the graveyard. And sure enough, we got a white sheet draped all over him, and the rest of us went along and crouchied down behind the headstones to see the fun.

Sure enough, a few minutes after, along come Jonas takin' his usual shortcut through the graveyard. What we didn't know was that, bein' as 'twas an airsome night, he'd persuaded Uncle Sol's daughter to give him a swig or two out of the moonshine keg. So with that under his belt and a picket off Uncle Sol's fence in his hand, Jonas was ready for anything.

To do Uncle Sol justice, says Grampa, he acted his part first-rate. With that big white sheet draped all over him, he stood up straight until Jonas was almost up to him, then he squat down on his hands and knees and begun to crawl round and round the grave groanin' somethin' dismal and sayin' over and over again, "I can't get back in. I can't get back in." To tell the truth, says Grampa, he almost had *us* frightened. But what effect did it have on that sleeveen*** of a Jonas Tacker?

He walked right up to the grave and we heard him say plain as anything, "What's the matter with you?"

And Uncle Sol groaned harder than ever. "I can't get back in. I can't get back in."

"A good reason for why," said Jonas, "'cause you got no business bein' out." And with that he give Uncle Sol a bang on the skull with the picket and went on his way towards Hartley's Harbour.

And we didn't even chase him, says Grampa, because we were too busy gettin' poor Uncle Sol untangled out of the sheet and up out of that grave. And even after we got him up, he was still groanin' about wantin' to get back in.

That's why, said Grampa, there's no spirits showin' their-selves nowadays. Why should they let theirselves be seen where people got no respect for 'em?

* lun: sheltered

** girt: great

*** sleeveen: rogue, rascal

KING DAVID'S
AFFLICTION

THERE'S ONE THING I'VE noticed about Aunt Sophy. Every year around this time, when Christmas is gettin' close, she's a changed woman, and whatever little grudges or hard feelin's she's picked up during the year, she sheds 'em just like a crackie* sheds his coat. I mentioned it to Grampa one time and he remarked on what a wonderful woman Aunt Sophy'd be if she was like that all the year, and he said he figgered that's exactly how Soph would be if she had her way. He said, although she was his own flesh and blood, he had to admit she was gettin' a big short-tempered of late years and he figgered 'twas a pity she wasn't married again, because, he said, that'd make a world of difference to her.

Well, that set me thinkin', and goodness only knows where my thoughts'd have led me, if I hadn't mentioned the subject to Skipper Joe the other evenin' when he dropped in to see me. Skipper Joe said yes, all that might be true, but he said 'twas a serious matter for whatever man would get married to Aunt Sophy. I asked him what was wrong with Aunt Sophy, but he said there was nothin' wrong with her personally. 'Twas just that she kept a boardin' house. He knew one man, he said, a good man, too, that married a widow who kept six boarders and this man come to a bad end. First of all, he got into the habit of sittin' around talkin' to the boarders when he should've been out fishin'. Then he give up fishin' altogether so as he could devote his full time to sittin' around talkin'. It ended up that he lost his independence altogether and had to ask his wife for money whenever he wanted to buy a plug of baccy.

Well, I dunno. Sometimes I think Skipper Joe'd rather see me bide single, so as he'd always have a quiet place to come to for a yarn. But to get back to Aunt Sophy. There's no doubt about it, the biggest row that took place so far this year was the row between Aunt Sophy and King David back there last March. Grampa thinks the row over the Suez Canal was an even bigger one. But like I always say, every man is entitled to his own opinion. I'm not goin' to repeat the story because I've told it before, how King David destroyed her tablecloth and then butted her when she bent over to get a rock to heave at him. She kept after our Council for months to have him barred up, and even threatened to go to a higher authority. She said she'd never forgive him as long as he lived. Well, she *did* forgive him, one day last week, and that's what I want to tell you about.

I was comin' down the hill from where I'd been in to my rabbit slips, when I saw Aunt Sophy away ahead of me. She'd just been across the road to get a head of cabbage out of her garden, and on the way back she'd laid the cabbage down and was bent over, back on to me, to pick up an apron full of chips from where the Council had repaired a little bridge across the ditch. Then, bless my soul, who else should I see but King David comin' down the hill towards her. I know I should've shouted out and warned her, but I was so interested in wonderin' what King David'd do that I had to let nature take its course. Besides, Aunt Sophy is not on the best of terms with me neither, so I figgered I might do better by rescuin' her afterwards than by warnin' her beforehand.

Then I got the surprise of my life. King David walked right along by her and the cabbage without payin' any attention to either one of 'em. When I saw that, of course I bawled out to warn her, to try and get some credit out of it.

"My goodness, Aunt Sophy," said I when I got down to where she was. "I thought for sure King David was goin' to do 'ee a mischief."

"Look," she said, "there's somethin' wrong with him. There's somethin' funny about the way he walks."

I looked at where King David was still strollin' down the path away from us and, sure enough, instead of walkin' straight ahead he looked like he was sidlin' – somethin' like a crab crawlin' out from under a rock. "Why," said I, "he's not walkin' the same direction he's lookin'."

"No," said Aunt Sophy, "he's walkin' on the bias."**

Well, I wouldn't have put it that way. It looked more to me as if he had his wheel hard down. But however you described it, 'twas strange. And then it dawned on me what it must be. King David couldn't see out of his left eye, and the reason why he'd passed Aunt Sophy like he did was because she'd been on his blind side.

"Oh, the poor darlin' thing," said Aunt Sophy. And nothin' would do her but she must break off the outside leaves of her head of cabbage and take down to him, makin' sure of course that she kept on his blind side. Isn't that a funny thing about women? About Aunt Sophy, anyway. There's nothin' appeals to her so much as helplessness and affliction.

There's a lot of interest bein' shown today in King David's welfare, and we're all hopin' his affliction is only a temporary one. Aunt Mary Bartle had half a bottle of eyedrops that Skipper Lige used before he died, and she give 'em to Jethro Noddy to try and see if they'd do any good. Aunt Sophy insisted on bein' the one that dropped 'em in his eye, so it looks for sure as if the only bit of bad feelin' in Pigeon Inlet is cleared up and nothin'll stand in the way of the true Christmas spirit.

* crackie: a small dog, of mixed breed

** on the bias: at an angle to direction of travel

ON THE HALVES

GRAMPA WALCOTT SAYS he's got misgivin's whenever he hears tell of two people, or, for that matter, two governments, doin' things "on the halves." And to back up this statement he can tell stories by the dozen, from his own experiences, of things that have happened in these parts all on account of people tryin' to do things or to own things on the halves.

For one thing, look at the time Jonas Tacker and his brother Bobby down in Hartley's Harbour bought a cow on the halves. Jonas, a connivin' man if ever there was one, contended that, because Bobby's name came first on the bill of sale, Bobby should own the front half, while he owned the hinder half.

Bobby was as patient a man as you'd care to meet, but he soon got tired of watchin' Jonas's family grow fat and Jonas's potato garden grow rich off the products of that hinder end. So he stopped feedin' the cow altogether. And Jonas had the gall to have court work over it. Poor Uncle Bobby was charged with cruelty to dumb animals for neglectin' to feed his own half and damagin' Skipper Jonas's half by shuttin' off supplies of nourishment from it.

Skipper Bob Killick was magistrate in those days, and the case lasted almost a week down in Hartley's Harbour Lodge.

Finally Skipper Bob ruled that Uncle Bobby was cruel to his own half for not feedin' it, and furthermore he ordered Uncle Bobby to give his brother Jonas a right-of-way through his half, through which Jonas could supply nourishment to his half. Uncle Bobby said the right-of-way was there every time the cow opened her mouth and Jonas could use it all he liked. But Jonas said if he used the right-of-way he wanted Bobby to pay for any nourishment his half might use up while 'twas passin' through. And that left poor Uncle Bobby no better off than ever.

It ended, said Grampa, when one day just before Christmas Jonas came out from where he'd been in cuttin' firewood and Bobby met him with a sad face. "You'd better come over to the stable," he said, "and look at the cow."

"Why, what's the matter with the cow?" said Jonas.

"Well," said Uncle Bobby, "I don't rightly understand it, but this mornin' I slaughtered my half for Christmas, and I do believe your half is perished."

But a sadder case still is the case of Lige Bartle's will and his tool chest that he left "on the halves" to his two sons, Sam and Luke. Even the law, said Grampa, couldn't settle that case, and 'twouldn't be settled yet only for a woman, which marks the first and only time a woman ever settled anything in these parts.

Skipper Lige's will, said Grampa, was wrote out plain as anything on the back of a calendar. He left Sam the house and land, and Luke his stage and fishin' gear. Then come the clause that started the trouble – "and as for my tools, I leave 'em to both Sam and Luke, on the halves."

Skipper Lige had one of about every kind of carpenter

tool was ever heard tell of, and kept 'em in a tool chest in a little workshop that was built on the edge of the bank across the road from his house. Trouble was, there was only one of each, but that didn't matter. For almost a year, when Luke wanted a tool he'd go and get it and Sam'd do the same. They were the best of friends, as brothers should be.

Then one day Luke forgot to put back the spokeshave after he'd used it, and Sam grumbled at havin' to walk all the way over to Luke's to get it. Another time, Luke wanted the auger, but 'twas gone, and when he crossed the road to Sam's house, Sam's missus told him that Sam had loaned it to Joe Prior, who lived right down to the far end of the harbour. Luke was too contrary to go for it, and the followin' Monday, Luke's missus, Emma Jane, was fit to be tied when her line full of clothes fell down in the backyard, and all because Luke hadn't bored a hole in a clothesline pole for her.

Emma Jane had words with Sam's missus over it, and from then on things went downhill fast. The upshot was that, before poor Skipper Lige had been in his grave twelve months, Luke and Sam were not on speakin' terms. Luke wrote to a lawyer in St. John's about it, and, actin' on the advice he received, he went and put a big padlock on the workshop door and kept the key to hisself. Leastways, he said, if tools went out, he'd know where they were goin'. Next mornin' he took the key and went down to get the claw hammer, only to find that Sam had put a second padlock on the door, a size bigger than Luke's. So, for almost five years, that little workshop bided there on the bank, and the two padlocks were never touched, and Luke and Sam got worse and worse.

And then along came this woman and settled it.

"What woman?" said I. "Emma Jane Bartle?"

Grampa snorted. "No," he said, "she was even nosier than Emma Jane, and that's sayin' a lot."

You see, he went on, all these years the poor little workshop was bein' neglected. There were shingles off the roof and the shores under it were gettin' rotten. Then, one night, when this woman (Hazel,* I think they called her) come up rip-snortin' down over the hill, picked up that workshop and pitched it right into the middle of the harbour. Next mornin' 'twas away over the rocks on the other side, smashed to smithereens.

As for the tool chest, said Grampa, I was lucky enough a few mornin's later to jig it up by the handle on the claw of my grapnel. I lifted it aboard unknownst to anybody and rowed out till I had sixty fathom under me, then I let it go. Skipper Lige and I were buddies all our lives and I know he'd have approved. Luke and Sam scoured the bottom of the harbour for weeks till they knew the tools'd be spoiled by rust anyway. Then they give up and become friends again.

* Hazel: Hurricane Hazel, which affected parts of Canada in October 1954

CRIME WAVE IN PIGEON INLET

A FEW NIGHTS AGO, I WAS up to Grampa Walcott's house cuffin' the yarn with Grampa while Grandma sat by knittin' socks. Grampa turned the radio on and we listened for a spell. 'Twas about a fellow tryin' to murder another fellow 'cause the second fellow had run off with the other one's wife. At last Grandma spoke up.

"Grampa," she said, "turn off that nonsense."

"Why," said Grampa, "that's supposed to teach us crime don't pay."

"Well," said Grandma, "it must pay them that puts it on the radio, or they wouldn't put it there. But," she said, "if everyone was of my mind it wouldn't pay, because no one would listen to the trash."

Grampa turned it off. Then he winked at me and said, "Grandma likes stories about love."

"Well," said Grandma, "they're better than the ones about crime. We've got to have love, but we can do without crime."

"You're right, Grandma," said I. "Like Pigeon Inlet, for instance. We haven't got as much love as we'd like to see, but one good thing about this place is that we've got no crime here."

"No," said Grampa, "we've got no crime here nowadays. But one time we had what the radio would call a real crime wave. A one-man crime wave, it was."

"Oh," said I, "you mean Uncle Solomon Noddy."

"No," said Grampa, "I don't mean Uncle Solomon. He was a hangashore, but he wasn't a criminal. What Uncle Sol did, he didn't care who knew about it. He'd brazen it out and argue that 'twas quite lawful. This other fellow was different. He used to do bad things and try to cover 'em up."

"Did he get caught?" I asked.

"Well," said Grampa. "In one way of speakin' he got caught, and in another way he didn't. What I mean is, we found out he was thievin' but we didn't let him know we found out."

"Why not?" I asked.

"Well," said Grampa, "we figgered 'twould be better not to let him know we knew he was a criminal. You see, sometimes when a man finds out that the neighbours know how bad he is, it makes him try to be better. But other times it might only make him worse. It might make him feel everyone is down on him anyway, and he might as well be hung for a sheep as a lamb."

"So you didn't punish him for his thievery? You let him get away with it?"

"No," said Grampa, "he didn't get away with it. We didn't punish but we did better. We corrected him."

"Tell me about it, Grampa," said I. So Grampa got his pipe goin' good and proper and started in.

"Uncle Jasper Stokey," Grampa began, "was a grown man when I was a boy. I didn't know his age. In fact, he didn't know it himself, although he always said his birthday come when the black currants were ripe. He had no family, and he lived by himself in a shack up behind where Pete Briggs lives now. In fact," said Grampa, "Skipper Jonathan Briggs, Pete's grandfather, was the first victim of Uncle Jasper's thievery."

"Why?" said I. "What did Uncle Jasper steal from Skipper Jonathan?"

"Birch billets," said Grampa. "Skipper Jonathan used to watch from his bedroom window night after night. Uncle Jasper used to go out every night when he thought Skipper Jonathan was in bed. He'd reach in over the fence and steal enough birch billets out of Skipper Jonathan's woodpile to boil his kettle next mornin'. Skipper Jonathan told me about, and one day he decided to correct Uncle Jasper so as he wouldn't do it again."

"How?" said I.

"Well," said Grampa, "he took a birch billet, bored a hole in one, and put some gunpowder in the hole and plugged it up. Then he laid the billet right by his fence, easy for Uncle Jasper to reach. Next mornin' at daylight, he noticed the billet was gone, so he come and woke me up so that both of us could be around when it happened. We didn't have a long wait before there was a puff of black smoke, and soot went up Uncle Jasper's chimney, and we heard a dismal screech as Uncle Jasper come through his door with another cloud of soot behind him. His face was the colour of thirty-for-sixty on spades. Skipper Jonathan looked at him for a minute to make sure he wasn't hurt, while I went into the shed. There was no real damage done, but the mess was pretty bad."

Grampa paused for a long puff and continued. "By that time the hullabaloo had woke up the neighbours and half of Pigeon Inlet come to see what had happened. Everyone took a sniff, and what do you think they smelled?"

"Gunpowder," said I.

"No," said Grampa, "they smelled brimstone. 'Twas the smell of brimstone that really did the correctin' on Uncle Jasper. He figgered Nick had come for him that mornin' but had gone away and given him another chance."

"But, Grampa," said I, "how did the smell of brimstone get there?"

Grampa chuckled. "Remember those old-fashioned matches we used to use years ago? Used to call 'em stinkers. Whenever you lit one you had to run away from yourself. Well," said Grampa, "when Skipper Jonathan put the gunpowder into the hole in the billet, I thought we might as well make a good job of it. I broke the heads of two or three hundred stinkers and put them into the hole too. What a smell!"

It seems that a finger or two of gunpowder and the heads of some stinker matches cured Uncle Jasper from stealin' birch billets, and, from then on, accordin' to Grampa, he boiled the kettle with his own wood like everyone else.

Goin' Home

ONE OF THE COMPLAINTS the Nova Scotia shipowners (or at least one of 'em) got against us Newfoundland fishermen is that, after bein' away from home fishin' from April until October, we want, for some strange reason or other, to go home. And 'tis true. I ought to know, bein' one of 'em. And although 'tis all right for outsiders to tell us about it every so often, the truth is that we don't need to be told 'cause we know all about it ourselves. And not only fishermen, but all Newfoundlanders. Why, ever since I can remember listenin' to stories, some of the best ones I ever heard were about Newfoundlanders wantin' to get home. I'd like to tell you a few of 'em, but for the life of me, I can't right now think of one that'd be proper to tell. Besides, bein' Newfoundlanders, you've probably heard 'em all anyway.

But, by all accounts, you never hear any stories about other people wantin' to go home. Only Newfoundlanders. That used to puzzle me one time, but I've got lots of time for thinkin' nowadays, what with Aunt Sophy gone to Corner Brook again to visit her daughter Soos who's expectin' again. And by the way, 'tis a awful thing to confess, and I hope Corner Brook won't be offended by it, but Aunt Sophy in her letters says she's fair dyin' to get home. But then, what can you expect, she's a Newfoundlander too. Anyway, I've been doin' a lot of ponderin' over this habit we Newfoundlanders got and tryin' to figger if there's any cure for it.

'Tis a problem, sure enough. Why haven't other places got it? Why is it you never hear any jokes about, say, Toronto people wantin' to get home? Well, perhaps the reason is that Toronto people are already home, such as it is. And that brings me to my first point. I don't suppose there is or ever was a race of people who spend so much time away from home as we Newfoundlanders. A man can only have his home in one place at one time, whereas his means of makin' a livin' is wherever he can find it. There are millions of people in the world who are lucky enough to have their homes and their jobs in the same place. That's what makes all these big cities that you see dotted all over the map of the world. An industry started somewhere, people got jobs there, and not wantin' to be away from home, just like Newfoundlanders, they shifted their families in. That's what makes Toronto, New York, London real cities with homes in 'em, instead of just collections of bunkhouses. So you can see there are millions and millions of people in the world who don't want to go home, and if that shipowner could get hold to a few of *them* he'd be all set. Trouble is, he can't get 'em, because they already got jobs. And besides, if he did get 'em to fish for him, then they'd be away from home and they'd likely be just as anxious to get back to it as the Newfoundlanders.

Know what I think? That there's only two kinds of people in this world who don't want to go home. Those that's already home, and those that got no home to go to. And I don't see that there's much we can do about it. Like Skipper Bill Bartle. He's doin' carpenter work these years up around St. John's, but he comes home for the winter and makes sure he gets home before navigation closes. His boss'd like for him to bide on a bit longer and teases Skipper Bill about wantin' to get home to see his missus. The boss, of course, got his missus up there with him. Skipper Bill, like a true Pigeon Inletter, owned up. Yes, he did want to get home to see his missus, but he also wanted to get home to remind his youngsters that they had a father. Skipper Bill thinks, and a million or so clergymen of all denominations'll agree with him, that growin' youngsters nowadays need a reminder like that every so often.

Now, mind you, Skipper Bill don't like losin' time from work. He put it to his boss fair and square. He said, "If you guarantee me steady work in here, I'll shift the family in." But the boss couldn't guarantee anything of the kind, which is one of the reasons Skipper Bill and a good many more of us are not too anxious to be centralized.

And now, you might say, there's the answer to that Nova Scotia shipowner's problem. Why don't he encourage these Newfoundland fishermen that leave him in the fall to go home, why don't he encourage them to come up there and live? Then they'd fish as long as there was a fish to catch and this shipowner's troubles'd be over forever.

But would they? No! 'Cause after they'd been up there a year or two, my guess is that they'd say to theirselves, "Hey, what's goin' on here? We've been fishin' for years. Why should we keep on fishin' all our lives while other people get the jobs on shore where there's less hardship and steadier pay?" And so they'd probably look for jobs in the plant or somewhere else on shore, and bein' Nova Scotians by that time, why shouldn't they? But then if they got shore jobs, who'd catch fish? Why, that'd be a easy question to answer. Get some Newfoundlanders to come up to catch 'em. And so we'd end up exactly where we is now. Which, when you come to think of it, is not too bad a place to be.

SALMON AND TROUT

BY ALL ACCOUNTS, IF HALF of what we hear is true, there's goin' to be some big doin's down here around Bartle's Brook this comin' summer. Bartle's Brook is a nice little river and hardly a summer passes but what we have one or two, or five or six, or sometimes a dozen or more sports down here salmon-fishin' in it. In that way, Bartle's Brook is a very fine thing for Pigeon Inlet, not for the salmon that we Pigeon Inlet people catch in it, but for the sports it brings here. They bring business to Aunt Sophy's boardin' house, to Levi Bartle's store, and many a five-dollar bill is earned by one or another of us that they take up to the river with them to show 'em the good places and sometimes to gaff their salmon.

There are five or six good pools on Bartle's Brook before you get up about two and a half miles to Pummelly Pool, at the foot of what we call the Big Falls. I've spent hours in August watchin' salmon tryin' to jump the Falls, but, to the best of my knowledge, no salmon ever quite made it. Pummelly Pool is as far as they can get, and whatever spawnin' they do in the river, that's where they've got to do it.

The Inspector, when he was here just before Christmas, told me that this comin' summer the Federal government (it seems that they got charge of the rivers since Confederation), they're goin' to fix it so that the salmon'd be able to get up over the Falls. I thought first that he was jokin' and asked him did they intend to empty some of Jethro Noddy's homebrew into Pummelly Pool to make the salmon livelier, but he said he was quite serious about it. What the government intended to do was to make a ladder so that the salmon could get up and go miles and miles further up the river to where there'd be better and quieter places for 'em to spawn.

Now, when he mentioned a ladder, I thought his idea was foolisher than the one about Jethro Noddy's homebrew, but after he explained it, I could see the sense of it. The way they make these ladders is by blastin' away the rock around one side of the falls so that it's like steps of stairs, a lot of little falls, instead of one big one. That way, the salmon go up with no trouble at all.

Like he said, that'd be a good thing in two ways. First of all, 'twould be good for us in Pigeon Inlet because, with four or five miles more river to fish in, there'd be more sports come here. And second, 'twould be good for the whole country because 'twould mean the salmon would have a chance to do a better job of spawnin' in the quieter pools further up the river. But who'd have ever thought there was such a thing as a fish ladder? Oh my, there's always somethin' to learn. Whatever the government thinks best'll suit us all right. We don't fish in the river, anyway. And whatever'll bring most people from outside to do their fishin' and spend their money here, that's what *we* want.

Mind you, now, I wouldn't like you to think that we don't like a bit of sport ourselves. We do, and we get plenty of it. What with birdin' and seal-huntin', I get sport that brother Ki up in New Brumsick'd give his eye teeth to have. And, as for sport-fishin', we've got all we want of that without payin' away a lot of good money for a license and all kind of expensive gadgets. We've got troutin', troutin' through the ice in the winter, and troutin' with a bamboo pole in the spring just after the ice goes out of the ponds. Troutin' in the summer? No siree! Not after the flies get around.

I love troutin' through the ice. After the season opens in January, I go about once a week in over the hills to one of the ponds in back of Pigeon Inlet. The trout are not very big, but I always manage to get a fryin' pan full for myself and a fry for Grampa and Grandma Walcott besides. Other winters I'd catch a few for Aunt Sophy, too, but this winter, as you know, poor thing, she's marooned up in a place called Corner Brook, eatin' her heart out with lonesomeness. In the winter, when there's no other kind of fresh fish to get, these trout taste good, especially with plenty of pork fat.

I asked Grampa Walcott once why he never goes in to the nearest pond to catch a few trout, and Grampa give me a surprisin' answer. "Mose," he said, "I lost interest in troutin' years ago."

"How come?" said I.

"They all got caught out," said he.

"But, Grampa," said I, "they're not all caught out. There's plenty of 'em in there still."

"Not like there used to be, Mose," said Grampa. "Years ago, when I was a boy," said he, "they were real plentiful in Birchy Pond, just over the hill."

"Were they?" said I.

"Yes," said Grampa. "We didn't use a trout line at all in those days, or a hook or bait or anything like that. No need to."

"What'd you use, then?" I asked him.

"Well," said Grampa, "my favourite outfit for troutin' through the ice used to be a piece of red flannelette and a copy of the *Family Herald* and *Weekly Star.* Yes," said Grampa, "I'd cut me hole and dangle this piece of red flannelette about a foot above the hole, and the trout were so plentiful that they'd jump right up in the air after it."

"What was the *Family Herald* and *Weekly Star* for?" said I.

"Oh," said Grampa, "I'd have that rolled up in a tight roll and use it to bat the trout to one side before they could fall back into the hole. The last time I was in troutin'," said Grampa, "I only batted about five dozen, so I figgered they were gettin' pretty well caught out, and I took no further interest in it."

LUKEY'S LABELS

NOW, DON'T MISUNDERSTAND me, I'm a great believer in radio. 'Tis a wonderful blessin', especially to out-of-the-way places like Pigeon Inlet. Everyone admits that, even Grampa Walcott who lived here over sixty years before radios were ever even heard tell of. He says to do without radio'd be almost as bad as havin' to do without Grandma.

Still and all, I suppose radio is like everything else. You can have too much of a good thing. Anyhow, that's the way poor Lukey Bartle feels about it. But then, Lukey is a special case, married as he is to Emma Jane Grimes from Hartley's Harbour. Lukey don't always have too pleasant a time. To tell the truth, and this might sound foolish, I sometimes figger it's a good thing when you've got an example like Luke Bartle right in front of you every day. It goes to show you that there's two sides to this gettin' married business, that it's wise to look before you leap and not rush into this "Here Comes the Bride" thing head over heels. But to get back to poor Luke's radio troubles.

Luke says it wasn't as bad when he used to use a dry-battery radio. Then, even Emma Jane had sense enough to try and make the battery last as long as they could so that they wouldn't be hung up too often waitin' for another one to come down from St. John's. But, he says, it got terrible after he bought a wet battery set and a wind charger to go with it. Ever since then, he says, Emma Jane got the radio goin' all day long.

She's a connivin' sort of a woman, is Emma Jane, right after the dollar. And with Luke's fish earnin's and what she gets for runnin' the Post Office, they're not too bad off. But Emma Jane is never satisfied. And when she listens to radio all day long, her mouth waters to hear about the money that the radio is tryin' to give away – the Jackpots and the Giant Jackpots and even the Super-Giant-Jackpots. And all you need to do to win all this bundle of money is tear the label off a can, write your name on it, and send it in.

Well, poor Luke has been livin' out of tin cans for the last two years. And for a man that likes his good plain home-cooked pork and doughboys like the rest of us, he's not too well pleased about it. He might have got the upper hand of Emma Jane and made her stop it, only for what happened last fall. Emma Jane actually got a prize. Fifty dollars, it was. Of course, that was only the little baby Jackpot, so Emma Jane spent the whole lot and another fifty dollars besides in buyin' a big outfit of canned stuff so that she'd have plenty of labels, for havin' a shot at the real big money. A few weeks later she'd sent in all the labels but she could still tell what was in the cans because she had 'em all put back in their proper cardboard cases. She didn't win any more Jackpots so far, but the storeroom is just about as full of tin cans (with no labels on 'em) as it can be, although poor Luke and the youngsters have been doin' their best all the winter to eat their way through 'em.

But that's not what made him mad. Luke is a patient man, and it wasn't until one day last winter that he lost his temper. The youngsters was playin' in the storeroom one stormy day, and like youngsters will, they got hold to all the tin cans, took 'em out of their cartons, and started to line them up row on row all across the storeroom floor. Their mother was at the Post Office sortin' the mail, when Luke came in and saw them with this pile of shiny naked tin cans out on the floor. He bawled at 'em and told 'em to put 'em back quick into the cartons before their mother caught them. They cried a bit over it because they said they were playin' a great game. They said they were buildin' a breakwater for the *William Carson*.* But Luke stood firm and ordered the cans all put back within five minutes. Sure enough, when he looked in the storeroom just afterwards, everything was tidied away, and Luke thought no more about it till next mornin', when he got up just before daylight to go in over the hill to cut a load of firewood.

Now, as you know, a man who wants to do a good day's work woodcuttin' should start off with some good solid grub in his belly. So Luke figgered on gettin' himself a breakfast of pork and beans. Years before, Luke would've been able to warm up some beans that'd be left over and lyin' in the bean crock, but nowadays he knew he'd find 'em in a tin can in the storeroom. Well that was all right, so he went in the store-room and got a can. There was no label on it, but the cardboard carton 'twas in said "Pork and Beans," so Luke used the can opener and opened the can over his fryin' pan. Well, he told me afterwards that pineapple chunks might be all right in their place, but certainly they're never meant to be fixed for breakfast on a winter mornin'. So he scrubbed the mess off the fryin' pan and tried again. The next was a can of milk, so he went to the back door and let the cat in. After all, he thought 'twas just as well for someone to get a breakfast out of it. Well, before he finished, he opened two cans of molasses, a can of green peas, and three or four cans of some kind of goo that he couldn't put a name on – leastways not a name I could repeat over the radio.

'Twas broad daylight by that time and the can opener was gettin' dull, so he had to hurry and make up a breakfast of bread and molasses, an all right meal for a cripple, but not what a man needs to cut firewood on. Luke figgers his only hope is that Emma Jane'll give up sendin' in labels and switch over to box-tops, or else the youngsters'll stop buildin' break-waters.

* *William Carson*: auto-ferry (built in 1955) which for many years operated across the Cabot Strait

BERRY JUICE

GRAMPA WALCOTT THINKS 'tis a cryin' shame that the youngsters in school nowadays should learn pages and pages about people dead and gone for hundreds of years and don't learn a word about a man who was better than any of 'em and who lived right here on this shore for over eighty years – Skipper Bob Killick. Skipper Bob, who mastered his own schooner for over thirty summers to the Labrador, and then was appointed to just about the highest position any man could ever get to – a magistrate.

Now, personally I never knowed Skipper Bob. Accordin' to those that did, I missed somethin'. 'Cause court work in his day was worth travellin' miles to go to. Nowadays 'tis different. Why, last summer, one day a boatload of us left fishin' – there was no fish anyway – and went to Hartley's Harbour to the court work there. But 'twas no good. Seven cases – and all over before noon. Why, there was one case alone where Jemima Grimes had Aunt Polly Tacker up for slander. 'Twould have lasted all day if Skipper Bob had had the tryin' of it. Because he was a great believer in gettin' at the roots of a case, and what he didn't know about law, which was plenty, he more than made up for by knowin' about people. And he give his judgments accordin' to it.

Like the time Uncle Paddy Muldoon and Aunt Biddy were up before him on account of alcoholic liquor – although, like Aunt Biddy told him right out in court, that was an awful unchristian name to give her drop of old berry juice.

You see, Uncle Paddy and Aunt Biddy were the last livyers in Muldoon's Cove, which was halfway between here and Hartley's Harbour. A lonesome life they must have had, except when travellers dropped in for a warm or a mug-up, and never was a traveller refused either or both of 'em.

The sample of her berry juice that the policeman sent in to St John's tested 32%. You see, it was from an old secret recipe that Aunt Biddy's grandmother had brought out with her from Ireland. And that's how she and Paddy Muldoon come to be standin' up before Skipper Bob Killick in the courthouse that day in Hartley's Harbour. And Skipper Bob, instead of mumblin' such things as "regulation" this and "clause" that, got to the bottom of the case and brought out the facts about Uncle Paddy and his heartburn.

Now, accordin' to Aunt Biddy, she wouldn't have bothered makin' the stuff at all if it hadn't been for Uncle Paddy's heartburn, a thing he suffered from somethin' awful. Why, there'd be nights when they'd be there alone and she'd ask him to take down his fiddle and play somethin', and he'd say he'd like to only his heartburn was so bad. Then she'd go and get him a mug of juice and he'd get relief and he'd start to play a jig or two. Then, after another mug or two, or perhaps three, he'd play beautiful pieces like "Danny Boy" and "The Wearin' of the Green" that'd bring tears to her eyes, and his too. And why, she said, the authorities should find fault with that and talk about ugly things like "alcoholic liquor" was more than she could understand.

Oh yes, she said, she remembered the evenin' the crowd of fellows come to her house from Hartley's Harbour and said there was a time on down there that night and did she have any stuff to give 'em. She said no, she had nothin' except berry juice and that was to be used for no other purpose except as a remedy for heartburn. And how they went off contented enough, but later they was all back to her door inside of an hour – the whole lot doubled up with the heartburn and sufferin' somethin' awful. And how after she'd cured 'em and they'd gone off, Obe Grimes come back hisself and asked if he could take away a bottle in case he had another attack later that night. And yes, she'd heard after that Obe made a show of hisself at the time that night. Next thing she knew, the policeman had come and taken away a sample in a liniment bottle.

Now there was some talk of Uncle Paddy payin' a fine, but of course cash was out of the question. Uncle Paddy said they could take his horse, but it turned out the horse he was talkin' about was just his woodhorse in his backyard. The policeman suggested maybe he could pay in berry juice, but Skipper Bob just glowered at him and said he hoped *he* wasn't gettin' heartburn.

Then Skipper Bob delivered his judgment. Uncle Paddy, he said, shouldn't be blamed too much for tryin' a tried-and-true remedy. And the law didn't want to prevent Aunt Biddy from hearin' such wonderful music as "Danny Boy" and "The Wearin' of the Green." However, he said, if Aunt Biddy ever again did find herself with any heartburn remedy on hand, she mustn't have any outpatient department. And on no account was she to operate a travellin' clinic.

Now, what happened in the matter of berry juice after that, nobody knows. One thing for sure – the public never knowed anything about it. And oh yes, Uncle Paddy certainly didn't die of heartburn.

MEN'S RIGHTS

THERE ARE ABOUT TEN OR A dozen families livin' along
the back road in Pigeon Inlet just behind Grampa Walcott's,
and whenever he's so minded, he lets 'em take a shortcut
through the backyard to get down to the landwash and to
Levi Bartle's shop. And they're only too glad to take advantage of his kindness. But I've noticed that, one day every
summer, he nails up his gate and stands there by it, turnin'
back anyone tryin' to get through. I asked him why, and he
said 'cause, after all, 'twas his property and he had a right to
stop 'em. If he didn't exercise that right, after so many years
he'd lose it, and then he wouldn't be able to stop 'em even if
he wanted to. He said that's how it was with people's rights.
You had to either use 'em or lose 'em, and to prove his point,
he brought up the subject of moustaches and pipes.

After all, he said, there's only two things left in this world
that a man can do and a woman can't copy. One is grow a
moustache, the other is smokin' a pipe. And, says Grampa, if
a man loses the right to do these two things, he might just as
well dress up in one of these sack things like Emma Jane
Bartle is fraped up* in.

Time was, accordin' to Grampa, when here in Pigeon Inlet
you could almost tell the independent spirit of a man by the

272

size of his moustache, and in every kitchen in the place the thing you'd spot first on every dresser was the moustache cup. "Now, Mose, me son," he says, "apart from the two of us, there's not a man in Pigeon Inlet that got one except Skipper Joe, and he uses it for a shavin' mug. There's no moustache cups left, 'cause there's no moustaches to use on 'em."

It started forty-odd years ago, says Grampa, when somebody (a travellin' agent I think he was) told Aunt Polly Bartle she didn't look a day over twenty. She was fifty at the time, but naturally she believed him, and then begun to wonder how in the world she ever got tangled up with an old man like Skipper Lige. He was fifty-two. She put two and two together and figgered that people'd never believe she was as young as she looked while she had to be seen in public with Lige. Then she remembered how young Lige looked when she caught him just before he had a moustache, forgettin' that was thirty years ago, and she come up with the idea that 'twas Lige's moustache that was holdin' her back somehow, and that 'twould have to come off.

Skipper Lige knew he'd be a laughin' stock on every net loft and stagehead in Pigeon Inlet, and he said afterwards he never would have given in only for the bullbird soup. He was awful fond of bullbird soup, and when Aunt Polly threatened not to cook any more, 'cause her soup was too good to be strained through *that* thing, he broke down and give in. That started it, and within ten years there wasn't a moustache left in Pigeon Inlet except one, and Grampa said he'd likely have lost that only Grandma is too fond of bullbird soup herself, and give in first. Them rights never come back, he said. Once you let go of 'em you've lost 'em for good.

Well, there's still one thing left – the pipe. And if we're not careful here in Pigeon Inlet, he said, we men'll lose that too. Poor Aunt Polly Bartle is not here to start the campaign this time, but Emma Jane Bartle, Luke's missus, is just as wily, and poor Luke'll never have the holdout that his father Skipper Lige had.

One night, a few weeks ago, she fired the first shot. She was readin' through one of those newfangled women's magazines, and Luke was lyin' down on the settle smokin' his pipe, when all at once she spoke up and said to him, "Luke Bartle, stop smokin' right at once and throw that dirty murderin' pipe in the stove."

Well, poor Luke looked at her like a fool, while she said, "Luke, you got somethin' growin' in your insides." He asked her what in the world she was talkin' about, and she said, right there in the magazine it said how smokin' made things grow in people's insides. Luke said, yes, he'd heard tell about it, but that was cigarettes. She said, yes, that was what the magazine said, but it must apply to pipes too. Otherwise, how would Luke have things growin' in his stomach when he didn't smoke cigarettes, only the pipe. Well, there was no answerin' an argument like that, and Emma Jane actually tried to take Luke's pipe to put it in the stove. Only, in wrasslin' with him for it, she got a finger jammed in the bowl on top of the ashes, and that took her mind off the subject for a spell. Luke told her then, that if pipe smokin' made things like that grow, Grampa Walcott's insides must look like a bunch of bananas. And there it ended, for that night.

But next day, Emma Jane went all around Pigeon Inlet showin' this article to the women and gettin' them organized.

And she done a good job too, because a few nights after, I went up to Grampa Walcott's place, and there was Grandma and Aunt Sophy givin' him dirty looks while he puffed away at his old pipe, and even dirtier ones when he invited me to light up too.

Then he tipped me the wink and said, "Mose, me son," he said, "in all fairness to the women, I got to own up that I did know one case where pipe smokin' shortened a man's days." The women cocked their ears at that, and Grampa went on, "Yes, he was Uncle Tobias Tacker from Hartley's Harbour, a pipe smoker if ever there was one. Smoked like a tilt from the time he was fifteen. Used the same match in the mornin' to light his pipe and the kitchen stove, and daytimes he begrudged havin' to take out his pipe to eat his meals. People used to warn him," said Grampa, "Just like Emma Jane is doin' now, that 'twould shorten his days, and sure enough it did."

"There," said Grandma, "I bet somethin' growed up in his stomach."

"Well, as to that," said Grampa, "I couldn't say. But what I know *did* happen was that, one night while he was smokin' in bed, he dozed off, and by the time the neighbours got to him, 'twas too late. It shortened his days all right, but bein' as how he was a hundred and two at the time, it couldn't have shortened 'em by much."

And so it looks as if pipe smokin' is one right we men might hang onto for a spell yet. Providin', that is, that plug tobaccy don't get too dear.

* fraped up: dressed in fancy, old-fashioned way

WHORTS

I SOMETIMES WONDER WHAT happened to that scheme that was on the go thirty or forty years back – that plan to get everybody in the world to talk the same language. Esperanto, they were goin' to call it – or some such name. There was a time when you could hardly take a trip on a coastal boat without runnin' across one of these fellows, generally tryin' to sell you a book on the subject and tryin' to make you believe that in a few years time everybody'd be talkin' Esperanto, and the world'd be a perfect place to live in because everybody'd understand what everybody else was sayin' to 'em. We never hear about it now. The promoters must've got discouraged and give up.

Perhaps 'tis just as well. Grandma says 'tis against scripture for people to all try and talk the same language and Pete Briggs says that 'tis a good thing the crowd on that foreign dragger didn't understand what he said to them when they carried away his trawl last year out on Ice Ledge. On the other hand, Jonas Bartle lost a summer's work down at Carol Lake on account of the same thing. The boss said good mornin' to Jonas in French, and Jonas quit and come home – said he was never so insulted in all his life. So, I s'pose there's two sides to the argument, like there is to everything else.

But what I would like to see is an attempt to get those of us who talk the same language to understand one another. 'Cause, unless we can understand our own lingo, there don't seem to be much sense in tryin' to learn someone else's. Although the education authorities won't agree with me, because by all accounts the youngsters here in the higher grades in Pigeon Inlet school spend a lot more time learnin' Latin and French than they do English. But the teacher tells me that's because they're supposed to know English all the time. They're supposed to learn it from listenin' to us older people talk it. See what I mean. How can they learn it from us unless we can agree among ourselves on what it is. That's why I'd like to see some sort of a Newfoundland dictionary. 'Cause we need it, if we're goin' to understand one another.

Take for example – whorts. They ought to be in our dictionary. But no. With millions of gallons of lovely whorts growin' on our whort bushes every summer, we got to call 'em by a foolish name like blueberries. I blame Aunt Sophy for the trouble I got into last summer. She's always after me to talk more refined when visitors come to the place and so, with this in mind, I happened to use the expression blueberries – just once. Here's how it happened.

The steamer was in to the wharf. She had about two hours' delay and the passengers were stretchin' their legs on shore. There was this nice oldish couple, man and wife, from somewhere in the States, they said, tourists, and they asked me if I'd show 'em in over the hill so as they could get a glimpse of the country. I was glad to do it, and we were goin' along the path almost to Bartle's Pond when she asked me what was the name of these berries growin' on all the bushes.

I remembered Aunt Sophy's advice and said, "Ma'am, they're blueberries." She looked puzzled but said nothin', just turned sorta pale, but he spoke up and said, "How is it they're blueberries when they're red?" So I, wantin' to be helpful as usual said, "Well sir," I said, "that's how it always is with blueberries, they're red now 'cause they're green." Then he turned white, grabbed her by the arm, and the two of 'em just give me one frightened look and hurried back along the path and down the road without lookin' back anymore till they was safe aboard the steamer. I spied the two of 'em on the top deck afterwards pointin' me out to some other passengers, and when I waved to 'em friendly like, they left the deck and kept out of sight till the steamer was gone. A steward told me next trip he'd overheard the woman say that man with the moustache ought to be locked up in a institution somewhere. So from now on, whorts is whorts. As far as I'm concerned, other countries can buy 'em for blueberries – but I'm pickin' 'em for whorts.

That's why I say we ought to have a dictionary of our own language. Perhaps this new university'll put one together and save us from the danger of forgettin' how to talk to one another, and our children from forgettin' their own language. Let's not let 'em grow up not knowin' a bobstay from a top 'n lift, or a killick from a piggin, a doughboy from a touten, a mashberry from a whort, or a mug-up from a scoff.

I can tell 'em this, it's a lot simpler callin' things by their proper names than tryin' to explain to somebody that somethin' blue is red 'cause it's green.

THE BULL MOOSE

AFTER HEARIN' THE UNKIND remarks that Grampa Walcott has made about the stupidity of such animals as the rabbit and the beaver, you might get the idea that he's a man with no respect for dumb animals. But don't get him wrong. You should hear him talk about what he calls genuine animals, ones that any up-and-comin' country like Canada might well be proud of to have as their national animal.

Take, for example, the dog hood. Now there's an animal with character. Why, a dog hood'll sit there on a pan of ice all day long, mindin' his own business. Leave him bide and he'll do as much for you. But molest him and see what happens – if you live to tell about it. Grampa says he's heard tell of animals in foreign parts that have been known to fight till they're dead. But the dog hood is different. Why, he'll fight *after* he's dead. Skipper Lige Bartle, out swilin' one mornin' years ago, shot and pelted one just after daylight, and comin' back that way late in the evenin' the carcass of that old dog hood, he said, snapped at him. And if Skipper Lige hadn't been so yary* he'd have lost a piece of his starboard leg.

But the noblest animal of them all, says Grampa, is the bull moose. And to prove his point he tells the story about Skipper Jonathan Briggs – that's Pete Briggs's father – and the experience he once had with a bull moose. Now, Grampa is not sure about the exact date. All he's sure of is that there was no war on at the time 'cause the price of fish was low and times were bad. So he figgers it was between forty-five and fifty years ago when Skipper Jonathan was in his prime, the spryest man with the longest legs that Pigeon Inlet ever produced.

Well, this day, accordin' to Grampa, Skipper Jonathan had an awful longin' for meat. Naturally, of course, with times bad, there was only credit for flour and molasses, and it was the wrong season for turrs. But he figgered if he took his muzzleloader and walked about two miles across Gull Mash into the low woods, he might spy a rabbit or somethin' that'd help keep body and soul together. So off he went, muzzleloader, powder horn, shot bag and all.

Now, as everybody knows, the shore between here and Hartley's Harbour is awful rugged, with cliffs about 200 feet high and a sheer drop to the beach below. There's not a tree to be seen all along that stretch of cliff, except one old pine tree right on the edge about a mile from here. Nowadays, with the frost eatin' away at the cliff every spring, that old tree is hangin' out over the water and likely to fall at any time. But in those days it was standin' straight up, right on the edge of that precipice, with the lowest limb about twenty feet off the ground.

Well, accordin' to Grampa's story, Skipper Jonathan left Pigeon Inlet that mornin', followed the dog-team trail along the edge of the cliff till he got to that old pine tree. Then, takin' his bearin's from it, he turned off and headed straight across Gull Mash towards the woods, about two miles back.

He stopped just before he got to the scrub timber and put about four fingers into his muzzleloader, about the right load for a rabbit. He put a cap on the nipple and went in, about half a gunshot, when what should he happen to bump into almost head-on but this bull moose.

For size, the like he'd never seen before or even heard tell of. It was so close he could almost reach out and touch him with the muzzle of the gun. Then, as Skipper Jonathan often admitted afterwards, he got excited and lost his head. He up gun and fired right into that bull moose's face, although he should have known that four fingers would have the same effect on that animal as a handful of pepper.

Well, the moose shook his head, gave a snort, and started towards him. Skipper Jonathan scooted out of that clump of trees in a hurry and headed back across Gull Mash with the bull moose right on his heels. The mash was dry, so Jonathan made good goin'. But so did the moose. Jonathan looked back once, but what he saw didn't look too pleasant so he hove away his gun and settled down to runnin'. He said after that he remembered seein' a rabbit or two on the mash, but they got out of the way to let somebody run as knowed how.

Then Skipper Jonathan remembered an awful thing. He was headed for the cliff, with a 200-foot drop and sure death ahead of him, and that bull moose, which was even worse, behind him. Then he thought of somethin' else – a hope. That old pine tree, straight ahead on the edge of the cliff. But the limb – the lowest one – twenty feet off the ground. Could he jump up to it? Well, just then the moose snorted right down the back of his neck, so he opened his throttle right to the last notch. The tree was just ahead. He judged his distance and jumped, with his hands above his head and his fingers stretched out, hopin' to clutch that limb.

"Did he clutch it?" said I.

"No," said Grampa. "He missed it. On the way up, that is. But he grabbed it on the way down. The bull moose went through the air like he was shot out of a gun and tumbled onto the rocks in the landwash below. Skipper Jonathan worked his way along that limb to the trunk of the tree, got down to the ground, and had that moose dressed and brought home to Pigeon Inlet before dark that evenin'."

If Grampa had his way, the bull moose would be the national animal of Canada. Then every Pigeon Inletter would be proud to be a Canadian.

* yary: quick, wary

Poppin' the Question

I'M FINDIN' OUT LATELY THAT there are a lot of nice, kind-hearted people in this world, both in Pigeon Inlet and outside of it. These are the people who tell me or write to me and advise me that I ought to pop the question to Aunt Sophy. They seem to think that all I've got to do is ask Aunt Sophy the big question and that she'll say "Yes." No more goin' home to a cold house in the nights, no more cookin' my own meals, darnin' my own socks, no more sewin' on my own buttons. Why, accordin' to them, all my troubles'd be over.

Besides that, they say, I'd share in the benefits of Grandma's double bed quilt that she's got for a weddin' present for Aunt Sophy. I'd find out how old Aunt Sophy is (a thing that's always troubled me), I'd knock out Josh Grimes, that Hartley's Harbour sleeveen that's after Aunt Sophy too. To top it all off, they say that the other woman – that Aunt Sarah Skimple from Hartley's Harbour – would leave me alone once I was married to Aunt Sophy. There's other things they told me, too, but they're not the kind of things a fellow ought to mention. It makes me feel bashful just to think of 'em.

Like I said, it just goes to show that these people who advise me to pop the question to Aunt Sophy are nice, kind-hearted people. But it also goes to show that they don't know what they're talkin' about. What they're sayin' might be true enough about other women, but not about Aunt Sophy.

Pop the question! How in the world am I goin' to pop the question at her, or pop anything else at her, when I can't get within' gunshot of her?

The latest trouble between us happened because I had a birthday present bought for Aunt Sophy, and by mistake I give it to Aunt Sarah Skimple in Hartley's Harbour. Aunt Sarah thought I meant it for her and she hugged me and kissed me on her front doorstep, with Josh Grimes takin' it all in from his backyard right alongside. Josh phoned the news up to Emma Jane Bartle in Pigeon Inlet and she, of course, told Aunt Sophy. Aunt Sophy hasn't spoken to me since.

I've tried everything. I even got Grampa Walcott (he's Aunt Sophy's father) to try to break the ice for me. It happened about three weeks ago.

"Grampa," said I.

"Yes, Mose, me son," said Grampa.

"Grampa," said I, "I suppose you see Aunt Sophy once in a while these days."

"Certainly I do," said Grampa. "Every day. Some days, three or four times. Why, Mose?"

"Does my name ever come up in the conversation?" said I.

"Yes," said Grampa, "I've brought it up myself. Somethin' about 'Uncle Mose is not lookin' so well the last few days,' or 'Uncle Mose is certainly workin' hard makin' his bit of fish.' Things like that."

"And what," said I, "does Aunt Sophy say when my name comes up?"

"Well," said Grampa, "in a way of speakin', she don't say anything, not in words, that is."

"Why, what do you mean, Grampa?" said I. "She either says somethin' or she don't say somethin'."

"There's only one way to describe it, Mose," said Grampa. "She snorts."

"Snorts?" said I.

"Snorts!" said Grampa.

"Then," said I, "you don't think 'twould be wise for me to pay her a visit?"

"No," said Grampa. "Fact is, Mose," he said, "I dropped a hint only last night that you had a mind to come up to see her."

"What did she say?" said I.

"She's my own daughter," said Grampa, "and I don't like to repeat it."

"I'll write her a letter," said I.

"That'd be a wiser plan," said Grampa.

So that night, I wrote this letter and, in order to show you that I'm doin' my best, I'll tell you what I wrote.

First I started off "My dear Aunt Sophy." Then I crossed out the 'dear' and on the line below that, I wrote "Aunt Sophy." Then I said: "I thought that bein' as how the fall weather was comin' on, you would soon be wantin' your storm windows put up and, bein' as how it's a man's job, the kind of a job a man likes to do for someone he's got a special regard for, I'd like, if I might make so bold, to put up yours whenever you want them put up."

Then I signed it "yours very truly, Uncle Mose." Then I crossed out the "very," sealed it in an envelope, and give young Bill Noddy five cents to take it up to Aunt Sophy's. Ten minutes later, he was back with a reply. It started off, "Mr. Mose Mitchell, Sir." Just like she was the Mounties and I was applyin' for a license to make moonshine. Here is the letter:

"Mr. Mose Mitchell, Sir: Am havin' my storm windows put up next week, but cannot accept your kind offer because I feel you will be too busy puttin' up storm windows in Hartley's Harbour. I agree with you, however, that it is a job a man likes to do for someone he has a special regard for and because of that, I am gettin' Mr. Josh Grimes of Hartley's Harbour to put them up next time he visits Pigeon Inlet." And then she signed it "Sophia Watkinson."

Bless my soul. Imagine "Sophia Watkinson."

That's why I say to all you people who tell me I ought to pop the question to Aunt Sophy, it just goes to show you might know other women but you just don't know Aunt Sophy. Or should I say you just don't know Mrs. Sophia Watkinson. And how in the world I'm goin' to pop the question without gettin' somethin' popped back at me is more than I can see.

THE CYNIC

THERE'S NO DOUBT ABOUT it, in late years the world is gettin' more opened up, and 'tis no trouble to see the results of it right here in Pigeon Inlet. During the run of a year we have a lot more visitors than we used to have, and they come from all parts, British Columbia, California, and even from as far away as Ottawa. Now don't misunderstand me, we're glad to see 'em not only for the bit of business they do here, but just as much for their company, and their conversation, and the new ideas they give us. I should say that in ninety-nine cases out of a hundred they're just as good a people in their way as we are. Of course, there's always the odd one or two, and we had one of these odd ones here late last summer. He spent a week salmon fishin' (off and on) up on Bartle's Brook.

He must've thought we were an odd crowd. Saturday night he tried his best to line up somebody to go guide for him next day on the river, but none of us would go, bein' as it was Sunday. Like we told him, it wasn't because we thought ourselves any better than he was, but there it was. It was not a habit we'd fallen into so far, and we were in no hurry to commence. So, next day, he idled around the place while the rest of us went to church, and that evenin' after service was over and a crowd of us were sittin' around on the bank overlookin' the harbour, he walked over from Aunt Sophy's boardin' house.

One of us asked him didn't he get an invite to church and he said, "Oh, yes." Then we said 'twas too bad it wasn't the same kind of a church he was used to and he said no, there's no difference, he wasn't much of a hand for goin' to church anyway. He said that where he come from was different from Pigeon Inlet. He said he's never run across a place in his life so much for this churchgoin' and religion as Pigeon Inlet was.

Now, I could see from the looks on the faces around that the boys didn't care too much for that kind of talk. Not, of course, that any of us would be ignorant enough to speak saucy to the man. After all, I suppose he was a bit cross over losin' his day up on the river and he had to take it out on somebody or somethin' and, bein' grown-up men, we didn't mind just so long as he didn't go too far with it.

Grampa Walcott asked him a civil question. "Sir," said Grampa, "if I might make so bold, what might you be – in the matter of religion?"

"Oh," said this fellow. "I'm nothin'. I guess I'm what you might call a cynic."

Jethro Noddy spoke up. "A what?" said Jethro.

"A cynic," said this fellow.

"Excuse me sir," said Jethro, "but you don't look like one."

"Why," said the fellow, "did you ever see a cynic before?"

"Yes," said Jethro, "I sees one every day. Up in our kitchen. The one the missus washes the dishes in."

The fellow gave Jethro a suspicious look, but Jethro's face

was as straight as it ever was, so the fellow went on talkin'. "Yes," he said, "why even your names around here are nearly all taken out of the Bible – names like Moses, Benjamin, Jethro, Luke, Joseph, Samuel."

Well, he had a good point there, even though I couldn't see much sense in whatever he was drivin' at. But just then Grampa Walcott chimed in. Like I've told you before, Grampa got a way of his own for dealin' with people like that, and when he's finished they never rightly know whether he was pullin' their legs or not.

"Well now, sir," said Grampa, "I'm glad you mentioned that about our Bible names, because late years I've been gettin' worried for fear we were gettin' away from that good old custom of callin' our children after Bible characters. You should have been here," said Grampa, "in the days of old Skipper Phineas Prior."

"Who was he?" this fellow asked, and Grampa was off under full sail.

"Skipper Phineas Prior," said Grampa, "was our lay reader for over forty years. He could barely read at all, but even at that he was away to wind of most of us, so he used to read services on all the Sundays except the four or five a year when the clergyman'd come here. He got to know the Bible almost from cover to cover and was what you might call a powerful man in the scriptures.

"Well," said Grampa, "Skipper Phineas had fourteen children and you might be sure he give 'em all (boys and maidens alike) good solid names straight from the scriptures. After the fourteenth one, Malachi I think it was, it began to look as if he wouldn't have any more and he was heard to say he was sorry because there was still one name he'd have liked to use. We often asked him what name he had in mind, bein' as how he'd used most of 'em but he wouldn't tell us. And then when Young Malachi was goin' on four years old, along come another one, a fine bouncin' boy, the spittin' image of Skipper Phin."

Grampa went on to tell that, as he was Godfather, he was right there when Skipper Phineas told the clergyman he wanted the boy named Psm Civ.

"What?" said the clergyman.

"Psm Civ," said Skipper Phineas.

"Where did you get that name from?" said the clergyman.

"Out of the Good Book, parson," said Phineas.

"But there's no name like that in the Bible," said the clergyman.

"Oh yes there is," said Phineas, "I'll find it for 'ee."

And sure enough, accordin' to Grampa, he found it. But the clergyman had to explain to him that Psm Civ was only the Latin way of sayin' Psalm 104. So they called the young fellow Zephaniah and let it go at that.

You'd think after hearin' that story, this tourist fellow would have had enough. But no. He had to make a remark about how he supposed Pigeon Inlet people even believed about Jonah and the whale. But that's another story that I'll tell next time.

JONAH AND THE WHALE

LAST WEEK I WAS TELLIN' you about that sport who was miffed 'cause nobody'd go up the river with him on a Sunday. Mind you, I'm not tryin' to make out that we people in Pigeon Inlet are any more God-fearin' than people anywhere else. Perhaps not so much so, especially someone like Jethro Noddy.

Except for that Sunday when it rained so hard, Jethro hasn't been inside the church door all summer. He goes in over the hill every Sunday mornin' and don't come back till after dark. What's he up to in there? Troutin', that's what. He don't want to shock people like Gramdma by carryin' a trout pole through the community in broad daylight on a blessed Sunday, so he keeps it poked away amongst the trees at the head of Bartle's Pond. The clergyman had his suspicions and once asked Jethro what was so interestin' in over the hill every Sunday. Jethro told him he was goin' in to see if there was any sign of the new highroad comin'.

So we don't pretend to be any more God-fearin' than any-one else. Still, we've got our beliefs and we're always ready to stick up for 'em. After church that evenin', that sport came along to join us. One thing led to another until he made a remark that he supposed Pigeon Inlet people believed everything – even about Jonah and the whale. It was the way he said it. The rest of us said nothin', figgerin' that this was a job for Grampa Walcott.

Grampa looked at the fellow respectful-like. "Don't you," said Grampa, "believe in Jonah and the whale?" The fellow laughed and said no indeed he didn't.

"I take it," said Grampa, "that you'm an authority on whales?" The fellow said no, not exactly, but then he didn't need to be – not for *that*.

"Well, then," said Grampa, "be you familiar with the girt whales we fellows see down in the Straits of Belle Isle on our way home from Labrador?" The fellow said no.

"Well, then," said Grampa, "I'll make you familiar." And Grampa told him this tale.

'Twas fifty-odd years ago, said Grampa, that his schooner – her name was the *Anti-Confederate* – was comin' home across the Straits. With a northerly behind her, she was comin' along wing-and-wing about twelve knots. Grampa was at the wheel and Uncle Joby Noddy was grindin' his axe about ten feet away, with his young fellow Sol turnin' the grindstone for him. There was a whalin' steamer about half-mile away and a few of those girt whales sportin' around, one of 'em close by off the starboard quarter.

"It must have been a little squall," said Grampa, "that made the schooner lurch. Anyway, the next thing I noticed was Uncle Joby, young Sol, grindstone, chocks, axe, and the whole she-bang goin' over the starboard rail, and that's the last we seen of 'em. That whale thrashed around for a spell, then he disappeared too. And after sailin' round and round the spot for hours, we had to give up hope. Lige Bartle put the flag half-mast, and we got the *Anti-Confederate* back on course. We happened to notice in the meantime," said Grampa, "that the whaler was killin' a whale, but we were too low-spirited to pay much heed."

Grampa paused right here to light his pipe, and that give us a chance to look around. The stranger was starin' at Grampa like he had two heads, and the rest of us were tryin' to look as if we knowed this story all our lives, although none of us had ever heard if before.

"Our course," said Grampa, "took us right to that whaler and we noticed they had the whale aboard by this time and they were signallin' us to heave to. Then the captain bawled out to ask us did we lose anything overboard and we told him. Then he said to lower a punt and come over."

When Grampa and Skipper Lige climbed up on that whaler's deck, there was all the crew standin' round that dead whale, and through its open mouth they could hear strange noises, the like they'd never heard before, inside a whale or out. "We listened," said Grampa, "and to us 'twas plain as anything. We could hear Uncle Joby cussin' on young Sol to turn the handle faster so as he could finish sharpenin' the axe and chop his way out. No wonder they couldn't understand it," said Grampa, "'cause they was all Norwegians and couldn't speak a word of English except the captain, and he certainly not the kind Uncle Joby was usin' right then.

"So," said Grampa, "they opened up the whale right careful, and the four of us went back to the *Anti-Confederate* and put the flag right to the top.

"And what I want to know," said Grampa to the sport, "is don't you believe *that*?"

What the stranger believed deep down we'll never know, but just then Pete Briggs straightened up from where he'd been sittin', took the boulder he'd been sittin' on, and tossed it casual-like over the bank. So the stranger said yes, of course he had to believe a thing Grampa had seen with his own eyes. Then he said somethin' about how 'twas gettin' chilly, and he headed off towards Aunt Sophy's boardin' house.

ROMANCIN'

TODAY I'D LIKE TO SAY A few words about this business of romancin'. You know the kind of thing I mean. Those stories that Grampa Walcott tells – stories like the one about the bull moose, or the time Grampa had the ride on the helicopter years before helicopters were invented – things like that. Well, what put it in my mind was a letter Grampa had not long ago from a fellow, a foreigner he must've been, who heard Grampa tell one of his stories on board the *Glencoe* last fall, and he wrote Grampa a letter suggestin' he ought to copy out the story and send it away to a place where they give prizes every year for the biggest lies. Grampa showed me the letter, before he tore it up and burned it. He said 'twas a good thing Grandma didn't lay her eyes on it or she'd have been shocked.

You see, the way Grampa looks at it, these stories are not lies at all. He said 'tis a wicked sin to tell lies, to deceive people, or to bear false witness, but romancin' is different. It deceives nobody. Even Grandma, who wouldn't wilfully tell a lie to save her life, doesn't think Grampa's stories are lies. She never says, "Grampa, stop tellin' lies" – she just says "Grampa, hush your romancin'."

Instead of doin' harm, I'm more inclined to think that

Grampa's romancin' does a lot of good. Time and time again, I've listened to people doin' a bit of braggin', till by and by they've got a little too far from Grampa's likin' and he chips in with one of these stories that'll take the wind right out of their sails. Like the time Josh Grimes from Hartley's Harbour was up here one night and was tellin' about the awful fight he'd had with a black bear one time when he was in the woods. Now, we had heard Josh tell the story so often we were tired of it, even though he used to add a bit to it every time. The only reason we could see for him tellin' it again was to impress Aunt Sophy, who happened to be in the room at the time. Josh Grimes already buried two wives and late years he's been comin' up from Hartley's Harbour hangin' around Aunt Sophy. And here's a funny thing that I don't understand. Aunt Sophy tells Grampa and Grandma that she can't bear the sight of Josh, but then she tries to make me believe that she thinks he's a fine man. Now, why is that? I'm sure I don't know.

Anyway, like I said, Josh was tellin' this again about him and the bear until Grampa couldn't abide it any longer and, when Josh stopped to catch his breath, Grampa said yes, 'twas an awful thing to be attacked by a vicious beast. He knew because he'd been attacked by four at one time in exactly the same place Josh was talkin' about. He said it took from just after daylight till nearly dark before he finally subdued the four of 'em. Then, he said, he brought the four of 'em home on his back.

That made Josh Grimes's eyes pop. "Bears?" said he. "No, rabbits," said Grampa – and Josh has never since been known to tell about his adventure with the bear.

But the story I had in mind to prove my point concerns one day early last fall. There was a few fish around to jig, but there was nobody out this particular day because we were all busy on our flakes. These two strangers come along to Grampa and asked him for the loan of his punt. They said they'd like to go out to see if they could jig a codfish. Grampa was all in favour of lendin' them his punt and a couple of cod-jiggers, but he had his misgivin's, especially when he heard one of 'em say to the other, "You sit in the sharp end of the boat and I'll sit in the blunt end."

So Grampa said, "Boys, have you fellows ever been cod-jiggin' before?"

"Oh yes," said one of 'em, "we're used to it."

"Ever jig anything?" Grampa asked.

"Oh yes," said this fellow, "why only last week we were jiggin' down off Hartley's Harbour. I jigged a big one."

"How big?" Grampa asked.

The two fellows looked at one another. Then one of 'em said, "Oh, about 200 pounds."

"Yes," said Grampa. "You must've jigged that one in the same place where I lost my lantern overboard last July. Lighted and all, it was. I was usin' it just before daylight to bait my hooks and I knocked it overboard accidental like. Never expected to see it again," said Grampa, "but three weeks later I was jiggin' on the same spot and I jigged up that lantern and 'twas still burnin' as bright as ever."

The two fellows looked at Grampa, then they looked at one another, then one of 'em said, "Oh, come now sir, that's not true."

"Why not?" said Grampa.

"Because," said this fellow, "even if the lantern hadn't gone overboard 'twould have burnt out by that time, but a lantern couldn't keep lighted under the water. You're tryin' to pull our legs."

"I wouldn't do such a thing for the world," said Grampa. "I'll tell 'ee what I'll do."

"What?" said the fellow.

"Well," said Grampa, "if you fellows'll knock fifty pounds off the weight of that codfish you jigged last week, I'll fix that lantern so that the oil was all burnt out and 'twas just on the hand of goin' out. And ..."

"Yes?" said the other fellow.

"If you'll knock another 100 pounds off that codfish, I'll dout* the lantern altogether."

One of 'em, the one sittin' in the blunt end, did jig a tomcod that mornin' and he was as proud of it as if it weighed half a ton.

* dout: extinguish

SMOKEROOM ON THE KYLE

WELL, 'TIS LIKE AUNT POLLY Bartle said when she finished unravellin' Skipper Lige's guernsey, "There's a end," she said, "to everything." And so like everything else, these Chronicles got to come to an end sometime.

It's almost nine years since I come to Pigeon Inlet, and I've tried to keep you up-to-date on the goin's-on in these parts. I hope you'll always keep a warm spot in your memory for Grampa, Grandma, Aunt Sophy, Skipper Joe, Pete, and all the others – includin', of course, King David.

But you know how it is. Nine years is a long spell for a single man still in the prime of life to bide in any one place, and to tell you the truth, I'm gettin' a bit fidgety. And so, I'm leavin' on the next steamer and goin' off on a trip. Where am I goin'? I don't know. Likely I'll spend a while with my sister Becky in St. John's or with Rachel who lives out round the bay. Perhaps I'll go up to New Brumsick to see my brother Ki. Maybe I'll come back to Pigeon Inlet again or maybe I'll get so used to pushin' buttons instead of workin' that I'll settle down in some other place instead.

They give me a farewell party here last night and Skipper Joe had what I thought was a good idea. He said, "Mose,

instead of sayin' goodbye, why not give us one of your old
yarns over again." When I asked which one, he said, "What
about the *Smokeroom on the Kyle.*"
And so, as a sort of a fare-thee-well, here it is.

Tall are the tales that fishermen tell when summer's work is done,
Of fish they've caught and birds they've shot, and crazy risks they've run.
But never did fishermen tell a tale so tall by half a mile,
As Grampa Walcott told last fall, in the smokeroom on the *Kyle.*

With baccy smoke from twenty pipes, the atmosphere was blue,
There was many a "Have another, boy" and "Don't mind if I do."
When somebody suggested that each in turn should spin,
A yarn about some circumstance he'd personally been in.

Then tales were told of gun barrels bent to shoot around the cliff,
Of men thawed out and brought to life who had been frozen stiff.
Of barkpots carried off by flies, of pathways chopped through fog,
Of Uncle Bill, who barefoot, kicked the knots out of a twelve-inch log.

The loud applause grew louder when Uncle Mickey Shea,
Told of the big potatie he'd grown in Gander Bay.
Too big to go through the cellar door, it lay at rest nearby,
Until one rainy night that fall, the pig drowned in its eye.

But meanwhile in the corner, his grey head slightly bowed,
Sat Grampa Walcott, eighty-four, the oldest of the crowd.
Upon his weather-beaten face there beamed a quiet grin,
When some shouted "Grampa, 'tis your turn to chip in."

"Boys, leave me out," said Grampa. "Thanks, don't mind if I do,
Well, all right, boys, if you insist, I'll tell you one that's true.
It's a story about jiggin' squids I'm goin' to relate,
It happened in Pigeon Inlet, in eighteen eighty-eight.

"Me, I was just a bedlamer, a-fishin' with me Dad,
And prospects for the summer were lookin' awful bad.
The caplin scull was over, it hadn't been too bright,
And here was August come and gone, and nar a squid in sight.

"Day after day we searched for squids till dark from crack o'dawn,
We dug up clams and cocks and hens till even these were gone.
But still no squids, so in despair we give it up for good,
And took our gear ashore, and went a-cuttin' firewood.

"One mornin' we were in the woods with all the other men,
And wonderin' if we'd ever see another squid again.
Father broke his axe that day, so we were first ones out,
And as we neared the landwash, we heard the women shout.

"'Come hurry, boys, the squids are in.' We jumped aboard our boat,
And started out the harbour, the only crew afloat.
But soon our keel begun to scrunch, like scrapin' over skids,
'Father,' says I, 'we're run aground.' 'No, son,' says he, 'that's squids.'

"Said he, 'The jigger – heave it out,' and quick as a flash I did,
And soon's it struck the water 'twas grabbed up by a squid.
I hauled it in, and what do you think – just as it crossed the rail,
Blest if there wasn't another squid, clung to the first one's tail.

"And another clung to that one – and so on in a string,
I tried to shake 'em loose, but father said, 'You foolish thing.
You've got somethin' was never seen afore in Newfoundland,
So, drop the jigger, grab the string, and pull hand over hand.'

"I pulled that string of squids aboard till we could hold no more,
Then hitched it in the risin's and rowed the boat ashore.
The crews were comin' from the woods, they'd heard the women bawl,
But father said, 'Don't hurry, boys, there's squid enough for all.'

"So Uncle Jimmy took the string until he had enough,
Then, neighbour like, he handed it to Skipper Levi Cuff.
From stage to stage that string was passed
throughout the whole night long,
Till daylight found it on Eastern Point with Uncle Billy Strong.

"Now Uncle Bill, quite thoughtfully, before he went to bed,
Took two half hitches on the string round the grump* on his stagehead.
Next mornin' Hartley's Harbour heard the news and up they come,
In trap skiff with three pair of oars to tow the string down home.

"When Hartley's Harbour had enough the followin' afternoon,
That string went on from place to place until it reached Carpoon.**
What happened to it after that I don't exactly know,
But people say it crossed the Straits, and ended in Forteau."

Tall are the tales that fishermen tell when summer's work is done,
Of fish they've caught, of birds they've shot, and crazy risks they've run.
But never did fishermen tell a tale so tall by half a mile,
As Grampa Walcott told last fall in the smokeroom on the *Kyle*.

* grump (gump): wooden pile protruding above a wharf for mooring vessels

** Carpoon: Quirpon, a small community on the tip of the Great Northern Peninsula

ACKNOWLEDGEMENTS

Many thanks go to Harry Cuff, the first person to recognize the potential of these stories for publication. As editor of the *Newfoundland Quarterly* in the 1960s, he selected and edited several of them, including the following that are part of this present collection: "Grampa and the Hockey Game," "Paddy Muldoon," "My Brother Ki," "Teachers," "Toutens," and "Youngsters." Tribute must also be paid to Peter Narvaez, who in 1982 launched the "Bring Uncle Mose Back Home" project, which followed the discovery in Halifax of sixty-nine previously lost recordings.

Others who have helped along the way include the following: Kelly Russell, Tonya Kearley, Grant Brown, Philip Hiscock, William Kirwin, Anne-Marie Finn, and Robert Hollett.

ADDITIONAL RESOURCES

Elizabeth Miller, *Uncle Mose: The Life of Ted Russell*. St. John's: Flanker Press, 2004. [A biography of Ted Russell, with extensive commentary on all of his writings.]

Tales from Pigeon Inlet: Original Recordings by Ted Russell as Uncle Mose. Produced by Kelly Russell. Pigeon Inlet Productions, 2004. [A three-CD set containing thirty of the original tales as read on CBC Radio.]

"Uncle Mose: A Timeless Legacy." Created by Christine Davies and Kathryn King, CBC St. John's. URL: www.cbc.ca/nl/features/unclemose/index_mose.html [Website devoted to Uncle Mose, with photos, biographical notes, sample recordings, and a commentary by Peter Narvaez.]

"Ted and Dora Russell Papers." Centre for Newfoundland Studies Archive, Memorial University.

Peter Narvaez, "Folk Talk and Hard Fact: The Role of Ted Russell's 'Uncle Mose' on CBC's 'Fishermen's Broadcast.'" *Studies in Newfoundland Folklore: Community and Process*, ed. Gerald Thomas & J.D.A. Widdowson. St. John's: Breakwater, 1991. 191–212.

Jim Wellman, *The Broadcast: The Story of CBC Radio's Fisheries Broadcast*. St. John's: Creative Book Publishing, 1997.

EDWARD "TED" RUSSELL was born in Coley's Point, Conception Bay, in 1904. At sixteen, he undertook his first teaching assignment at Pass Island. For the next twenty-three years he worked in outport communities as a teacher and later a magistrate. In 1943 he moved to St John's to accept the position of Director of Co-operatives for the Commission of Government.

After a brief stint in politics (a member of the first Smallwood cabinet), Ted returned to teaching. But he also found a new opportunity to give expression to the more creative side of his nature. In 1953 he was offered a spot on CBC Radio's *Fishermen's Broadcast* as Uncle Mose. The highly successful "Chronicles of Uncle Mose" continued until 1962. During this period Ted also wrote several radio plays, all of which were broadcast by CBC. The last years of his working life were spent on the faculty of Memorial University (English Department) from which he retired in 1973. He died four years later.

Ted married Dora Oake (of Change Islands) in 1934. They had five children: Rhona; Elizabeth "Betty"; June; Margaret "Peggy"; and Kelly.

Photo by Jason Nolan

Daughter of Ted and Dora Russell, ELIZABETH MILLER spent much of her life as a teacher, first in Joe Batt's Arm (Fogo Island) and then at Memorial University. During the 1970s and 1980s she published widely in the field of Newfoundland literature. Since 1990, she has gained international recognition for her research on the novel *Dracula*. Her biography of her father, first published in 1981, was revised and reissued in 2005 as *Uncle Mose: The Life of Ted Russell*.

Elizabeth has one son (Dennis) and currently lives in Toronto.